"If I weren't a gentleman, this would be the opportunity for me to say I could help keep you warm."

"You're *not* a gentleman," she replied with a nervous giggle.

He had walked up to the circle of pines and was using one foot to scrape the pine needles into a pile. "You'd better hope I'm a gentleman, Hannah Forrester, because it's going to be one hell of a long night."

Something in his voice told her that he was not teasing. She walked timidly toward him and began to push the needles from the other side of the "bed."

"So are you, or aren't you?" she asked softly.

"A gentleman?"

She nodded.

He squinted to see her better in the dark. He spoke slowly. "I...don't think so...."

Dear Reader,

Ana Seymour has been delighting readers and editors alike since her first book, *The Bandit's Bride*, was published by Harlequin Historicals in 1992, and this month's *Frontier Bride* is bound to do the same. It's the story of a woman torn between her affection for the man who bought her indenture and her growing love for the rugged frontiersman who is guiding them to a new life in the territories. We hope you enjoy it.

And don't miss the third book in award-winning author Theresa Michaels's Kincaid Trilogy, *Once a Lawman*, featuring the oldest Kincaid brother, a small-town sheriff who must choose between family and duty as he works to finally bring to justice the criminals who've been plaguing his family's ranch.

This month, Miranda Jarrett has written another of her delightful Sparhawk titles, this one, *Sparhawk's Angel*, about a captain tormented by a meddlesome angel bent on matchmaking that *Romantic Times* calls "delightful, unforgettably funny and supremely touching." And a sensible novelist brings love and laughter to the wounded soul of a neighboring earl in Deborah Simmons's new title, *The Devil Earl*.

Please keep a lookout for Harlequin Historicals, available wherever books are sold.

Sincerely,

Tracy Farrell
Senior Editor

Please address questions and book requests to:
Harlequin Reader Service
U.S.: 3010 Walden Ave., P.O. Box 1325, Buffalo, NY 14269
Canadian: P.O. Box 609, Fort Erie, Ont. L2A 5X3

Ana Seymour

Frontier Bride

Harlequin Books

TORONTO • NEW YORK • LONDON
AMSTERDAM • PARIS • SYDNEY • HAMBURG
STOCKHOLM • ATHENS • TOKYO • MILAN
MADRID • WARSAW • BUDAPEST • AUCKLAND

ISBN 0-373-28918-9

FRONTIER BRIDE

This edition published by arrangement with Harlequin Books S.A.

® and TM are trademarks of the publisher. Trademarks indicated with
® are registered in the United States Patent and Trademark Office, the
Canadian Trade Marks Office and in other countries.

Printed in U.S.A.

Books by Ana Seymour

Harlequin Historicals

The Bandit's Bride #116
Angel of the Lake #173
Brides for Sale #238
Moonrise #290
Frontier Bride #318

ANA SEYMOUR

says she first discovered romance through the swashbuckling movies of Errol Flynn and Tyrone Power and the historical epics of Thomas Costain and Anya Seton. She spent a number of years working in the field of journalism, but she never forgot the magic of those tales. Now she is happy to be creating some of that magic herself through Harlequin Historicals. Ana lives in Minnesota with her two teenage daughters.

To my dear friends...
Bronwyn, Jan, Jeanne, Karen and Debi...
Frontierswomen all!

Prologue

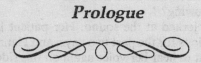

Philadelphia—December 1762

Priscilla Webster was finally going to die. Hannah wiped cold sweat from the woman's forehead, then straightened up, rubbing her own back. She looked out the window at the late afternoon darkness.

Through the thick panes of glass, the first storm of winter was howling, but inside, the small room was sweltering. Randolph Webster had insisted on keeping the fire stoked to the maximum all this week as they waited for his wife to take the last of her short, tortured breaths.

Hannah gave a deep sigh. She would miss Priscilla. When Hannah had arrived at the Webster household almost two years ago, she'd been apprehensive and weak from poor food and bouts of seasickness that had plagued her during the six-week crossing. She and the other hundred indentured servants on the *Constant* had been forced to remain below decks almost the entire trip, leaving her pale and dispirited. Priscilla Webster had greeted her more like a lost relative than a woman her husband had purchased. She had

insisted that Hannah get sufficient rest and food those
first few weeks until her spirits and her health were
fully restored. After months of injustices and mis-
treatment, Hannah had drunk in the woman's kind-
ness like sweet water after a drought.

"Is it snowing?"

Hannah jerked at the sound. Her patient had not
been conscious for the past two days, and Hannah had
not thought to hear her voice again on this side of the
grave. She looked down at the sick woman. Priscilla's
eyes shone unnaturally blue next to the red flush of her
face.

"Aye, mistress. There'll be snow for Christmas, I
reckon." The Websters were among the few in Philadelphia who celebrated the holiday, Hannah had been
delighted to discover. The past two Christmases had
been full of all the merriment that she had once longed
for as a child back in England. But there would be little celebrating this year.

Priscilla gave a barely perceptible nod. "The bairns
will like that." Her voice was faint.

"Will you take some broth, mum?" Hannah asked,
reaching for the bowl that had been sitting untouched
on the bedside table.

Priscilla swallowed, and her chest moved in a fee-
ble reminder of the violent coughs that had racked her
for so many months. She looked up with a serene smile
that made Hannah's heart ache. "No, Hannah, lass.
No food," she said slowly, laboring over the words.
"I'll need no...earthly...sustenance...where I'm
going."

Tears stung Hannah's eyes. When Priscilla's
coughing had become so bad that Mr. Webster had
quietly moved his things to the spare sleeping room,

the sick woman had not uttered a word of complaint.
When her lace handkerchiefs had revealed a terrible
black sputum, she had merely apologized to Hannah
for the extra laundry. And when the delicate hankies
had been replaced by rough cotton towels that more
and more often showed bright splotches of red, she
had gripped her servant's hand with weak fingers and
told her how grateful she was that Hannah had come
from afar to take care of her family. Hannah had
never met a sweeter soul.

"Let me call the master," she said.

Priscilla's eyelids drooped, shuttering her bright
eyes. Hannah quickly crossed the room and opened
the door, admitting a whoosh of cold air. She didn't
have to call. Randolph Webster was waiting in the next
room and was on his feet the minute he saw her.

"What's happened?" he asked, moving toward her.

"She's come 'round a bit. She spoke to me."

Hannah turned back to her patient with Mr. Webster close behind her. "Priscilla?" he said in a voice
barely above a whisper.

His wife's eyelids fluttered and she answered
weakly, "It's snowing, Randolph."

"Yes, love." He moved around Hannah to sit in the
chair at the side of the bed. Taking his wife's hand, he
asked tenderly, "How are you feeling?"

Her lips moved, but no sound came out. Randolph
looked at Hannah. There was anguish in his brown
eyes. His hair had pulled out of its binder and hung
unkempt around his gaunt face. He leaned closer to
his wife. "What is it, my love?"

"Dress...the bairns...warm." The strength seemed
to flow out of her body with each word. She looked up

at his confused expression and desperation flickered in her eyes. She turned her head toward Hannah.

"It's the snow," Hannah explained gently. "She wants us to dress the children warmly."

Randolph nodded briefly at his servant, then turned back to his wife. "Don't fret yourself, Priscilla. Peggy and Jacob'll not be going out in this weather. It's blowing up a storm."

Priscilla's chest moved with another ghost of a cough. "Then...every...thing's...just...fine."

Her eyes closed, and her hand fell from Randolph's to the coverlet. He quickly retrieved it and leaned over to bring it up against his cheek. "Everything's fine, love," he repeated, his throat sounding full.

Hannah blinked hard and turned to tend the fire. It was a moment before she felt she could speak. "Shall I leave you with her, sir?" she asked without turning.

There was no answer from behind her. She put another log on the huge blaze, then moved around to the opposite side of the bed. "Do you want some time alone, Mr. Webster?" she asked again.

Still clutching Priscilla's hand, he looked up at her, and Hannah was shocked to see that his cheeks were wet with tears. She averted her eyes. "I'll just wait in the next room," she said.

She leaned over to tuck the coverlet around her patient. The body underneath it had become so frail these past few weeks that it was sometimes hard to tell the bed was occupied at all. Hannah's hand hovered, then froze. There was no movement. The almost undetectable rise and fall of Priscilla's sunken chest had ceased. A feeling of dread settled in Hannah's stomach. She glanced at Mr. Webster, but his head was bowed.

She turned to the mistress's wardrobe chest behind her and, with suddenly cold fingers, grasped the ornate handle of Priscilla's prized silver mirror. Slowly she brought it back to the bed and held it over Priscilla's mouth. There was no cloud. Hannah closed her eyes, and instantly the tears poured down her cheeks.

An anguished sound from Mr. Webster made her look up. He reached across the bed and snatched the mirror from her fingers. "Priscilla," he said, then repeated his wife's name, almost shouting.

"She's gone, sir," Hannah said, choking on a sob. "She's gone to her Maker."

The mirror fell from his hand and slid down the covers to the floor. He grasped his wife's shoulders and pulled her inert body into his arms, rocking back and forth in silent agony.

Hannah's own grief subsided for a moment as she witnessed her employer's pain. Randolph Webster was not a warm man, and she had not grown close to him as she had to Priscilla. He had never made an effort to help her forget that she was his bondwoman, bound to him body and soul for three more years. But he was a good man and had loved his wife dearly. If Hannah dared, she would move to the other side of the bed and put an arm around his shaking shoulders. It was one of those moments when it seemed as if only physical contact could serve to comfort.

Her torrent of tears dried as she stood watching him, unsure of what to do next. "Shall I fetch the children?" she asked finally.

He shook his head without looking up, still cradling his wife's body. "No! They'll not see her this way." His harsh voice ended Hannah's urge to touch him. She took a step back from the bed.

"Do you want me to go for the MacDougalls?" Priscilla's parents owned a public house just down the lane from the Webster home.

Randolph didn't reply for a moment. He placed Priscilla's body tenderly back down against the pillow, then looked up at Hannah and spoke in a weary tone. "I've lost my wife, not my wits, girl. I'd not send you out in a storm like this."

"It's not far. I'm willing to go."

Randolph stood. "I'll go myself. They'll want to come be with the children. Then I'll go on to Newbury."

Hannah's eyes widened. "All the way to Newbury... in this weather?"

He glanced at the bed. "She'd not want any but her brother to perform the service."

"But the storm..." Her voice trailed off as Randolph's expression hardened.

Neither spoke for a moment. Then Randolph bent to kiss his wife's forehead. Without looking at Hannah, he said. "You will... tend to her?" His voice broke.

"Aye."

Without another word, he was gone.

Chapter One

Philadelphia—April 1763

"I declare, Hannah lass, Randolph's gone soft in the head. But ye do *not* have to go along with him." The burr of her Scottish homeland gave Jeanne MacDougall's speech a pleasant softness, in spite of her adamant tone.

Hannah shook her head and gave a swipe with the towel to the dish she was drying. She was helping Mistress MacDougall with the washing up in the big kitchen of the MacDougalls' inn. "I've a contract, mum. With three more years to run."

"There's nothing in that contract that says he has the right to drag ye off to live in the wilderness with no one for miles around." Mistress MacDougall's ample chest heaved with indignation. In the past her relations with her son-in-law had always been cordial, but she was furious over his plan to take her grandchildren away from the culture and civilization of Philadelphia for an uncertain existence on the frontier.

"There are four families going," Hannah replied gently. "I'm sure we'll stay nigh one another."

"And what about the savages?"

"Savages," Hannah repeated under her breath, tightening her grip on the pewter bowl. She had dealt with savages before. The debt collectors back in London who had seized her mother's bed from beneath her as she lay dying. The doctor who had refused to give Hannah even a little bit of physic to ease her mother's pain. The magistrate who had declared that an eighteen-year-old girl who had just buried her only parent should be imprisoned or transported to pay the costs of her mother's illness. "I'm not afraid of the savages," she said with a grim smile.

"I can't believe Randolph's serious about this venture," Mistress MacDougall said, wringing out a towel as if she wished it were her son-in-law's neck.

"It's hard to lose the children," Hannah agreed. "But you should hear him describe the lands they're opening up along the Ohio River—rich green meadows crisscrossed with silver rivers. The fish practically jump into your boat as you glide along, he says, and the crops grow themselves."

"I suppose the deer shoot themselves, too," Jeanne MacDougall huffed. "Ye'd better hope so, or ye'll all starve to death. Randolph knows nothing about hunting."

"I expect we'll all help each other, at least until we get through the first winter."

Mistress MacDougall shuddered and her voice became teary. "Sometimes I just don't think I can bear it. First we lose Prissy. . . and now the children."

Hannah dried one hand on her apron and put it on the older woman's sleeve. "I'll bring them back with me for a visit when my term's done," she said soberly.

She leaned over to look through the door to the front tavern where Peggy and Jacob were playing precariously on a hogshead of ale. She and the children had spent a lot of time at the MacDougalls' these past months. The Websters' roomy house at the end of the lane, which had seemed so welcoming to her when she first arrived in America, was now full of shadows and grief. The children preferred to be here in the bright, busy inn with their grandparents. Especially since their father was rarely at home these days.

"Mind that doesn't tip over on your little brother," she called to Peggy. The girl's laughter stopped abruptly. She jumped to the floor and steadied the wobbling barrel. Hannah bit her lip and immediately regretted her words of caution. It was so seldom that Peggy played these days. Losing her mother at the age of eleven had given her an instant boost into adulthood.

"Go ahead and climb, if you like. Just have a care." Hannah smiled at the towheaded pair then turned back to Mistress MacDougall. "They're fine children. You should be proud."

"They're all I have left of my Prissy," Jeanne MacDougall said. "'Tis unjust of Randolph to take them so far."

"Mr. Webster says that he needs a new start—that they all do. Or they'll never get over Priscil...Mistress Webster's death."

Jeanne MacDougall's mournful expression turned sharp. "Ye seem to be very well versed on what my son-in-law is feeling and saying."

Hannah felt her cheeks flame. She hoped she was misinterpreting the direction of Mistress MacDougall's comment. "I've heard him talk with the children. And with the other gentlemen who are joining us with their families. They've met often at the house these past months.''

Mistress MacDougall's face softened. "Ye've had a lot of work, Hannah, and no female in the house to give ye a kind word.''

"Mr. Webster has been gone so much that it's mostly been just the children and I. In truth, 'tis not so hard as . . .'' She stopped.

"As when ye was nursing my daughter day and night and caring for the bairns, as well.''

Hannah nodded. "The sadness weighed us all down those last weeks.''

Mistress MacDougall took the towel from Hannah's hand and pulled her over to sit beside her on the rough wood settle by the fire. "I was going to have Mr. MacDougall talk to ye, Hannah. But ye know how men are—great for blathering until ye have something you really want them to say.''

Hannah hid a smile. She had never heard dour old Mr. MacDougall "blather.''

"The fact is, lass, it's just not right,'' Mistress MacDougall continued.

"Not right?''

The older woman looked down at her hands and shifted her bulky form on the hard bench. "When Randolph hired ye to care for Priscilla, that was one thing. But now, he's a lone man, a widower. And ye are an attractive young woman. It's not a proper situation.''

The color returned to Hannah's cheeks. So she *hadn't* misunderstood Mistress MacDougall's earlier remark. She had no idea how to reply. The idea was so absurd. Mr. Webster scarcely spoke to her, rarely looked at her. When he noted her presence at all, it was to give some kind of order about the children.

"Forgive my speaking plain, Mistress Mac-Dougall, but you're very mistaken. Mr. Webster pays me less mind than he does one of his horses. He was devoted to Priscilla, and I warrant it'll be a long time before he cares to cast his eye on any other woman."

"I'm not questioning his integrity, Hannah, nor yours. It's just that if ye head off together alone, folks are bound to talk."

"We'll not be alone..."

Mistress MacDougall held up a hand to ward off Hannah's protest. "And so, Mr. MacDougall and I have decided to buy your contract from Randolph. We can use ye here at the inn." She gave Hannah's hand a pat. "We're not as young as we used to be, ye know."

Hannah sat back hard against the straight back of the settle. The offer was a surprise, and she was not at all sure that it was a welcome one. When Mr. Webster had first talked of journeying west, she had been disappointed and concerned. But now, after weeks of listening to him and the other men talk of their hopes and dreams for the new land, an odd anticipation had begun to smolder in her middle like a poorly banked fire.

"It's overkind of you, Mistress MacDougall..." she stammered, then paused as loud male voices interrupted from the front room. "You have guests. I'd best see to the children." She stood and picked up a tray of clean mugs to carry out to the taproom. Mistress MacDougall's words had left her feeling dizzy. It was disconcerting to be presented suddenly with a choice about her own future. Her life had not been her own to manage for so very long.

She stopped in the doorway. Her glance went immediately to Peggy and Jacob. She had promised Priscilla to care for them. Could she bear to send them off by themselves into an uncertain wilderness?

"Strike me blind, Webster! You didn't tell me that in Philadelphia the barmaids wear the faces of angels."

The smooth, deep voice made Hannah's head jerk toward the group of men who had just entered. Randolph Webster was there, and some of the other men she had met at the Webster house. But it was the unshaven stranger standing at the front of the group who held her gaze. His dark eyes surveyed her with undisguised admiration.

"And not just the face. The whole of her is of divine making, I'd wager." His smile flashed white against several day's growth of dark beard.

He took two long steps toward her, then swept off his fur cap and gave her a little bow. "These gents need ale, mistress, if you would be so kind. And you may bring me a tankard, as well, though, I swear, a mere drink of your beauty could quench a devil's thirst."

Hannah's eyes went past the man to seek out Randolph Webster, who was listening to the newcomer with a look of surprise. The other men in the group were grinning. She recognized Amos Crawford and Hugh Trask, a burly fellow who always made Hannah feel vaguely uncomfortable when he visited the Webster household.

She was about to make a reply to the stranger's request when Trask shouldered his way through the man and put an arm around her waist, almost toppling the heavy tray to the ground. His body pressed heavily against the thin muslin of her dress. "The captain's right," he said, leaning over her. "We've a powerful thirst, sweetheart. For ale . . . and mayhap something more if the tap's runnin'." He looked back to the other men with a leering smile.

Holding the tray awkwardly, Hannah pulled herself out of his grasp. "I beg your pardon, sir!" she said with a grimace of disgust. The words came out less forcefully than she would have liked.

Suddenly the tray was plucked from her by the bearded stranger, who shot Trask an angry look, then steadied Hannah with a gentle hand on her elbow. "It appears you could use some lessons in treating a lady, Trask. Are you all right, mistress?" he asked.

Belatedly Randolph Webster shook off his dazed expression and came over to join Hannah and the two men. He moved between Hannah and Trask, then addressed the stranger. "She's not a barmaid, Reed. She's . . . ah . . . she lives with me."

One of the stranger's dark eyebrows went up. Then he smiled and threw his hands up in a gesture of apology. "I'm sorry, mistress. I just assumed . . . I had been told that you were a widower, Webster."

"Yes, that is . . ." Randolph cleared his throat.

Hannah took a step back into the relative security of the kitchen, then tipped her head up to look the tall stranger directly in the eyes. "My name is Hannah Forrester," she said with quiet dignity. "I am Mr. Webster's servant."

The man shot a look back at Randolph, then said slowly, "Mr. Webster is a lucky man."

He was different from the other men in the room. It wasn't just the beard, since there were two or three others who looked as if it had been awhile since they'd felt the sharp edge of a blade. It was something about his height and the way he was...filled out. Hannah didn't know exactly how to describe it. His shoulders almost blocked her view of the rest of the room. His breeches were not the customary wool or linsey, but rather a fine doeskin that clung to muscular thighs in a way Hannah had not seen in the ordinary gentleman who frequented the tavern.

She retreated one more step into the kitchen. The stranger hadn't stopped looking at her. "I believe you wanted ale," she said, trying to keep her voice even.

Randolph Webster had recovered his poise. Still blocking Trask, he clapped a hand on the stranger's back. "An honest mistake, Reed," he said heartily. "And I'm sure Hannah would be happy to bring us something to drink if my mother-in-law is busy in the kitchen. Would you be so kind, Hannah?"

Hannah took a deep breath and looked down at the floor. "Of course. If I may, Mr....er...Reed?" She reached to take back the tray he'd been balancing easily on one arm.

"Ethan Reed, ma'am, at your service. I'm most pleased to make your acquaintance."

He bowed to her once again, a formal bow as though they were standing in the middle of St. James's palace. Then his eyes sought hers once more. Hannah was sure that her face was the color of Mr. Mac-Dougall's finest claret.

She turned quickly back into the kitchen. For once the steamy room seemed cooler than the front taproom. Mistress MacDougall had removed her apron and was drying her hands. She had witnessed the exchange and said in a low voice, "I'll see to them, Hannah, if you prefer."

Hannah shook her head. "No." She would just as soon stay busy. With Mistress MacDougall's help, she prepared a tray of cheese, cold chicken and bread.

Her heart had resumed its normal beat, and she decided that her overly strong reaction to Mr. Reed had been due to the fact that she was tired. She'd been up much of the night tending to Jacob's croup. "Who *is* that man?" she asked Mistress MacDougall.

"Marry, girl. That's Captain Reed. He was with Rogers's Rangers, you know. We had some of them here at the inn a couple years ago, and a rowdier bunch of wild men you've never seen."

"He's a captain?"

"Well, not anymore. The war's over now, of course. The French have hightailed it up to Canada and the Indians have calmed down—except for that Pontiac fellow."

Hannah lifted the heavy tray and glanced toward the door to the front room. "Were the Rangers all so... big?" she asked.

Mistress MacDougall chuckled. "Captain Reed's not big, lass, he's just bonny. A fine specimen of manhood, if ye ask me."

"What's he doing with Mr. Webster?"

The older woman's smile died. "Well ye may ask, child. I'm very much afraid the captain is here to take ye, Randolph and my dear Prissy's bairns so far from here that I'll never gaze upon ye again."

It was long past sundown. The evening had grown so cool that it felt as if winter were attempting to sneak back. Hannah got up to close the tavern windows, then returned to her rocking chair with a yawn. At the far end of the room, the men were still poring over Captain Reed's drawings and maps. Randolph Webster sat with Jacob on one knee and Peggy clinging to his side. The children had had so little time with their father lately that they both looked as if they would be willing to stay in his company all evening. But Hannah could see dark circles of fatigue on their pale cheeks. She wanted to take them and head back up the lane to the Websters'. Perhaps Jacob would sleep through the night tonight after taking some of his grandfather's posset. The warmth of the fire felt good against her face. Her eyelids grew heavy.

"They've worn you out, Mistress Forrester."

Again the rich voice jolted her. She straightened and twisted her head to find its owner. "It's late for the children," she managed to say.

"It's not the children who I see dozing by the fire like a well-fed kitten." His dark eyes teased.

Hannah was at a loss for words. She was not used to carrying on a conversation with a male. Though she had spoken a few times to the gentlemen who had visited Mr. Webster at his home, the conversation had always been circumscribed to her duties as a servant. Before that . . . well, her mother had made certain that Hannah's exposure to men of any age was as limited as possible.

Hannah could still hear her voice. "I'll not see you follow in the path of yer wretched mum, girl—flowery in the head after a few pretty words from a fine-looking gent, then thrown over as neatly as an apple core pitched into the gutter. With a babe in my belly and not a farthing in my purse."

It had been the litany of her childhood.

Captain Reed leaned closer. "They do feed you well, don't they, mistress?"

Hannah found the question absurd. She straightened the rocker, almost knocking him in the chin. "I feed myself, Captain Reed. Now if you'll excuse me, I think I'd best bundle up the children and take them home."

He stepped around her chair and crouched down next to the fire. The position looked natural to him, as though he spent many hours in places where there was not a chair to be had.

"I was hoping to talk with you, mistress. It's been a long, dry spell since I've been in feminine company."

The words cajoled, but it was his smile that kept her rooted to her seat. She glanced across the room to where the other men still seemed engrossed in their papers. "Don't you need to be over there—planning or routing or...something?"

"My routes are in here," he said, tapping the side of his head with his finger. His hair was a deep, rich brown and he wore it long, not pulled back into the customary queue. His short dark whiskers emphasized the rugged line of his jaw.

"You know the wilderness well?" she asked after a moment.

He grinned. "Well now, I'm not a man to boast. Let me put it this way. Before I round a bend of the Ohio, I can tell you how many marsh rats we'll find nesting on the other side."

Hannah laughed. Ethan Reed's utter lack of humility both irritated and fascinated her. Some of her nervousness subsided. Here was a man who actually knew this land Mr. Webster had described so glowingly and in such detail. "Is it as rich as they say? As beautiful?"

"The Ohio River valley's richer than anything these colonies have seen. One of these days people will be clamoring to own a piece of it. You folks are lucky to be among those getting there first."

"Do you 'own a piece of it,' Captain?"

He shook his head. "I'm not exactly the settling-down type, Mistress Forrester. I figure, why should I limit myself to a little piece of paradise when I can freely roam the whole thing?"

"But, surely, now that families are moving into the area, you'll not feel quite so independent?"

"The tiny little chunks of land you folks will hack out of the wilderness won't change things much."

Hannah looked puzzled. "I thought Mr. Webster said that the tracts would be upward of two hundred acres."

Reed laughed, rich and low. "There's hundreds of *thousands* of acres out there, mistress. Your little portion of it won't amount to more than a fly speck."

Hannah shifted her eyes to the fire. "Not *my* portion, Captain Reed. I'm just going along to care for Mr. Webster's children. At the end of three years I'll return here to the city to seek employment."

Reed was silent for a long moment. When Hannah turned back to him, he was looking at her with a half smile and eyes that had grown suddenly intense. "I'd not place a wager on that, mistress," he said softly.

She wanted to look away again, but his gaze held hers. "Why not?" she asked. Her mouth suddenly felt dry.

"Webster's not that big a fool."

It was the second time that day she'd had to listen to insinuations about her relationship with Randolph Webster. Hannah gripped the arms of the rocker and said stiffly, "Mr. Webster is my employer, Captain Reed. He has just lost his beloved wife. And if we're all to be traveling together, I'll thank you not to embarrass the poor man with your preposterous comments."

Reed was unruffled. "If not Webster, then some other man will snatch you up, Mistress Forrester. There's a sore need for women on the frontier."

Hannah stood briskly, setting the rocking chair swaying. "I'm not available to be 'snatched,' as you put it, Captain. I'm contracted to Mr. Webster, and that's the end of it. In the future I'd appreciate it if you kept your speculations about my destiny to yourself."

With no visible effort, Reed went from his easy crouch to a standing position. His broad chest was just inches from her face. "Yes, ma'am," he replied with a grin.

"Thank you. I'll bid you good-evening, sir." She turned away with a flounce of her skirts.

Reed watched as she crossed the room to lift a drooping Jacob from Randolph Webster's lap.

Hannah had cleaned the tiny office in the back of the Webster house many times, but this was the first time she had ever sat there in the stiff horsehair chair across the desk from Randolph Webster. It was after the noon meal. Peggy and Jacob were playing blindman's wand with a group of children from the neighborhood. Hannah had been watching them from the front window, thinking that soon they would be leaving all their friends behind, when Mr. Webster had come up quietly behind her.

"Are you busy, Hannah?"

She'd jumped and a guilty flush had come over her. It was seldom that she could be found idling thus in the middle of the day. But Mr. Webster looked distracted and didn't seem to be chiding her for her lack of activity.

"I wonder if I might have a moment of your time?" he'd continued.

He'd led her into the office that he used to keep his accounts and those of his in-laws and many other friends and neighbors. The neat rows of books and ledgers made Hannah question once again Mr. Webster's decision to leave his home and comfortable city life. What did Randolph Webster know about carving a farm out of the wilderness? She sighed. It wasn't her decision. And she supposed someday the frontier would need accountants, too.

Mr. Webster appeared to be studying her from his deep leather chair, and Hannah was just beginning to grow uncomfortable when he said, "I've not been the most attentive employer these past months."

The remark surprised her. It had sounded almost apologetic. "You've had your grief to bear, Mr. Webster. 'Tis understandable."

"You've done a remarkable job with the children. They miss Priscilla, but I can't imagine how they'd be faring if you hadn't been here for them."

"They're very dear." Hannah smiled uncertainly.

"Yes, well..." Randolph reached out to roll a marble blotter back and forth under his hand. "It's been brought to my attention that it might be unfair of me to ask you to join us on the trip west.''

Hannah let out a breath. So this was what was on his mind. "My contract doesn't specify where my services will be performed, Mr. Webster. I consider that you and...Mrs. Webster...have always been fair with me."

Randolph gave the blotter a spin, then stopped the motion with a smash of his hand. "The MacDougalls want me to sell them your indenture."

Hannah swallowed. She had thought of little else all morning. It wouldn't be a bad life. The MacDougalls were honorable people, and Hannah had no doubt that her three years would pass pleasantly enough. But if she stayed in Philadelphia, she'd never see those silver rivers....

Randolph Webster watched her silently. His stern features had softened, and he looked almost like a little boy making a silent plea for permission to embark on an adventure.

All at once Hannah realized that her decision had already been made. "Mr. Webster," she started slowly, "back in London when my mother became too ill to work, we moved to an almshouse. I lived with forty other people in a room the size of your Sunday parlor. On the crossing, there were over a hundred of us in a smelly ship's hold not as big as this house. Now you tell me about a rich land where you can walk all day in the sunlight and never see another living soul. Just imagine!" Her blue eyes sparkled. "If you and the children want me, I'll go west with you."

Randolph seemed to let out a breath he'd been holding. He didn't smile, but the tenseness left his face and he leaned back in his chair. "We do want you, Hannah." The slightest bit of red began to show from underneath his stiff white collar. "Er...that is...the children are very fond of you."

"Then it's settled," Hannah said briskly. "Please thank the MacDougalls for their offer and their concern."

Randolph nodded. He didn't speak further, but continued studying her.

"Was there anything else, sir?" she asked.

"No. Ah...thank you, Hannah."

She got up and started to leave, but Mr. Webster's voice stopped her at the door.

"Hannah, there is one more thing. Would you please prepare the back room?"

She turned back to him. "The back room, sir?"

"Yes. Captain Reed will be joining us tonight. He has accepted my offer to stay here until we're ready to leave."

Much to her annoyance, Hannah realized that her heart had given a thump inside her chest at the mention of the man's name. "Very good, sir," she said a little sharply.

Randolph looked up at her curiously. "Reed seemed taken with you last night at the inn."

"He said it had been a spell since he'd been around women, and judging from his manners, I believe he was telling the truth."

Randolph smiled. "It's hard to fault a man for noticing a pretty girl, Hannah."

Hannah's cheeks grew hot. It was the first time that Randolph Webster had made the slightest comment on her person. His eyes had an odd expression, too, as he watched her from behind his big desk. She dropped her gaze to the floor. "I'd best see to getting his room ready, Mr. Webster." Then she gave a bob of her head and escaped down the hall.

Chapter Two

Ethan Reed had spent the entire past year with a
government survey party mapping the unknown territory along the Monongahela River north of the
Ohio. The winter before that, he'd spent at Fort Pitt,
the rough frontier stronghold that the English had
built to replace the burned-out French Fort Du-
quesne. As he had told Webster's servant yesterday, it
had been a long spell since he'd been around a lot of
women. It had been an even longer one since he'd seen
any as pretty as Mistress Hannah Forrester.

He stood framed by the open doorway of Webster's house and watched her as she bent dipping candles in a pan of tallow. She was too intent on her work
to notice his arrival, and he took advantage of the
moment to let his eyes roam over her long, slender
body. Too slender, perhaps, for the rigors of the West.
But with a willowy grace that put a hollow in his mid-
section. She wore no cap, and her bright blond hair
hung in a thick braid down to the middle of her back.

She turned to hang a dripping row of candles on the
drying rack, then stopped as she spied him. Her body
stiffened. She was a skittish one, that was for sure.
Like the fawn he'd tried to tame last fall when one of

the members of the survey party had killed its mother. Ethan had patiently attempted to convince the little animal to trust him, but it had looked at him with big fearful eyes and jumped every time Ethan came near.

Mistress Forrester's eyes were not fearful, but they were full of mistrust. He wondered if she'd been telling the truth about Webster's lack of interest. The man must be daft ... or blind. Of course, as she had said, Webster was still grieving for his wife. Ethan shook his head. If he had a woman like this living under the same roof, he'd do a lot more than notice.

"You startled me, Captain," she said, putting the candles in their place.

"I beg your pardon, mistress. I should have announced myself. But you were standing there in that shaft of light, and I was trying to decide if that was your real hair or a halo of sunbeams wreathing your pretty face."

Hannah wiped a wisp of hair from her forehead. "Captain Reed, it's not seemly for you to address such remarks to me. I'm Mr. Webster's servant."

Ethan stepped inside the door and removed his felt tricorne. "I believe you're going to find that west of the Ohio those kind of labels don't make much difference anymore. Everyone's as good as a servant out there. Those who don't work hard won't make it."

Hannah's eyes widened as he approached. He was clean shaven now and dressed in a well-tailored suit, tapered at the waist in the current style. He still looked big. His shoulders filled out the jacket in a way that she'd never noticed with Mr. Webster or his friends. With his whiskers gone and clean clothes, Captain Reed suddenly looked as if he could be one of the fine gents who had sauntered into Piccadilly back home in search of a good time and easy women. Her mum had always scurried away when one approached, dragging Hannah behind her. "They'll not be after you with their fancy words, luv," she'd say with that distressing look of desperation in her eyes.

"Perhaps you're not aware that I'm indentured to Mr. Webster," she told the captain. "I'm his servant not by choice, but by contract."

His potent dark eyes watched her. "Contracts don't mean a hell of a lot out West, either."

"Nevertheless," she said with quiet dignity, "I intend to honor my commitment to the Websters—Mr. Webster and the children."

"It'll not be a picnic." He finally broke off his gaze and began looking around the large kitchen. "You'll not be able to take much of this with you."

Relieved to turn to a less personal topic of conversation, Hannah said, "The MacDougalls will be selling most of these things after we're gone. Mr. Webster has spent the past few weeks packing up the essentials. We're taking very little."

"I saw his bundles out in the carriage house and told him to reduce the amount by two-thirds."

"But surely..."

Ethan gestured impatiently. "As I told Webster, we'll be traveling over little more than a mule track as far as Fort Pitt. From there we'll move onto the flatboats, which will be a sight easier on everyone. You might be able to pick up some extra supplies at the fort."

"We were hoping to take Priscilla's vanity for Peggy," Hannah said with a frown.

Ethan shook his head. "Tell her grandparents to save it for her. Someday the roads west will be broad enough to move a whole house, but not yet."

Hannah nodded. She felt sorry for the little girl, who had lost her mother and must now leave almost every trace of her behind. But Hannah herself had gone through worse sacrifices during her childhood. Her mother had always said what didn't kill you, made you strong.

"I'll talk to the MacDougalls. They've plenty of room to save some of Mrs. Webster's things for a future date."

Ethan gave a smile of approval. "I like your attitude, Mistress Forrester. Most women put up a fuss about leaving their precious belongings behind."

"I only asked for Peggy's sake, Captain Reed. For myself, I've nothing precious to take or to leave."

She spoke the words matter-of-factly, Ethan noted, without a trace of self-pity or bitterness. Webster's servant was not only beautiful. There was an underlying strength to her character that would serve her well on the frontier.

Hannah's back hurt again. She'd spent all day trying to prepare enough candles to last for the unknown number of weeks before she would be able to make more, and the bending and dipping had her muscles aching. Her unpredictable back was one of the curses of being tall and slender, her mother used to say. Of course, her mother had measured little more than a yeoman's yard, which meant that Hannah's height had to have come from the deserting blackguard who had fathered her. Her mother would see naught but ill in the trait.

"You've put in a long day, Hannah." Mr. Webster stepped in the front door and clapped his hat on the wall peg.

Hannah smiled at him. Since their conversation in his office this morning, Mr. Webster's remarks to her seemed to be subtly different. The day had gone much as most days, a busy combination of household chores and children, but more than once she had caught his eyes on her, and he had complimented her warmly on the supper, which had been nothing but an unpretentious beef stew. Of course, the presence of Captain Reed had made the meal more festive than usual. He'd regaled them with stories of the West until both Peggy and Jacob had jumped around in a circle and declared that they wanted to leave that very minute.

"I thought you would be staying up at the tavern with Captain Reed and the others," she answered.

"The noise was giving me the headache. I decided I'd rather come home and tuck the bairns in their beds."

Hannah's smile dimmed at his use of Priscilla's word for her children. It wasn't a fair world that took a mother away from her little ones. "I'm afraid Jacob's asleep already, but Peggy may be awake. She was working on her sampler."

"I'll just go upstairs and see. And then..." He glanced at the hand Hannah still held at her aching waist. "Are you too tired for a bit more work tonight?"

Hannah removed her hand and tried to straighten the crimp out of her back without being obvious. "Of course not. What would you like me to do?"

"Help me. We need to go through the household items I had planned to take and decide which ones can be left. Captain Reed claims that we'll not be able to take such a load."

"Aye. He told me the same thing."

Webster looked annoyed. "When did he tell you that?"

"This afternoon. He surprised me in the kitchen as I was making the candles."

"There's no call for Reed to be telling you what to do, Hannah. He's our trail guide, nothing more. If you wish, I'll ask him not to speak to you unless necessary."

"Oh, please no. He's not a bother to me, Mr. Webster."

"If he should become one, Hannah, kindly let me know. Mayhaps I shouldn't say this to you, but I believe Captain Reed has something of a reputation with the ladies."

"The ladies? To hear him talk, he's spent the past two years with bears, wild Indians and even wilder soldiers."

"Perhaps that's all the more reason I should tell him to stay clear of you," Randolph said grimly. "All I know is that they say he was raised in Boston of a good family and he left under somewhat cloudy circumstances that concerned a woman."

Hannah sighed and stretched her back one more time. "I appreciate your concern, Mr. Webster, but I don't believe I need protection from Captain Reed."

"Yes, well . . ." Mr. Webster looked at her with the odd expression that seemed to have developed since the incident in the tavern last night. "It's my responsibility to take care of you, Hannah. If *anyone* tries to bother you, you must tell me about it forthwith."

Hannah was bewildered by the proprietary tone. For almost three years she'd lived in the same house with this man, feeling of no more importance to him than a sack of turnips. Now all at once he seemed concerned about her. Mistress MacDougall's comments came back to her, but she dismissed them impatiently. "I was raised on the streets of London, Mr. Webster, not at a convent. I can take care of myself."

Webster nodded. "I believe you. God knows, you've taken care of all of us well enough these past months."

"Yes, well..." Hannah felt her cheeks grow warm. "I'll just go on out to the stable and start looking at the packs."

"You're sure you aren't too tired?"

"No, I'm fine."

"You're a hard worker, Hannah. But I intend to take a little bit better care of you in the future."

She didn't know what to reply, so she nodded and turned toward the door. But she felt Randolph Webster's eyes follow her all the way out to the yard.

Hannah always felt a stitch in her heart when she walked by the big stone kiln at the corner of the Baker brickyard. It had been at that site over a year ago that carefree, young Johnny Baker had lost his life when an unbalanced load of bricks had fallen on him, crushing his throat. Johnny Baker had bantered with Hannah when she had first arrived in Philadelphia, and Priscilla had teased her that the handsome young man was sweet on her. But Hannah knew that Johnny flirted with every young maid in the area. He wasn't likely to set his heart on an indentured servant with five long years to serve. Still, his death had shocked and saddened her. Johnny's mother, Eliza, had been nearly crazy with grief, and Hannah had taken to spending some of her free moments with her. Johnny had been Eliza and Seth Baker's only child, and in many ways it seemed as if their very future had died along with him.

Hannah walked up the neat brick path to the Baker cottage. Eliza's beloved crocuses were making their first brave appearance, in spite of the continuing cold weather. The cheery splotches of yellow brought the natural smile back to Hannah's lips. The Bakers would miss their home, she thought. When a recent German immigrant had made an offer to buy the brickyard, it had seemed to be the opportunity to flee from their grief. Some of Seth's natural enthusiasm had returned as he joined in the plans to head west with the Websters, the Trasks and the Crawfords. But Hannah knew that Eliza would miss her crocuses in the spring, and she'd especially miss her daily climb up to the small cemetery behind the church.

"Hannah, my dear. What are you about so early?" Eliza's kindly, weathered face poked out the front window.

Hannah smiled at her. "I'm just bringing around a message from Mr. Webster."

The head disappeared and the cottage's bright green door opened. "Come inside, girl. The morning's still got a chill on it."

Hannah ducked under the portal to enter the Bakers' immaculate kitchen. It smelled of herbs and fresh bread. "Take off your bonnet and have some warm cider," Eliza urged, bustling around to fill a mug with steaming liquid from the black kettle and slide a pan from the warming oven. "And you'll take some bread, as well. It's just baked."

Hannah laughed and shook her head, but took a seat on one of the stools. "I can't stay, Eliza. I have yet to visit the Crawfords and the Trasks."

"You'll stay long enough to put some warmth in your middle," Eliza said firmly, handing Hannah the mug.

"Mr. Baker isn't at home?" Hannah asked.

"He's out in the yard with Herr Gutmueller." Eliza's expression dimmed. "I hope we're doing the right thing. It's tearing Seth apart to leave the business to a stranger. Yet, how could he stay on when every day he has to face that horrible spot where Johnny..."

Hannah gave a nod of understanding. "You've been over it a hundred times, Eliza. You yourself have said that Seth is feeling better now that he's making plans for a new life. It's probably for the best."

Eliza sat across from Hannah, her full skirts puffing up around her. "I know, I know. I'll not bother you again with my worries."

Hannah reached out to take the older woman's plump hand. "You never bother me, Eliza. I just wish I could do something to make the leaving easier on you and Mr. Baker. After all the help you gave me when Mrs. Webster died. I'd never have managed all those relatives and neighbors without your assistance."

The two women shared a smile of friendship. "It was a heavy burden for a young thing like you, Hannah. Still is... the children to manage, and Randolph moping in his beer every night."

"Mr. Webster's doing better, too, I think, keeping busy with all the plans and preparations."

Eliza withdrew her hand from Hannah's and reached over to slice off a golden crust of bread. "Well, you see, that's men for you. Give them an adventure and they're willing to forget everything else. We womenfolk are left to grieve by ourselves." Her eyes went to the back wall of the house, as if she could see beyond it to the brickyard where her husband was in the process of disposing of his life's work.

"Perhaps their way is better," Hannah said gently. She, herself, had found that learning a new land had helped her deal with the crushing loss of her mother. And she found herself looking forward to the westward adventure as much as the men did.

Eliza's eyes had misted over. "Perhaps. I'll do my best to make this work for Seth."

"From what Captain Reed says, we'll all have to do our best."

The tone of Hannah's voice had changed subtly and Eliza looked up sharply. "Captain Reed's a spellbinder, isn't he?"

"The children certainly seem fascinated by his stories." Hannah looked away from her friend.

Eliza cocked her head. "Indeed," she said dryly.

Hannah picked up the piece of bread Eliza had pushed toward her and jammed it into her mouth. "I have to be on my way," she said between chews. "I just came to tell you that we'll all be meeting tomorrow evening at the MacDougalls' for a farewell party."

"Good. We'll bring Herr and Frau Gutmueller."

Hannah jumped up from her seat and reached out to give Eliza a quick hug. "We're all going to be just fine, Eliza. You'll see."

* * *

Hannah waved to Mr. Baker as she hurried along the east edge of the brickyard to the Crawfords' tiny house. It was in need of paint and the front stoop had been broken since Hannah had first arrived in town. The boards slanted to one side at an odd angle that forced Hannah to hitch up her skirts and look down to keep from falling. She had wondered about the ability of Amos Crawford to keep up with the hard work of a wilderness farm, but at least he would be another man to serve as protection. There was safety and comfort in numbers, she supposed. Besides, young Benjamin Crawford was Jacob Webster's best friend, and the two boys had been playing at being frontiersmen for weeks.

It was Benjamin who answered her knock, but as he started to open the door he was pushed out of the way by his seven-year-old brother Thomas. "I said *I* would get the door, Benjie," he shouted, giving his older brother a push that sent him sprawling into the cluttered room.

Benjamin leapt up and dove for Thomas's knees, which put both boys on the floor, pummeling each other.

"Mama, Tom and Benjie's fightin' again," cried little Patience Crawford, while her twin sister, Hope, jumped up and down in excitement.

Martha Crawford appeared in the doorway to the back room. She was a slender woman who had been one of the town beauties a few years back, but who now looked drawn and weary. She clapped her hands together and yelled, "Stop this!"

The words had no effect whatsoever on the commotion, but the woman didn't appear to care. She made her way around the tumbling boys and gave Hannah a tired smile. "Good morrow, Mistress Forrester."

Hannah glanced at the floor where both girls had now jumped into the fray, and quickly relayed her message. As she finished, Amos Crawford came out of the back room. Without so much as a glance at the fighting children, he said heartily, "Aye, we'll be there. We're chomping at the bit to get started, I can tell you. Out on the trail...out where a man has room to breathe."

His wife didn't look his way. "Should I bring something for the party?" she asked Hannah softly.

Hannah shook her head. "The MacDougalls will be fixing the victuals," she said, her voice raised to carry over the children's shouts. "Ah...fine, then. We'll see you tomorrow. Good day to you all."

Hastily she backed out the door and down the precariously tilted stoop.

Hannah had left the Trask house for last. She was not looking forward to seeing Hugh Trask after his insulting gesture at the inn the other night. She could still feel the man's sweaty hand pressing painfully into her waist. It was not the first time Trask had made her feel uncomfortable. It seemed that every time he came to the Webster house, he had taken some opportunity to make a sly comment or look at her with a lewd expression. She couldn't help but be sorry that the Trasks would be accompanying them on this journey. Nancy Trask appeared to be a nice enough woman, though, and their two daughters, Janie and Bridgett, would be good company for Peggy. The poor child needed the diversion.

Hannah was relieved to find Nancy Trask alone at her home. She relayed her message quickly, then hurried away with a sigh of relief. But her relief was short-lived. As she started up the small hill that would lead back to the Websters' road, she saw that Hugh Trask was coming down the path directly toward her. There was no way to avoid an encounter.

"Halloo, Hannah," he called. "What were you doing at my house?"

He planted himself in front of her in such a way that she couldn't continue on up the path without pushing against him, so she stopped. "I just came to tell you that we'll all be meeting tomorrow night. Mistress Trask has the message." She kept her eyes down.

"You needn't run away so fast. My wife could use some company these days with another brat growing inside her."

Hannah had suspected that Nancy Trask was with child, but the quiet woman kept so to herself that it seemed no one in town knew for sure. Now that it was confirmed, Hannah was appalled. How could Hugh Trask bring his wife on the dangerous journey ahead of them in such a state? If she weren't an indentured servant, she would give the man a piece of her mind. As it was, she just wanted to make her escape. "I . . . I'm sorry," she said, trying to edge around him up the hill. "I have a lot to attend to yet . . . the packing . . ."

Trask grabbed her elbow. "You don't think you're too good to set awhile at my house, do you, missy?"

Hannah tried to pull away, but his hold on her was firm. She could feel the warmth of his pungent breath. "Of course not, Mr. Trask. But we have only two more days to get ready. I'm sure you and your wife have much to do, as well.''

Trask pulled her a step closer and moved his leg so that his thigh touched hers. "I'm never too busy for the right kind of company," he said with a chuckle that gurgled in his throat.

Hannah felt sick. She swallowed hard and said, "Please let me by, Mr. Trask."

He leaned his face nearer and she closed her eyes. "I'm not sure I want to do that...."

Suddenly Trask's hand was jerked from her arm. He went stumbling several steps down the path. Hannah opened her eyes and found herself looking up at the handsome, angry features of Ethan Reed.

"What's going on here, Trask?" he asked.

Trask rubbed his shoulder where Reed had wrenched it. "Nothing's going on. What the hell're you shoving me for?"

Ethan turned to Hannah. "Was this man bothering you, Mistress Forrester?"

Hannah looked from Reed to a sullen Trask. She wanted to say yes, but a servant had no right to complain about a man taking her arm. She'd heard tales of many who'd suffered much worse than that. "I'm fine, Captain Reed," she said finally. "Thank you for your concern."

Trask glowered at Reed. "Why don't you mind your own business, Reed? We're paying you good money to guide us on the trail, not to interfere in our lives."

Reed took a step toward Trask. "Once we get on that trail, Trask, your life and the lives of everyone in your party will be in my hands. You play by *my* rules. And my rules say that you'd better mind your manners."

Trask looked as if he were about to make another retort, but in the end he just turned and stalked away down the path to his house.

Ethan watched him go, then smiled at Hannah. "Now, tell me the truth. Are you all right?"

She nodded and made an attempt to return the smile.

He reached out to take her hand. "You're shaking," he said with a frown.

"No...it's just..." She couldn't come up with the right words.

Ethan slipped an comforting arm around her shoulders for just a moment, then stepped back. "If that man bothers you, I want you to let me know."

"Yes, sir," Hannah said, her voice shaky.

"Do you want me to see you home?"

"No, thank you. That won't be necessary."

He tipped his hat. "Until this evening, then," he said, and started off down the road.

Hannah turned toward home with a bemused expression. It was ironic. She'd never looked to a man for protection in her entire life. Now she had Ethan Reed offering her protection from Trask and Randolph Webster offering her protection from Reed. But as her mother used to say, Hannah could do just fine on her own. She didn't intend to take either gentleman up on his offer.

Chapter Three

Peggy Webster carried the basket of fritters into the public room, the proud tilt of her head showing that she felt grown-up serving as hostess along with her grandmother and Hannah. Janie and Bridgett Trask were watching her closely. They all attended the same school over on Mulberry Lane, but the Trask sisters rarely played with the other children, and Peggy had never gotten to know them well. The two sisters sat demurely on a low bench alongside their mother, Nancy, none of them saying a word. No one except Peggy seemed to even notice that they were there. Hugh Trask, as usual, was noticed by everyone. He'd already had several pints of Ian MacDougall's corn ale. Peggy wished the Trask family was not going west with them.

"The beans are ready, Peggy," her grandmother called from the kitchen doorway. "Just give them a final stir and bring them on out to the table. Mind your hands on the pot."

Peggy smiled shyly at Janie Trask, the older sister, and turned to go back to the kitchen. Her brother, Jacob, tugged at her skirts as she passed. "Where are the Crawfords?'' he asked. ''Benjie and I were gonna build a fort out back. Now it's almost dark.''

''I don't know where they are, Jacob. Probably busy with last-minute packing.''

''Do *you* want to build one?'' he asked without much hope.

''I'm serving the supper, helping grandmother.''

''Can I, too?''

Peggy was usually patient with her eight-year-old brother, but tonight there was too much anticipation, too much uncertainty in the air for patience. ''You're too little, Jacob, and, besides, you're a boy,'' she said shortly, stepping over him to make her way to the kitchen.

Jacob looked around forlornly. His father was busy in conversation with Mr. Trask, Mr. Baker and Captain Reed. That's where he should be, Jacob thought—with the men.

He jumped to his feet and walked over to the group who stood around the fireplace smoking long pipes that sent trails of blue smoke drifting up into the rough beams of the public room ceiling. The four men were laughing at something Captain Reed had said. Captain Reed was just about the most fascinating person Jacob had ever met. He'd been everywhere. And fought the Indians and the French and even a bear.

''Will there be bears?''

The four men looked downward at the sound of Jacob's puny voice. His father picked him up and balanced him on one arm, which Jacob felt was not at all a dignified posture for a boy who was about to become a frontiersman. He squirmed until his father put him back on the floor.

"There are lots of bears, Jacob," Reed answered, giving him a serious man-to-man look that made Jacob feel good. "We'll have to be on the lookout, because it will be up to us men to be sure that none of those bears come near our womenfolk."

The other three men smiled down at Jacob, but Reed stayed serious, and Jacob directed his answer to him. "I'll be a good lookout, Captain. I'll be looking out all the time."

Reed nodded his approval, then motioned with his pipe. "I don't suppose you smoke quite yet, Jacob?"

Jacob shook his head, his eyes fixed on the pipe. Ethan nodded once again. "Probably just as well. It's not such a great habit anyway."

In the kitchen Eliza Baker and Jeanne MacDougall were taking the turkey out of the big roasting oven built alongside the huge kitchen hearth. Hannah lifted the bean pot off its hook with her apron. "I'll carry these," she told Peggy, "and you bring out the crock of turnips. It's not quite so heavy."

"The Crawfords aren't here yet," Peggy informed the women.

"Well, the food's ready, so we're just going to have to eat," Jeanne MacDougall said. "I've never known Amos Crawford to be on time for anything in his entire life."

Jeanne had been snapping all night, Hannah thought sadly. She was fighting their departure up to the very last minute. Hannah couldn't blame her for her resentment. It must be terrible to lose your only grandchildren this way. But in some ways it was hard for Hannah to identify with the forceful Scotswoman. Except for her mother, who had sometimes lived in a dreamworld where Hannah could not reach her, Hannah herself had never had a family to cling to. She had tried over these past few days to be tolerant of Mrs. MacDougall's bad humor, which had worsened when Hannah had turned down the MacDougalls' offer to buy out her indenture. Hannah suspected that Mrs. MacDougall had secretly hoped that when Hannah refused to go west, Randolph would abandon the idea.

She left the kitchen and started toward the tables, holding the solid iron bean pot awkwardly with both hands. Ethan Reed's eyes went to her instantly, and he stopped in midsentence to cross the room to her. "I'll take that, mistress. It's too heavy for a slender young lady like yourself. And, besides, you'll ruin that lovely pinafore."

His hands brushed hers as he took the pot from her. "It's just an old apron," Hannah murmured in embarrassment, noting that every head in the room was turned to watch them.

Randolph set his pipe deliberately in its holder on the mantel, then walked over to Hannah. "I didn't realize that you needed help, Hannah. Just let me know what you would like me to do."

"Goodness, Mr. Webster. We've more than enough hands in the kitchen as it is. Everything's ready as soon as we bring out—"

The door opened and the tardy Crawford family came trooping in. Amos held one of the twins in his arms. Hannah didn't know if it was Hope or Patience. It was impossible to tell them apart. Benjamin and Thomas followed him, their expressions glum, and Martha came last, holding the other girl. Jacob ran immediately over to Benjamin and thumped him on the back. "We're going to be lookouts for the bears," he blurted to his friend.

"Evening, Amos, Mrs. Crawford," Randolph said with a nod. "Come on in. We're just ready to eat."

None of the Crawfords returned Randolph's welcoming smile. Amos's eyes darted nervously around the room. "I reckon there's something I need to tell you all first," he said.

"What's the matter?" Randolph asked, immediately alert. He and Amos had been schoolboy friends together and knew each other like brothers.

"There's no easy way to say it." Amos set his daughter down, then straightened up slowly. "We're not going to be able to go along with you."

There was a moment of silence, then Hugh Trask said loudly, "You'd better be joking, Crawford. There's no way you can pull out of this now."

Amos kept his eyes on Randolph, who looked as if he shared Trask's sentiment. "What's the problem, Amos?" he asked quietly.

Martha Crawford had let down the other twin, and the two little girls went running over to Peggy, who was their particular favorite. "Mama was crying," one of them said before Peggy motioned them to be silent.

"We just can't do it," Amos said, his own voice breaking. "I was fooling myself to think we could handle this. The girls are no more than babes, and the boys aren't old enough yet to be of much help. Martha says she's tired all the time as it is."

Seth Baker was still leaning against the mantel with his pipe. "You signed on like the rest of us, Amos. We agreed to pay the captain, here, among the four families."

"We'll pay if we have to," Martha Crawford said, coming forward to support her husband. "But we'll not be going. I'm not taking my babies out to be slaughtered by wild Indians."

"That's exactly what I've been saying," Jeanne MacDougall hollered from the kitchen.

"Well, why didn't you say that months ago when we started making all the plans?" Trask asked Martha, his face florid.

She took her husband's arm. "We didn't think it through. I'll admit it. And if we have to pay the price, then so be it. But we're not going west."

Amos looked helplessly at Randolph, who tried to reason with her. "The Indian problem is mostly over now, Martha. The killing was back when the French were out there urging the Indians to kill the English, sometimes paying them to kill."

"Well, the French are gone. Nobody's paying them now," she retorted. "But they say that Pontiac's Ottawa warriors seized a British fort just last month."

Ethan had been listening to the exchange in silence, but now he stepped forward. "The British wouldn't be allowing settlers to stake out land if they didn't think it was safe, Mrs. Crawford. Though I grant you, there's always a risk. Pontiac's the strongest leader the Indians have had in some time. And he's unpredictable."

"They can't back out now, can they, Reed?" Hugh Trask asked him.

"I don't see how you're going to force someone to enter into an expedition like this one," Ethan answered calmly. "You need to have people who are able and *willing*."

Trask looked around the room. "My wife's got a kid in the oven, but you don't hear us bellyaching about how tough it's going to be."

Everyone except Hannah looked over at Nancy Trask in surprise. "You're with child, Mrs. Trask?" Randolph asked.

Nancy turned beet red and looked down at the floor.

"Is this wise, Trask?" Randolph asked. "Are you sure you want to take your wife away from civilization at a time like this, away from all medical care?"

Trask shrugged. "I reckon the tyke'll be born just as well there as here."

Randolph shook his head and turned back to the Crawfords. "All the more reason we need you folks. Isn't there anything we can say to change your minds?"

Hannah felt a pang of sympathy for Amos Crawford, who looked as though his life's dream had just been ripped away from him. But she had had her misgivings about the Crawfords from the beginning, and the haggard circles under Martha Crawford's eyes attested to a hard-fought decision made over many sleepless nights. She hoped Randolph would not press his friend too hard.

"We've decided," Amos said firmly. "I'm sorry to leave you one family short on such little notice, but I'm afraid our decision is final."

Ethan looked around at the solemn faces. "Do you want to postpone the trip until we recruit another family?" he asked. "It might mean waiting until next spring."

Randolph was already shaking his head. "No. We're all set to go. The Bakers and the Trasks have already sold their places. We'll just have to make do with the ones who are left."

"I'm sorry," Amos said again. Martha gripped his arm more tightly, and he patted her hand. The two boys looked down at their shoes, and Tommy wiped his hand across his nose.

Ethan broke the silence. "If it's all decided," he said, giving Hannah a quick wink, "then I say it's time to eat."

It was more wrenching than any of them had anticipated to leave the rambling white clapboard house at the end of Stratford Lane with all its memories of Priscilla and happier times. Peggy had clung to her grandmother with heartbreaking sobs. Jacob, whose dreams of conquering the West with his friend Benjie by his side had been abruptly crushed, had been sullen and untalkative. Randolph had spent a few last minutes in the bedroom he had shared with his wife and had emerged with red eyes.

They'd ridden all day mostly in silence—a motley-looking train of horses and mules and one jackass that Randolph had purchased, claiming that he had heard of the animal's reputation as a strong pack animal. It pulled a small two-wheeled cart that they had decided to bring along against Ethan Reed's recommendations. Hannah thought the beast looked mean and did her best to stay out of its way.

Their midday rest had been brief, so Ethan had allowed them to stop and make camp early in deference to those who were not used to an entire day on the trail, which was all of them.

Hannah stood looking out at the small river they'd been following and pulled her cloak more securely around her. It was a wool cloak that had belonged to Priscilla. She'd been reluctant to take it, but Randolph had told her that if they were to be pioneers, they couldn't indulge in foolish sentiment. The cloak was practical and warm and would serve her well on the trail.

The sun had already set on the other side of the river, and the night promised to be chilly. Randolph had explained that it was necessary to leave as soon as possible so that they would have plenty of time to build secure cabins before the next winter, but Hannah was wishing that they'd been able to wait at least until May.

She supposed if she got busy, she'd warm up. There was firewood to gather and food to prepare and tents to pitch. But for just a moment more she wanted to stand and watch the rushing waters—waters that were rushing west. To a wide open land where perhaps no white woman had ever trod. It raised bumps on her skin just to think about it.

"Hannah, are you all right? You're not too weary from the ride?" Randolph came up beside her. His voice sounded tired.

She turned to smile at him. She was starting to get used to this new, more solicitous side of her employer. "I'll admit that I'm a bit sore...er...where one might expect after all day on a mule, but other than that I'm fine. It's all of you I'm worried about."

Randolph rubbed two fingers along the bridge of his nose. "It's been a wearying day, I vow. The bairns have held up bravely, but it's hard..."

"I know," Hannah said softly, putting her hand on his sleeve. "'Tis hard to leave behind the memories. I had the same problem leaving England. But soon the children will be involved in their new life—and so will you."

"And we'll be so blamed busy we won't have time for self-pity," he said with a sad half smile. "It's too bad about the Crawfords. Jacob was counting on being with Benjamin."

"Aye. We didn't need another disappointment."

Their gazes went over to the camp fire. Ethan was showing Jacob how to tie up a turkey by the neck and hang it over the open fire. "Now take this piece of bark, Jacob," he told the boy. who seemed to hang on his every word. "Try to catch the juices as they drip off and then pour them back over the bird."

"What's that for?" Jacob watched intently as the big man who knelt beside him demonstrated his basting technique.

"It makes the turkey tender and juicy. Your sister and Mistress Hannah are going to be downright pea green with envy when they taste what a bird you've cooked."

Jacob grinned and took the curved piece of bark from Ethan.

Hannah turned back to her employer. "At least it looks like he's happy for the moment."

Randolph was watching his son and their guide with a frown. "He'll burn his hand off if he doesn't have a care."

Hannah was surprised at his hostile tone. "Captain Reed appears to be watching him closely enough."

"It's not Captain Reed's job to be watching my son," he snapped.

Hannah's jaw dropped. After all his kind remarks to her, she couldn't believe that Randolph meant his comment as a reprimand from employer to servant.

Yet it *was* her responsibility to be watching his children.

"Would you like me to tell him to move away from the fire?" she asked, her voice tightening.

Randolph looked down at her in surprise. "No! That is ... I didn't mean to imply that you aren't doing your duty, Hannah. What a preposterous idea. I've told you before—the children and I would be lost without you."

"I thought you sounded irritated, sir."

Randolph looked over again at Jacob and the captain. "I'm just tired, Hannah. I'm sorry. It's been a difficult day."

"I'm sure we'll all feel better as soon as we leave the goodbyes behind us and get farther down the trail."

Randolph smiled at her. "Just talking to you makes me feel better, Hannah."

By the third day out, Hannah started to wonder if her prediction would ever come true. Instead of leaving behind the memories, it seemed as if they were becoming stronger. Much of the talk around the camp fire that evening had been about warm home fires and soft beds and Jeanne MacDougall's apple pies. Hannah had assured the children that they would be picking up such supplies as flour and lard at Fort Pitt before they started down the Ohio. She promised them that when they had their own homestead they would make pies of their own. She didn't know about apples. How long did it take to grow an apple tree, she wondered?

The truth was that, with the possible exception of Ethan Reed and young Jacob, all of them were in varying degrees of physical misery.

Peggy and the two Trask girls giggled over their oddly placed pains in secret, and Hannah could see that a slow bond was beginning to form among them in the way that it does with young girls. The friendship was good for Peggy, who had been isolated for too long, but it left Jacob more alone than ever.

Seth and Eliza, by far the oldest members of the group, had ridden along without complaint, quietly protective of each other and unfailingly cheerful with everyone.

Nancy Trask had also made no protest at the long hours on the trail. The previous afternoon Hugh had loudly proclaimed to the entire party that his "arse" was as raw as a skinned chicken and he wasn't going another mile. Ethan had calmly invited him to follow at whatever pace he liked and then had continued on up the trail with the rest of the group following docilely behind.

As for Randolph, Hannah wasn't quite sure what to think about her employer's condition. He had not complained, certainly, but neither had he been the buoyant adventurer who she had watched plan this journey. His enthusiasm for the trip seemed to have disappeared, and when he spoke to her at all, it was with a diffidence that she had never before noticed in him.

She didn't know exactly when it was that she had begun to suspect that Randolph's uncharacteristic churlishness toward Ethan came from a kind of jealousy of the frontiersman's attention to Hannah herself. It was hard to believe, because it implied that Randolph held some sort of regard for Hannah beyond that of an employer, which he had never before given her reason to suppose. And, of course, any thought of jealousy was absurd, because Hannah was sure that Ethan Reed's compliments to her and smiles and winks meant nothing. He treated gray-haired Eliza Baker with the same mockingly flirtatious manner.

"A penny for your thoughts, mistress."

Hannah jumped as Ethan's voice came out of the darkness. Most of the group had retired for the night. Hannah had tried to go to sleep earlier in the little tent she shared with Peggy and Jacob, but had been unable to find a comfortable position for her jolted bones. Finally she had given up and come out to sit by the fire. She turned as Ethan approached carrying two logs, each one as big around as her waist.

"These will burn through the night," he said, putting them on the fire. He dusted off his hands, then dropped down beside her. "Now, tell me. What has put that furrow into your lovely brow?" His hand neared her face but didn't touch her.

Hannah tried to pull her thoughts away from her speculation about Randolph and Ethan. She hoped mind reading was not among the captain's many talents. "I didn't know anyone was awake," she said, avoiding his question.

"So why are you still up?"

Hannah shrugged. "I couldn't sleep. Too sore, I think. I've never ridden before, at least not like this."

"You've been a brave girl about it. All of you have done well, really. Before long you'll all have calluses in the places you need them the most."

"I never thought I'd find that idea attractive," Hannah said with a little chuckle, "but I can't wait."

Ethan laughed. "I've a bottle of whiskey that could ease some of those aches, but I'm afraid if I bring it out there'll be no handling Trask."

"You seem to handle him well enough."

"I've dealt with his type before along the trail. I can't imagine how a woman as sweet as Nancy Trask ended up with a lout like him."

Hannah felt a sudden unfamiliar twist. She'd just been thinking about jealousy, but that surely could *not* be what she was experiencing at this moment. Nancy Trask had a kind of fragile beauty that she imagined was appealing to men. Her glossy black hair and creamy white skin made her stand out among people whose coloring was not so extreme.

"Mrs. Trask is lovely, isn't she?" she commented, looking back at the fire.

Ethan turned his head toward her sharply. "She's fair enough. I just hope she's a lot stronger than she looks, and that her babe holds off until we reach our destination."

Hannah gave an exclamation of dismay. "Oh, but it must! She'd not have the baby out here on the trail."

"Babies have a way of coming into the world on their own schedule."

The very idea of Nancy Trask giving birth in the middle of the wilderness drove all thoughts of jealousy out of Hannah's head. "What would we do?"

"How many babies have you helped birth?" he asked her.

Hannah's eyes grew round. "None. I suppose Eliza may know more about it."

"Well, we menfolk aren't likely to be of much help, so it will be up to you two."

For the first time it really hit Hannah what it meant to be leaving civilization. In London she and her mother had often had to forgo necessities for lack of money, but at least she had known that help was available if it came to an emergency. And in Philadelphia, caring for Priscilla, she had lacked for nothing, except the divine power to overcome an incurable disease. "We'll just have to make do," she said, trying to sound confident. "I'll talk things over with Eliza tomorrow."

"Good. As I've said before, Mistress Hannah. I like your attitude. It will serve you well in the West."

Unlike the frivolous compliments the captain was wont to disperse, this one seemed sincere. "Thank you," she said, her voice grown hushed.

He had leaned close to her. "I find that I like lots of things about you, Mistress Hannah."

The fire grew brighter as the bark burned off the giant logs. She hoped the sudden blaze was the reason why her cheeks had grown so warm. But the height of the fire would not explain her cold hands. Hannah rubbed them together. "Now you are bantering with me again, Captain, and as I have explained before, it's not seemly."

An expression of annoyance flickered briefly in his eyes, then passed. He leaned even closer to her, until she could see the reflections of the flames in the dark centers of his eyes. "Do you like sweets, mistress?" he asked very softly.

"I beg your pardon?" Hannah was finding it hard to breathe normally with his face just inches from hers.

Abruptly he sat back and pulled a paper packet from inside his buckskin coat. "Horehound drops," he said. He pulled something out of the paper and reached over to her. His fingers pushed the candy into her mouth, then lingered ever so briefly on her warm lips.

The slick, minty candy felt good against her tongue. After a moment of surprise, she smiled.

"The Creeks say that if you fall asleep with something sweet on your lips, you'll have sweet dreams the whole night through," Ethan said, popping one of the drops into his own mouth.

"I thought we were only supposed to bring essentials along on this trip, Captain Reed," Hannah said with mock disapproval.

"Horehound's an essential as far as I'm concerned. It's the main reason I head back east every now and then. There's not much else in so-called civilization that interests me."

"You have a sweet tooth?"

"Yes, ma'am."

"But surely there are *some* other things you miss from the city?" she asked, talking around the piece of candy still in her mouth.

As she waited for his answer, a log cracked, sending sparks up into the velvety blackness of the sky. Her gaze followed them upward, then scanned the clearing Ethan had chosen for their campsite. The woods seemed to enclose them in their own little world, smelling of smoke and moist, spring-scented earth.

"No, I can't say that I miss much," he was saying, his eyes on the fire. "Sometimes I miss reading. Books are hard to come by out West, and newspapers are already history by the time we get them."

"Don't you have family, friends that you miss?"

Ethan's head came up. "I have friends at Fort Pitt. They're all I need."

His tone had grown colder, as if closing off discussion about anything personal. Hannah sat uncertainly for a moment, then said. "I should try to sleep now."

Ethan stood with her and offered the paper of candy. "Would you like another one?"

Hannah took one of the drops. "Thank you. So now we're guaranteed to have sweet dreams tonight. Is that the idea?"

Ethan's dark eyes held hers. "I already have mine planned."

Chapter Four

Ethan had driven his inexperienced party from Philadelphia as hard as he thought possible over the past two days. He knew that tempers were growing short. Both the people and the animals needed a rest. But this particular section of the trail was Seneca territory, and he wanted to get through it as soon as possible.

The Seneca had been peaceful of late, but just before he'd left Philadelphia, he'd had word from an old Rogers's Rangers comrade that Pontiac was urging the Seneca to join with his Ottawa and the Potawatomi in an alliance against the increasing numbers of British settlers moving into the Ohio River valley. He hoped the report was just another alarmist account like the ones they constantly used to hear at Fort Pitt. He certainly was not going to frighten his charges with vague possibilities. But he wasn't willing to completely ignore the report when the lives of women and children could be at stake. Once they were out of range of the Susquehanna River and closer to Fort Pitt, he'd slow down the pace.

In the meantime, he made it a point to be in the lead during the day with his musket close at hand and to sleep as little as possible each night. He had hopes that

Hannah Forrester would have a another attack of insomnia and join him at the camp fire late at night, but he had seen no sign of her for the past four evenings. It was just as well. His mind was sharper when it wasn't fixed on an attractive woman. And Hannah was definitely attractive. Even after more than a week on the trail, her hair shone as bright as a field of spring buttercups. And each morning she awakened fresh and blooming, her eyes sparkling like the waters of the river they followed. He had not heard a single complaining word from her. When the others became sullen as he urged them on for an additional mile at the end of a long day, she did her best to put heart back into the group.

As if his thoughts had conjured her up, Hannah suddenly appeared at the edge of the circle of firelight. Her thick blond hair was out of its customary braid, falling loose around her shoulders. Ethan had an almost uncontrollable urge to touch it.

"Do you ever sleep?" she asked.

Ethan smiled. "Fits and starts. You get used to it out on the trail. A full night's sleep is rare."

Her hands were at her waist, pulling on her shawl, unconsciously stretching it tightly across her full breasts. Ethan felt his body stir. "Would you sit with me a spell?" he asked.

She nodded and stepped around the fire to sink down next to him on a large log. "I see you here every night, long after everyone else has gone to sleep. Yet you're always the first one up in the morning, though I myself have awakened before dawn."

He shrugged. "We've an eternity to sleep, I reckon. No sense trying to get it all in at once."

"I thought perhaps there was some reason you were keeping watch. Some danger?"

He could tell her the truth. She didn't seem to be one of the hysterical-type females he'd known so well in Boston. But she might feel it her duty to tell her employer, and before long he'd have a whole train of overly skittish charges ready to shoot off their rifles at the belching of a squirrel.

He grinned at her. "Mayhap it's those sweet dreams of mine that are keeping me awake."

"Captain Reed . . ." she began in an admonishing tone.

Ethan held up his hand. His face became serious and he said, "Actually, I do have a problem."

Hannah was instantly attentive.

"I've finished my horehound drops," he said. His eyes fixed on her mouth. "I've nothing sweet to put on my lips before I sleep."

Hannah had seen Captain Reed sitting by the fire each evening since their first late-night encounter, but she had deliberately kept to her bed to avoid another meeting. She was afraid of him. Or rather, she was afraid of the odd feelings he engendered in her head and in her body. Her mother had warned her off all men, and since her mother's death her status as a servant had precluded any kind of relationship. She was twenty-one years old. By that age most of the girls back on the East End had half a dozen babies to raise.

The captain closed the distance between them on the log and kissed her lightly on the cheek. "There," he said, now smiling. "That should be enough to sweeten my dreams this night."

The press of his lips lingered on her face. It had been her first kiss from a man, and it hadn't been the least bit evil, as her mother had always warned. It had been gentle and tender and made her feel pleasantly quivery inside.

Unconsciously she lifted two fingers to touch the spot he had kissed.

"Your skin is softer than a babe's," he said, his hand lifting to cover hers.

She jumped back. She hadn't come out to the camp fire for more of Captain Reed's audacious flirting. She had wanted to talk with him seriously. But around this man her normally intelligent conversation turned to mush.

"Please, Captain Reed. I must ask you once again to behave more decorously. I'm not used to...this kind of teasing."

"You've had too serious a life, Mistress Hannah. I could see that from the first day I met you there in the tavern. You'd the look of a beautiful lass who was living away her life doing for other folks without ever knowing—without ever exploring—what it would be like to live for herself for a change."

"I find a great deal of satisfaction in 'living for others,' as you put it. And even if I didn't, I'm bound by contract to do so for a good long time yet."

"How long?"

"My indenture with Mr. Webster runs another three years."

Ethan gave a low whistle. "You'll be an old woman by then. You'd better start doing a few things for yourself right away."

"I'm perfectly satisfied with my life the way it is, Captain Reed." She made her voice aloof, trying to put an end to the direction of their conversation.

He went on as if she hadn't spoken. "Things such as not feeling guilty about wanting to come sit out under the stars with a fine fellow like myself. And giving yourself the liberty to feel the pull between us. It's one of the oldest feelings of mankind, and it's tugging mightily at my innards right now. Tell me you don't feel it, too, Hannah."

She sucked in a gulp of smoky air. "Captain, I came here tonight because I needed to talk to you—no other reason."

Ethan pulled back and surveyed her. Her expression was hostile and, yes, afraid. It was hard to believe that a beauty such as Hannah Forrester had reached this age without becoming involved with any men, but he didn't know what else to make of her fear. She was not shy in any other aspect of daily life that he had seen of her. In spite of her status as a servant, she had no trouble speaking her mind to him or any other member of the expedition on any number of subjects. A dark thought entered his head. Perhaps some unscrupulous lout like Hugh Trask had hurt her in the past, and that was what made her look at him like a rabbit caught in a trap.

"What was it you needed to talk to me about?" he asked gently.

"Nancy Trask. This pace is too much for her. She's growing weaker each day, and Eliza says if she doesn't rest, she'll not have the strength left for the birthing when the time comes."

Ethan tore his thoughts away from Hannah and her past. "I warned the Trasks before they came that it would be difficult for her."

"Perhaps it was a mistake for them to come, but that doesn't alter the fact that she's wearing out, and we have to do something about it."

Ethan stood and paced to the other side of the fire. "We can't stop yet. I have to think of the welfare of the whole group."

Hannah stood up, indignant. "So ask them. I'm certainly willing to stop. And I'm sure Mr. Webster and the Bakers will not object."

He shook his head. "I'm sorry."

Hannah couldn't believe what she was hearing. Just a few moments ago Ethan had sounded caring and tender. He'd implied that he had some feelings for her, and she had begun to believe that those feelings involved more than the male lust her mother had talked about. But perhaps her mother had been right, after all. She glared at him across the flames. He looked big and menacing as the firelight flickered red across his dark face. "I can't believe you won't stop and let her rest for just a day. Why should there be such a hurry?" Hannah asked, her voice pleading.

"I told all of you who signed on this trip that my authority on the trail has to be absolute. We head out tomorrow as usual."

Hannah would have shouted at him if she hadn't been afraid of waking up the entire camp. Instead she put her hands on her hips and said as forcefully as she could, "Mrs. Trask's life is in your hands!"

"All of your lives are in my hands," he replied with irritating calmness.

Hannah removed her hands from her hips and crossed her arms. Then she uncrossed them. She tried to think of something more to say. Ethan continued to watch her silently. Finally she gave a huff of irritation and marched back to her tent.

Hannah was not willing to give up and let Captain Reed have the final word. He might be their guide, but he evidently didn't have the humanity to see that one of their group was suffering. She approached Randolph as he was leading two of the horses down to the river for a drink. He turned to her with the new, special smile that seemed to be just for her and that still startled her each time she saw it. "Good morning, Hannah. Did you and my bairns sleep well last night?"

"Good morrow, sir. We slept fine, but I've a concern I'd like to discuss with you."

Randolph dropped the horses' leads and let them move to the river's edge. "What is it? You look upset."

"It's Mrs. Trask. She needs some time to rest before we move on. I talked to Captain Reed about it last night, and he absolutely refuses to stop."

Webster frowned. "You talked to Reed?"

"Aye. He gave me no reason whatsoever, simply refused to slow down our progress for any cause."

"When did you talk to him, Hannah?"

Hannah had the impression that her employer was more concerned about her conversation with the captain than about the health of Mrs. Trask. "Last night by the camp fire. I couldn't sleep, so I decided to take the opportunity to approach him after everyone else had retired."

"I don't like you talking with him alone."

Hannah shook her head in exasperation. She had yet to sort out her feelings about her meeting with

Ethan Reed. But it frustrated her that Randolph was
focusing on that rather than the matter at hand. First
the captain, now Randolph. Why was it so difficult for
them to pay attention to the health of a pregnant
woman? They seemed to have everything else on their
minds but what she was telling them.

"Mrs. Trask is too weak to travel," she repeated in
a slow, deliberate voice. "I'd like your help to convince Captain Reed that we should take a day of rest."

Finally Randolph seemed to grasp what she was
telling him. "Is she sick?" he asked.

"No. But the babe is weighing heavily on her. Eliza
says that if we're not careful, she could have it right
out here on the trail."

Randolph grew pale. Hannah remembered that in
the first year of her indenture Mrs. Webster had suffered a miscarriage. Her disease was already in evi-
dence by then, and Hannah had privately thought the
loss was a fortunate thing for the health of her mistress. But Mr. Webster had been extremely upset.
"Then we must stop and let Mrs. Trask rest," he said.

Hannah gave a wan smile. "That's what I've been
saying."

They left the horses drinking and went to find
Ethan, recruiting Eliza along the way. The captain was
at the back of the campsite fixing a broken cinch. He
looked up as the three approached him, his smile fad-
ing when he saw the determined expressions on their
faces.

"Good morning," he said mildly.

"I understand that Hannah talked with you yesterday about Mrs. Trask's condition and you refused to
listen," Randolph started out bluntly.

Ethan put the saddle to one side and stood, towering over all of them, even Randolph. "I listened to her. I just wasn't able to accede to her request."

In the harsh morning sunlight he looked every inch the woodsman, his broad chest filling out his buckskin jacket and his dark brown hair flowing freely down to his shoulders. Hannah felt her pulse quicken as she watched him facing her employer, his full mouth set in a pleasant smile that did not reach his eyes. She couldn't believe that last night he had pressed that mouth to her skin.

Randolph appeared not the least intimidated by the captain's size. "It so happens, Captain, that *we* are paying *you,* not the other way around. Which means if we want to stop a day, then that's our decision."

Ethan's eyes narrowed almost imperceptibly. "You're wrong, Webster. I take it you've never been in the army? You can think of this as a campaign. You all are the soldiers . . . and I'm the general."

"You can call yourself a captain if you like, Reed, but we're not in any damn army. You're a hired hand, and we're your employers. You'll do as we say."

There was no longer any pretense of a smile. "That's not the way it works, Webster. If you feel that way, I have no choice but to take you all back to Philadelphia."

The two men sized each other up like rival bulls, but Hannah could see that, whereas Randolph was losing his temper, Ethan kept his on a careful leash. There was no doubt in her mind who was the more dangerous. And she was not about to let their antagonism flare into open combat.

"Gentlemen," she said sharply. "It's not doing any good to have the two of you glaring at each other.

Can't we sit down and discuss this like civilized people?"

Ethan turned to her. His voice was calm enough, but it was obvious that his irritation now extended to her. "There's nothing to discuss, mistress. Perhaps I should have explained to you more fully last night, but it seemed I had other things on my mind." His eyes skimmed briefly over her face. Hannah tried to hold steady, but finally dropped her gaze and engaged herself in smoothing her cotton skirt. After a moment, Ethan continued, "I also did not want to alarm the group."

"Alarm us about what, Captain Reed?" Eliza Baker asked.

Ethan turned toward her, instantly respectful. "There are Seneca through this stretch of the trail, ma'am. They aren't normally any trouble, but there've been a few rumors lately, and I didn't want to take any chances."

"Of course not," Eliza said. She had the slightly quavery, calming voice of the grandmother she would now never be. "How much longer will we be at risk, Captain?"

"We should be out of their territory within two days, maybe three."

"Let's get moving then," she said briskly. "I'll give Nancy Trask some of my tonic this morning, and tonight I'll brew her some sassafras tea to make her sleep. We'll keep her going until you decide on a safe place for us to stop."

Ethan gave the round little woman a grateful smile. Then he nodded curtly to Randolph and Hannah and strode briskly away.

* * *

Randolph kept his horse in line next to Hannah's mule all that day, except for a short time around noon when he rode back to inquire as to the condition of Nancy Trask. The pregnant woman had appeared to be embarrassed that an argument had taken place on her account, and before they started out that morning she had assured everyone that she was perfectly fine. And, indeed, whether it was sheer power of will or Eliza's tonic, her cheeks did have a bit of color for the first time in several days. Hugh Trask had been irritated at all the fuss, apparently feeling that it implied that he couldn't take care of his own wife. He told Randolph as much when he came to inquire, and said brusquely that he'd thank him and the rest of the party to stay out of their affairs.

Hannah also found herself regretting the morning's confrontation, and she wanted to find a moment to talk alone with Captain Reed. She did not intend to apologize exactly. After all, if he had explained to her about the Indians when she had first come to him with the issue, she would have understood and would never have gotten others involved. But she did feel bad that the morning's incident had not helped the frosty relations between the captain and Randolph. An unspoken rivalry had grown between them even before they had left Philadelphia, and Hannah was still hoping that it had nothing to do with her. Both men were capable and intelligent. Both had congenial personalities and got along well with others. She couldn't understand why the antagonism had developed.

The long day passed with Captain Reed pushing the party an extra hour to try to cover as much territory as possible. It wasn't until they had pitched camp and eaten a cold dinner of salted pork and corn cakes that Hannah finally was able to talk with their guide. He was alone staking down the animals for the night. Randolph was busy in the tent playing with his children before saying good-night. Hannah walked in the darkness over to Ethan.

He smiled at her as she approached, but his welcome was not as warm as it had been on their previous meetings.

She did not waste time on preliminaries. "I'm sorry about the problems this morning," she said. "You should have explained to me about the danger right from the beginning."

It was hard to see his expression in the darkness. "Perhaps I should have," he said simply.

"I . . . it's possibly my fault for becoming agitated. I didn't wait for an explanation."

He leaned to pull a saddle off a speckled gelding that Peggy and Jacob had been riding together. Hannah had helped Peggy split her skirts so that she could ride a straight saddle without sacrificing her feminine modesty. "You became agitated, mistress, but that wasn't why you didn't get your explanation. I didn't want to create alarm about the Indians, because most likely we won't even encounter any."

"You yourself said I was not a hysterical female, Captain Reed."

Ethan came around the front of the horse and stood close to her. "Yes. But you are a stubborn one. Next time I'll thank you not to question my decisions. The welfare of the group is the first thing on my mind. I know what I'm doing."

The rebuke was probably deserved, but it stung. "Are we to understand that you are perfect, then, Captain?"

"I'm as damn near perfect a trail guide as you're going to find in these parts. And in your case, I'm the *only* trail guide you're going to find. So you'd better start listening to what I say, because your lives may depend on it."

Hannah considered his words. "It might help matters if you would defer a bit to Mr. Webster. After all, he was the one who organized this expedition and hired you."

"And hiring me was about the only thing the blamed fool has done right. He plans a settlement made up of one family with a sick, pregnant woman, two old people who should be sitting in rocking chairs back on their porches in Philadelphia, and a third family who backs out at the very last minute." He shook his head and gave a soft slap to the flank of the horse next to them.

Hannah found herself wanting to defend her employer. "He couldn't know that the Crawfords would withdraw from the expedition, or that Mrs. Trask would end up with child."

Ethan bent toward her, continuing his criticism. "And then he endangers everyone by questioning my authority, just because he doesn't like the fact that, unlike him, I have good enough eyes in my head to see the kind of woman he's had living under his roof."

Around them the night had closed in again. Out in the trees the insects were celebrating the first warm night of spring with their rhythmic chirping. From the river came the call of a wild duck. Over at the campsite she could hear a low hum of voices punctuated with muffled giggles from inside the tent she normally shared with the children.

A shiver went up Hannah's back, in spite of the warm night. Her hopes that the antagonism between Ethan and Randolph had nothing to do with her died. She had tried to discount the notion as absurd. She couldn't deny that Ethan had taken notice of her, but she had the impression that he was the kind of man who would take notice of almost any woman who happened to be at hand. And it was true that she had had more attention from Randolph in the past two weeks than in the two years that she had worked for him, but it was surely not attention of a romantic nature.

"Mr. Webster just wants this venture to be a success," she said at last. "To suggest that he would jeopardize it because of some sort of competition over me or any woman is ridiculous. And, as I explained to you before we even started this journey, Mr. Webster has no feelings of that type for me."

"You're sure about that." He moved so close that, in spite of the darkness, she could see the stubble of his beard.

"Absolutely," she said firmly.

"He has no romantic interest in you?"

"None whatsoever." She tried to take a step backward, only to find that her back was smack against the long neck of the horse.

"Then he won't mind if I do what I've been thinking about since last night at the camp fire." He lifted her against him, the muscles of his arms hard across her back. His lips were soft, gently compelling. They were warm and dry at first, but then drew moisture from hers with a half nibble and the tentative noninvasive stroke of his tongue.

Hannah felt her body turn to jelly inside, pleasantly, amazingly. He was the one to pull away.

"He won't object?" Ethan asked again, a husky undertone to his deep voice.

Hannah blinked hard, trying to comprehend what he had asked her.

"Your employer," Ethan prodded.

She pulled away from him, jostling the horse who tossed its head and gave a throaty rattle of protest. "My employer has nothing to say about it," she said, trying not to sound as breathless as she felt. "But I do. I'm the one who's objecting, Captain Reed."

She turned and stumblingly made her way in the darkness back toward her tent. Ethan looked after her with a half smile on his face. He had done his share of kissing. More than his share, some might say. And he knew one thing for darn sure. There had been not the least objection in the kiss he'd just shared with Hannah Forrester.

Chapter Five

Both Hannah's and Ethan's fears came to naught.
The Philadelphia party crossed the Susquehanna River
out of Seneca territory without incident, and Nancy
Trask seemed to have finally adapted to the trail. She
attributed her recovery to Eliza Baker's tea, and the
two women had formed a friendship. Hannah had
never been able to get close to Mrs. Trask. The woman
was unfailingly polite to her, but Hannah was unable
to forget her servant status with Mrs. Trask, the way
she was with Eliza.

As a result, Hannah felt a little shut out by the new
bond between Eliza and Nancy. It added to the low
spirits that had plagued her in the two days since her
private encounter with Ethan Reed. She found herself
spending an inordinate amount of her time thinking
about the minute or so that his mouth had been in
contact with hers. In all the times she had listened to
her mother talk about the unspecified seductive wiles
of the male animal, Hannah hadn't a clue what she
had meant. Well, now she knew. She decided she
would keep her distance from both Ethan and Randolph and concentrate on making the children happy,
especially Jacob.

After supper when they all sat around the fire, it seemed that she and Jacob were the two odd ones. Nancy and Eliza talked together about their mutual friends back in Philadelphia. Peggy huddled with Janie and Bridgett to speculate about the soldiers they would meet at Fort Pitt. And the men, in spite of a continuing reserve between Ethan and Randolph, always seemed to have some topic of vital importance to discuss, such as the value of the bayonet in armed conflict.

The feeling of isolation concerned her more for Jacob's sake than her own. Her life with her mother had been a solitary one. The circumstances of her birth had precluded their entry into certain levels of society. Friendships had been discouraged. But Jacob had always been a gregarious, sunny child, and she didn't want him to end up changing into a loner. She tried to engage him in conversation as often as possible, and she was grateful for the times when Ethan would turn to him and include him in the men's conversations. Their guide seemed to remember the boy's presence more often than his own father did.

"Would you like to go on a hunting party tomorrow, Jacob?" Ethan asked on the night they finally reached the place where he had declared that they could stop and rest a day.

Jacob's cheeks grew pink with pleasure. "Shooting? Shooting bears?"

Ethan laughed and reached over to ruffle Jacob's shaggy blond hair. "Probably not bears. I don't think we'd be able to carry a whole bear along with us on the trail, and a good woodsman only shoots what he can eat or carry."

Jacob scrambled to his feet and went to stand beside his father. "I can go, can't I, Papa?" He held on to his father's shoulder and did a little dance with his feet as he asked Ethan, "What will we be hunting, then?"

"Grouse, most likely. Ducks, turkey, quail. Maybe a squirrel or two."

The list evidently did not quite fit Jacob's hopes, but in a minute he had regained his enthusiasm.

"Will you be using the Sure Shot?" he asked, using Ethan's pet name for his long rifle. He had told the children a number of stories about how the gun had saved his life during his time with Rogers's Rangers.

"I wouldn't go hunting without it," Ethan replied.

Jacob turned to his father. "May I go, Papa? I want to see Captain Reed fire the Sure Shot. And may I try shooting, too?"

Randolph looked as if he were about to deny his son's request, but then he took a good look at the boy's eager face and said, "You may try one of the fowling pieces. Not a rifle quite as yet."

Jacob beamed. "May I load it and everything?"

Randolph nodded. "But if you're to be a hunter tomorrow, it's to bed with you now."

Hannah rose to her feet immediately. "I'll take him. But first . . ." She looked over at the men, keeping to the side of the circle where Randolph sat with Hugh Trask and Seth. She avoided meeting Ethan Reed's gaze. "Do you think I might go with you tomorrow, too?"

"Hunting?" Randolph asked with a little frown.

"Yes. I . . . I was thinking it would be a good thing for me to know, now that we'll be living in the wilderness."

"Hunting is for menfolk," Trask said.

Hannah looked at her employer. "I'd like to learn," she said.

Randolph's expression was doubtful, but before he could say anything, Ethan answered for him. "I don't see any reason why Mistress Forrester shouldn't join us if she wishes."

Randolph's eyes went from Hannah to Reed, then back to Hannah. "All right. I have no objection."

Ethan ignored the slight strain in Webster's voice and turned to Jacob, whose happy grin was starting to droop with sleepiness. "So, no slugabeds tomorrow morning, lad. Those birds won't wait for us."

"I'll be ready, sir," Jacob said, standing straight. Then he put his small hand into Hannah's and turned with her toward their tent.

It felt good to be walking instead of rocking in a saddle, Hannah thought as her skirts swished against the tall marsh grasses. She lifted her head to breathe in the spring air. It smelled like freshly cut hay. They'd started out early that morning, leaving the three girls and Nancy Trask sleeping. Only Eliza had been awake to bid them good luck. They'd traveled downriver until they'd reached a wide slough that stretched out to the south. Now they were following along its edge. Jacob barely reached above the weeds at times, but he marched proudly forward, carrying a small fowling musket that Ethan had lent him for the day.

Hannah, herself, carried no gun. It appeared that none of the men had actually taken her desire to learn to shoot seriously. But she didn't intend to let the day go by without giving it a try.

Seth Baker had bagged the first prize of the day, a homing pigeon that had sat prettily in a tree for him without moving a feather. But the grouse that had been flushed out of a clump of bushes by the sound of their arrival had gotten away. Randolph had shouted that the bird was his, and then had badly missed his shot. Hannah remembered Jeanne MacDougall's comments about her son-in-law's hunting ability, and she hoped her employer would do better as the day went on.

"There are too many of us," Ethan said as they came to the edge of a brackish pond. "We're making too much noise." He pointed to the other men's boots. He, himself, had switched from his riding boots to a type of moccasin that was bound around his legs up to the knee. "Stay here and let me circle around the pond. Then I'll scare whatever's there over in your direction."

They nodded agreement and watched as Ethan made his way without a sound to the other side of the water.

"Can I shoot now, Papa?" Jacob asked in a loud whisper.

"Not yet, Jacob," his father answered. "Let us get a few birds first, and then I'll help you with your gun."

When Ethan was directly opposite them, he took a large stick and threw it into the middle of the pond. Immediately came the sounds of splashing and squawks and three blue-black teal lifted from the water flying toward them.

Seth, Hugh and Randolph all raised their rifles at once. "That one's mine," Randolph hollered as one of the birds veered to the left. The three blasts were deafening, and sent smoke billowing around them. When it had cleared, Jacob said, "Yours kept on flying, Papa."

Seth and Hugh had each hit their mark and were walking to retrieve their game at the edge of the marsh, just where the grasses started to get mushy.

Randolph pounded the butt of his rifle into the ground and looked over at Hannah, his face chagrined. "I never was any good with these blamed things," he said.

Jacob looked up at his father, "You could use my musket, Papa. Maybe you'd have a better chance—one of the pieces of shot might hit something."

Randolph smiled. "Maybe I'll give it a try, Jacob."

But as the day wore on, it became obvious that Randolph's skill with the fowling pieces was little better than with his rifle. Ethan tried to give advice. "The birds will want to take off into the wind," he told his charges. "So you can anticipate where they'll be heading and shoot just in front of them."

The day was made for Jacob when he was able to take a pheasant at point-blank range. "I don't know if we'll ever get all the pieces of lead out of the poor bird," Ethan had whispered to Hannah, "but at least the boy's happy."

They had plenty of birds to take back when Hannah finally got up the courage to say, "Now it's my turn. Who's going to lend me a gun?"

Randolph, trying to maintain a facade of good humor in spite of his poor performance, said, "I'd *give* you mine. It's surely not doing me any good."

Ethan was just coming back from the woods where he had gone to pick up a grouse he'd shot. "A rifle would be quite a kick for you to start out. We'll use the little gun I lent Jacob."

Ethan retrieved the small musket from Jacob and tamped in a light load of shot. "Have you ever done this before?" he asked her.

Hannah shook her head. Then before she knew what was happening, Ethan had moved behind her and put his arms completely around her, holding the gun angled toward the ground. Hannah started as his body moved against hers. Her eyes went to Randolph, who was watching them with a fixed smile.

Ethan's voice was impersonal as he showed her how to position the gun against her shoulder and sight a target, but Hannah found it hard to concentrate on his instructions. His body felt warm and solid against her, bringing flashes of memories of the other night when he had held her against him and kissed her.

"Do you think you want to try it by yourself or should I help you out the first time?" he asked her, his voice deep in her ear.

Hannah wet her lips. "By myself, I think," she said, hoping her voice sounded more normal to the others than it did to herself.

Ethan stepped back. "All right. There's a wood duck in that tree yonder. See what you can do. Squeeze, don't jerk. Slow and steady."

Freed from Ethan's unsettling proximity, Hannah focused on the task at hand. She tightened her body in concentration and tried to remember everything Ethan had told her. The gun's kick was more than she had bargained for and sent her reeling backward. But she didn't fall, and when she straightened up Jacob shouted, "She got it! Hannah got it, Papa!"

Sure enough, Seth Baker was coming toward them, waving the dead duck above his head. "Nice shot, Hannah girl," he called.

"I knew you'd be a fast learner," Ethan said softly in her ear, as he took the gun from her to reload.

"Congratulations, Hannah," Randolph said. "It looks like we'll have to depend on you to bring home the food for our family."

Hannah couldn't remember having been included before as part of the "family," and she had the feeling that Randolph's words were for Ethan's sake as much as for hers. But she could also tell that Randolph's ego had taken a bruising this day, and she wished she could make him feel better. Besides, Ethan had a smug look on his face that Hannah did not like. What was it about men that made the failure of one so satisfying to the others?

She relinquished the gun and walked over to Randolph. "You've done a fine job of providing for your family for many years, Mr. Webster, and I'm sure that's not going to change. And anyway, I declare, that blast blew two years off my life. I hadn't realized."

Ethan had reloaded the gun and held it out to her. "Care to try again?"

"No. I've had enough for today, thank you."

Ethan looked around at the group. "I think we all have." He pointed at the stack of birds on the ground. "We'll dine well tonight and for some time to come."

"And I helped, didn't I, Papa?" Jacob asked proudly.

Randolph slung his rifle around to the back of his shoulder and gave a sigh. "Yes, son. You surely did help."

* * * *

The day's rest had done everyone good. Spirits were high as they sat around the fire eating their fill of the fresh meat the hunters had brought back. Jacob was happier than Hannah had seen him since they had started the trip. He had spent several minutes recounting his hunting adventures to his sister and the Trask girls, who obliged him with all the praise he had hoped for. With Peggy's help, Janie and Bridgett had started to overcome some of their shyness. Now when asked questions, they gave soft answers instead of looking down and scuffing their feet. They had started to accept Jacob in their circle and tonight were treating him very much like a little brother. Hannah watched with satisfaction as the four children laughed and began a game of shadows, using the light of the fire, which had been built higher than normal to accommodate the extra food.

Even Hugh and Nancy Trask seemed to be enjoying themselves this evening. Nancy had actually laughed out loud a time or two. And it was she who suggested that Seth bring out his fiddle after the food and dishes had been cleared away. When she smiled and the color was in her face as it was tonight, Hannah noted, she was quite beautiful. Her husband must have thought so, too, because for once he seemed to be paying her some attention and even refilled her plate when she asked for seconds. "You're eating for two now, wife," he'd said, much to Hannah's surprise. Nancy had been surprised herself, judging from the pleased, shy smile that had crept over her face.

Eliza had backed up Nancy's suggestion about the fiddle. She'd given her husband a squeeze and said, "Oh yes, Seth. You've played so little since . . ." The smile almost faded from her mouth, but after a slight adjustment she kept it firmly in place and continued, "Oh please, do play!"

It appeared to Hannah that the only person who was not in a good humor was Randolph. He ate plenty and joined with the children in a couple of rounds of shadows, but Hannah could tell that his mind was elsewhere. She was reminded of the days following Priscilla's death when he had walked the house like a blind man, not even noticing that other people were present. It was likely that seeing the Trasks together talking about their coming child, and the Bakers, who were always so tender with each other, had made him miss his wife this evening. Hannah's heart ached for him. Through the many months that she had watched him plan this trip to the West, she had held a secret fear that he was trying to run away from his grief. She knew from her own experience that it didn't work. The grief simply followed you along wherever you went.

When the children added their pleas to those of his wife, Seth unlaced one of the packs and retrieved his fiddle and bow. He unwrapped it reverently from the layers of lamb's wool he had packed it in. The girls and Jacob crowded around, and Jacob asked, "How'd you learn to play, Mr. Baker? D'you think I might be able to learn sometime?"

Seth smiled as he lovingly smoothed his hand over the polished wood. "This winter, when we're all tucked safe into our homesteads, I'll teach you, Jacob. By next spring you'll be playing a reel for our first barn dance."

Randolph had left the circle around the fire. Hannah saw that he was standing a few yards away looking out at the dark river. Quietly she walked down the bank toward him.

"Aren't you going to come listen to the music?" she asked.

He turned toward her. Even in the darkness she could see that there was pain in his eyes.

"What's wrong?" she asked.

He cleared his throat before he spoke. "I'm not much in the mood for music tonight, I guess."

"Sometimes when I'm in a bad mood, I force myself to do something cheerful, and before long I'm feeling better in spite of myself."

He attempted a smile. "You never seem to be in a bad mood, Hannah."

"Oh, but I am," she assured him. "After my mother died, I was in nothing but a bad mood for so long, I wondered if I would ever be happy again."

"But now you are?"

"Why, yes."

"Even though you are under indenture, not free to do as you please?"

"I've been very happy in your household, Mr. Webster. You know that I love the children dearly." When she had come over to comfort him, she hadn't expected to be discussing herself. "Of course, I still miss Mrs. Webster, and I know that her absence must weigh on you heavily at times."

Randolph stared out into the darkness. "Aye. It weighs on me. We had such plans, she and I. We would have taken over the inn, you know. The MacDougalls are getting too old to handle it. And we thought we'd add a relay station. This country's growing, and Philadelphia is getting more important all the time," he added, sounding wistful.

"But now you'll be part of opening up new lands to make the country even bigger."

He looked back to her. "Sometimes I wonder if I've made the right decision. Look at what happened today. Perhaps I have no business thinking that I can make a go of it on the frontier."

"We're all going to have a lot of learning to do."

"If we don't all starve to death first." He gave a disgusted kick to a log at his feet. It rolled down the bank and fell into the river with a dull plop.

Hannah felt slightly guilty that the same thought had occurred to her as she'd witnessed Randolph's struggles on the hunt today. "I don't suppose you wanted to think about operating the inn without Mrs. Webster."

Randolph shook his head. "It will go to her brother now, of course, though what he'll do with it I don't know. He has his own parish to tend, and I don't think he'd ever give up the church to become a businessman."

"Well, I'm sure everything will turn out for the best. You and the children will have a grand new life in a wonderful new land."

"We all will, I hope," he said. He put his hand around the upper part of her arm. "I wouldn't even have the heart to try it if you weren't going to be with us, Hannah. You give us all strength."

He had touched her many times, taken her arm to help her in and out of a carriage or wagon, but tonight his hand seemed to burn against her. She wanted to pull away from his grasp, but she forced herself to stay still. "Strength comes from within each of us, Mr. Webster. No one can give it to us. You and the children have all had to be strong since losing their mother, and the strength has been there when you needed it. I had nothing to do with it."

"You're wrong about that, Hannah." Finally he dropped his hand from her. "One of these days I'm going to show you how wrong."

For a moment he stood looking at her intently. Then he took a step backward and said, "Let's go listen to Seth's fiddle and see if your cheering-up system works."

Seth was talented. It hardly seemed possible that such a varied collection of sounds could emanate from a few little pieces of wood and string. Ethan sat clapping along with the rest of the group, but beyond the firelight he could make out Webster and Hannah in earnest conversation down by the river. Was the man finally beginning to realize what a prize she was? He'd been a widower for several months, and Ethan supposed that by now the grief had dulled enough for him to start looking around again. In Webster's case, he didn't have far to look. He had a beauty living right under his own roof. The man wasn't stupid.

Out of the corner of his eye he saw Webster put his hand on her. He noticed that she didn't pull away. They stayed like that for several moments, their heads bent close. It was to be expected, he told himself. And a lucky thing, too. It would make one less complication in his own life. He could concentrate on getting this pack of greenhorns out to their settlement. Then he could put them all out of his mind, including Miss Hannah Forrester. She did funny things inside his head. Inside the rest of him, too, for that matter. When he'd felt her soft roundness pressed up against him today as he taught her to use the musket, he'd been afraid his hand was going to start shaking like a schoolboy's.

It would be good to get to Fort Pitt. In the meantime, he didn't intend to give Randolph Webster's servant any more shooting lessons.

Chapter Six

It didn't take long for the energizing effects of the free day to wear off. By the end of another five endless days in the saddle, tempers were frayed and the faces around the nightly camp fire looked drawn and weary. Nancy Trask had been too weak to sit up for her supper. She had retired to her tent the minute it was pitched. Left to himself, Hugh had broken a bottle out of his family's packs and was soothing his fatigue with liquor.

Janie and Bridgett, normally so reserved, had had a fight, complete with hair pulling, and when Peggy had attempted to intervene, both sisters had turned upon their new friend and on Jacob, who had come to his sister's defense.

Hannah heard the ruckus as she sat with Nancy Trask in the Trasks' tent. She had been trying to urge Nancy to take at least a little broth so she would have strength for the trail. The pregnant woman had refused until Hannah had told her that Ethan had predicted that they would be at Fort Pitt by tomorrow. This brightened her spirits enough so that she was able to sit up and eat a little.

"I'd best go see to the children," Hannah said.

"I can't believe that's my Janie and Bridgett hollering like that," the sick woman said. "I should go out to them." There were great dark circles under her eyes, and in the light of the lantern her features looked sunken and ghostly.

"I'll see to it, Mrs. Trask. You lie back and rest. We still have one more long day to go tomorrow."

Nancy gave Hannah a wan smile. "You've mothered Priscilla's children, now mine, Hannah. I reckon we're mighty lucky that Randolph brought you on this trip."

"I'm happy to help, Mrs. Trask."

Nancy put her hand in Hannah's. It seemed to Hannah that she could feel each one of her bones through the tissue-thin skin. "I'd be pleased if you'd use my given name, like you do with Eliza," she said.

The shouts from the children grew more strident. "I'd be pleased, too, Nancy," Hannah said. "Now you lie back, and I'll go see what's going on with those youngsters."

She crawled under the tent flap right into the middle of the fracas. Janie and Bridgett were heading toward their mother's tent in search of a referee. Hannah shooed them all to the other side of the campsite, then gathered them around her in a circle. "You four have been brave and cooperative this whole trip," she told them. "It's been a great help to all of us. Now let's not spoil the record our very last night on the trail. Tomorrow night we'll be at the fort, and you'll have several days to play and meet new people and see lots of new things before we start downriver."

All four were listening to her intently. The quarrel seemed to be forgotten. "Can I count on you all to be mature and helpful for one more day of riding?"

One by one the heads nodded. Jacob was the last. "But Janie called Peggy a twit," he said.

"When we're tired we all do and say things we don't mean, Jacob. What we need is to all get a good night's sleep and start fresh in the morning."

"I didn't mean it, Peggy," Janie said timidly, her long brown hair falling over half her face.

Peggy turned to give her new friend a hug. "I'm sorry," she said.

"I'm sorry, too."

"Me, too," Bridgett added. And suddenly there were smiles all around and the four ran off to check on their squirrel trap before they went to bed. They had built a trap each night, but so far had not caught one.

"You're wonderful with them, Hannah." Randolph came up behind her.

"They're good children. The Trask sisters are really quite nice."

"I'm glad to see Peggy with some friends."

"It would be nice if all the children could do their schooling together once we get settled. We could all take turns teaching them." Hannah had had some basic schooling in London when she was a child, but her mother's continuing illnesses had forced her to spend more and more of her time at home. She was able to help Jacob with his sums and his writing, but she felt that Peggy was reaching a level beyond her. Nancy had had much more education, and had actually been a teacher before she married Hugh.

Randolph nodded. "That's a good thought. I'll talk to Mrs. Trask about it when she's feeling better."

"I've just given her some soup. I think she'll be all right for one more day. Then she can get some good rest at the fort."

"It's amazing that Mrs. Trask and the girls are so sweet with the loudmouthed father they have."

"Mr. Trask makes me feel uncomfortable," Hannah admitted.

"Has he been rude to you, Hannah? He's not bothered you certainly?"

Hannah hesitated, then said carefully, "Not any more than one should expect in my position."

To Hannah's surprise, he suddenly took her hands.

"I don't like to hear you talk that way, Hannah. You don't have to think of yourself as a servant anymore."

His hands closed warmly around hers, drawing her just a step closer. Hannah tried to think of something to say. For two years she had given this man the deference due an employer. Now he was holding her hands and looking down at her with an expression that was anything but impersonal.

"But..."

His thumbs moved back and forth across her palms. "We don't need to go any further than that as yet. It will take some getting used to, I know."

After a moment's embarrassment, it didn't feel so awkward to have her hands in his. She'd been taking care of him and his family for so many months, it seemed almost natural that their relationship would deepen. He was kind and considerate and attractive. In the depths of her despair before she got on the ship in London, she had never imagined that her indenture would bring her into a family where her labors would be rewarded with so much affection and even love.

"In truth, I hardly think of myself as a servant, sir," she said.

Randolph dropped her hands. "Then why do you call me sir?"

Hannah blushed. "I'll not do so anymore if you don't like it."

"I'd prefer just plain Randolph," he said. "Do you suppose you could manage that?"

"But what would the others think?"

"They'll think just what I want them to think. That things are changing between Randolph and Mistress Forrester. And people like Hugh Trask will realize that you are more to me than an indentured servant."

Hannah tried not to interpret his declaration too broadly. "When you purchased my contract in New York, you offered me your protection, and it seems that you are offering it once again. I'm very grateful."

Both looked a little uncomfortable at the apparent change in their relationship. Randolph was the first to speak. "So one more long day on the trail," he said briskly.

"Aye, I'd better go see to it that the children are getting to bed."

"Sleep well, then. I'll see you in the morning."

She bobbed her head and walked away, leaving him gazing after her. Her bright blond hair shone in the darkness long after he couldn't see the gentle sway of her hips. He had loved Priscilla more than he had ever thought a man could love a woman, but she'd been gone now many months. Even his memory of her dear face had begun to fade. The sharp cut of grief was dulling, and nowadays when he watched Hannah laughing with his children, a new kind of ache had begun to grow in his middle. It had grown stronger during this trip, being around her all the time, next to her at the camp fire, behind her on the trail. She was grateful, she'd said. But it was more than gratitude he wanted from Hannah Forrester.

The last person Hannah wanted to run into after her unsettling conversation with Randolph was Ethan Reed, but he was leaning casually against a tree alongside her tent as she approached.

"It looks like you and Webster are getting more chummy every day," he noted, chewing nonchalantly on the end of a stubby clay pipe.

Hannah was disconcerted. A few nights ago this man had kissed her, and she had let him. Now he had witnessed her holding hands in the dark with Randolph. For a girl who had lived her life more protected from men than a cloistered nun, it had been quite a week. Would she now be accused of being the loose woman her mother had always claimed she would be if she paid the least attention to a man?

"If you'll excuse me, Captain Reed. I have to find my children and get them to bed."

"*Your* children?" The pipe in his mouth tilted up as he grinned at her.

"My *charges,*" she amended. "The Webster children."

"Indeed. Don't let me keep you, Mistress Hannah."

Flustered, she turned the wrong direction in confusion, then recovered and headed toward the rear of the encampment.

The four youngsters had made their peace and were talking together happily when Hannah found them. They made no fuss about being told to come to bed. She crawled into the tent after Peggy and Jacob and gave them each a hug and kiss good-night, as was her custom since the time when their mother had become too weak to go to their bedside and do so herself.

"Will there be Indians at the fort tomorrow?" Jacob asked. He had a special skill for coming up with questions just at bedtime that required elaborate answers, but this time Hannah would not let herself be led into the game.

"I guess we'll find out when we get there, won't we?" she answered. Then she brushed the hair back from his forehead and gave his chest a little pat. "Go to sleep now, dearlings."

As she turned to go, Peggy said, "Hannah?"

"Yes, dear?"

"This trip would have been awful without you along."

For a moment, Hannah didn't reply. She wondered if the children had heard that the MacDougalls had tried to persuade her to stay in Philadelphia. In particular she wondered if Peggy, who was old enough to speculate about such things, had been aware of her grandmother's feelings about Randolph and Hannah. Children often knew more than one gave them credit for. "Your father would have taken fine care of you even if I'd not been here," she said.

"But all the same, we're glad you're with us," Peggy said firmly. "May I tell you a secret?"

"Certainly."

"Sometimes when I see you riding along in Mama's cloak, I pretend to myself that you really are Mama going west with us."

Hannah's throat closed. She leaned to give the girl a hug. "Your mama will always be with you, Peggy.

No matter where you go. But I'm happy that I can stand in for her in some ways with you children.''

"I love you, Hannah," Jacob murmured in a voice that sounded already half-asleep.

"I love you, too," she whispered. "Now go to sleep. Happy dreams."

She sat for a moment listening as the children's breathing evened out into slumber. They *were* her children in many respects, and she had grown to love them both dearly. More than a servant, their father had said. Yes, she certainly felt that way with Peggy and Jacob. And now it seemed that she would be given the opportunity to see if she could feel that way with their father, as well.

Her thoughts were still on this startling idea as she walked down to the river to wash before going to bed herself. They had chosen to stop at a spot where a flat bar of sand rimmed the river's edge, forming a little beach. Hannah was tempted to remove some of her clothes so she could really get herself clean, but decided it was too risky. When they got to the fort she would find a way to take a real bath.

She knelt in the gravelly sand and bent over the edge of the river. By now she was used to the icy water and didn't even flinch as she splashed it over her face and neck. She lifted her skirt to dry herself, then turned abruptly as something gave her a sudden, uneasy chill.

Hugh Trask was standing at the edge of the beach, silhouetted in the moonlight. He had a bottle in his hand and a nasty grin on his face.

"Don't let me interrupt you, Hannah," he said, holding his bottle aloft in a mock salute. "I was just enjoying the view."

She jumped to her feet. "I was about to retire," she said hastily. "I'll bid you good-evening."

"Not so fast." He came toward her with a lurching walk. Hannah's heart began to beat as she realized that he was drunk. She'd seen drunks before on the streets of London and had learned to stay away from them. Her shoes slipping on the sand, she started to dart around him, but his free hand shot out and took a painful grasp on her shoulder. "What's yer hurry?" he said, weaving slightly as he held her fast.

Hannah's mouth went dry. Randolph may be telling her not to consider herself one, but that didn't change the fact that she was a bonded servant. There was very little protection under the law against all variety of indignities that a free man might want to inflict upon her. "Please excuse me, Mr. Trask," she said, trying to sound as haughty and unconcerned as possible under the circumstances.

But his hold on her shoulder only became tighter. His thumb pressed cruelly into her shoulder blade and she buckled under the pressure. "I think we should have a li'l moonlight shh...troll," he said.

"Please, Mr. Trask, you're hurting me!" Hannah could no longer keep the panic out of her voice.

"Get your damned hands off her, Trask, or I'll ram that bottle down your ugly throat."

Trask's grasp on her shoulder loosened and Hannah sank to her knees in relief as Ethan came out of the shadows and strode toward them across the beach. He pulled the bottle from Trask's hand and flung it out into the middle of the river. "You're drunk, Trask, and this is my last warning. If you want to continue on with this expedition, you'd better sober up fast and stay that way."

Trask blinked hard as though trying to focus on his antagonist. "You ain't got no right to be telling me what to do, Reed," he said. "You heard what Webster said the other day—we're paying you, not the other way around."

Ethan took hold of Trask's shirt and pulled him within inches of his face. He spoke in an undertone that Hannah could barely hear. "If you lay a hand on her again, Trask, you'll see just what kind of bloody rights I have. I'll be eating your liver for breakfast."

Trask turned his head to one side and looked as if he were about to be sick. "Do you understand me, you miserable sot?" Ethan asked. He gave Trask a push that sent him stumbling up the sand toward the woods. Then he dropped to the ground next to Hannah. "Are you all right?"

"Thanks to you. This is the second time you've rescued me from a disagreeable encounter with Mr. Trask."

"I should skewer the bastard."

Hannah shook her head. "I don't want trouble on my account."

Ethan turned to look at her. "You're shaking," he said with concern. Before Hannah knew what was happening, he had lifted her in his arms and held her cradled like a babe against his broad chest.

"I'm fine," she protested.

"Your heart is beating like a moth's wing." He put one hand on her soft muslin dress, just above her right breast.

"I'm fine," she said again, but it came out as a whisper.

His hand stayed where he had placed it, which meant that her heart continued its erratic dance. Hugh

Trask was forgotten, and both had become aware that she was sitting in his lap on a darkened beach. "Let me see for myself," Ethan said. He moved his hand finally, but only to bring it up to cup her chin as he turned her face toward him.

She knew that he was going to kiss her. She tried to think about Randolph and how steady his hands had felt around hers earlier that evening. About Jacob's tiny voice saying "I love you." She tried to think of anything but Ethan's strong arms moving around her and his warm lips descending on hers. But the battle was lost before the soldiers had taken the field.

Unlike the gentle caress they had shared the other evening, this kiss was demanding from the start. His hand held the back of her neck as his mouth molded itself to hers, then skillfully, patiently, explored and teased and aroused until Hannah's entire world was reduced to this incredible union of lips and tongues.

"I'm sorry, lass." Ethan's shaky voice reached her through a haze. "I fear you've robbed me of my senses."

Slowly the earth tilted back into place. Hannah opened her eyes to see Ethan watching her with a rueful smile.

"I had just planned on a simple kiss," he said.

"It wasn't." Hannah stated the obvious. She might be untutored, but even she knew that something special had passed between them. Her rapid heartbeat had been replaced by a slow, steady throb, and her body felt warm all over.

Ethan shifted her in his arms to widen the distance between them. He took a long breath. "I'm not sure what I intend to do about it."

His words made Hannah feel uncomfortable for the first time since he had taken her in his arms. He sounded as if this were an entirely one-sided proposition. *He* decided. *He* intended. What about *her?*

"You needn't do anything at all." She pushed herself off his lap and turned on her knees to face him. "You rescued me, comforted me. That's the end of it."

Ethan made no move to retain his hold on her. "I think we both know that that's probably *not* the end of it, Hannah."

Hannah folded her hands in front of her and pressed them down on her knees. This would be easier if she didn't still feel so unsteady. First Trask, then the captain. All at once she wasn't sure which man had upset her more. "As I believe I have explained to you, Captain Reed, I've not had a great deal of opportunity in the past for—" she gave a vague wave of her hand back and forth between them, then cleared her throat and continued "—for dealings with men. Nor do I intend to have for some time in the future, at least for the duration of my contract."

He frowned at her. "Don't you think you could call me Ethan, considering what has happened between us—twice now, by my count? And what is likely to happen between us again, no matter how many damned contracts you sign?"

Hannah stood, looking down at him. "No, Captain, I don't. I must admit that I'm not unaffected by you. But all things considered, I believe it would be best if we kept our distance from one another."

Ethan didn't stand. He'd wanted to kill Trask when he'd seen him hurting her. Then he'd wanted to lay her down on the beach and make her forget that she'd ever been touched by any man but him. His body was only now easing the stridency of the desire their kisses had generated. He couldn't remember when he had wanted a woman as much, but he tried to tell himself that it was because he knew deep down that she was unavailable.

"Very well," he said, forcing his tone to a lightness he did not feel. "I'll keep my distance."

"Thank you." She turned to leave, but he called her back.

"Hannah!" When she paused he said softly, "I promise to keep my distance, but only as long as you keep yours."

By the next morning Hannah thoroughly regretted her actions of the previous evening. She had not only submitted to Ethan's advances, she had participated, had indeed been quite swept off her feet. He was the one who had called a halt. Who knows what might have happened if he hadn't. For the first time, Hannah had the sick feeling that her mother had been right when she had warned that Hannah had inherited her own "weak blood."

"We're just the kind men prey on, Hannah," she would say. "Women who enjoy wickedness."

Hannah had not felt the least bit wicked when she had been in Ethan's arms in the moonlight, but in the harsh light of day, she wondered and she hurt.

Ethan had not spoken to her as they made preparations for their final day. She had seen him turn his head sharply once in her direction when she had called her employer "Randolph." She had done it in a deliberately loud voice, she admitted to herself, as if making some kind of proclamation, but no one except Ethan seemed to pay attention to the change, not even Randolph himself.

The day was uneventful and seemed to drag on endlessly. Everyone kept waiting for the welcome sight of the fort to appear over the next rise. Ethan had told them that they would be able to see the fort from atop a bluff and at the same time would have their first glimpse of the great vee where the Monongahela and the Allegheny Rivers joined to form the mighty Ohio.

When the dramatic time finally came, there was a moment of silence before Ethan called, "We'll dismount and rest here awhile. It's still a good piece down to the fort—farther than it looks from here."

Hannah wondered if the rest of the party shared her brief twinge of misgiving at the first sight of Fort Pitt. It was a stout, five-sided structure built on the point of land formed by the rivers. All around the current buildings, the ramparts of the old French fort lay in ruins. It was much smaller than she had imagined. The trading post beyond was a tiny village of ramshackle huts that had not the least resemblance to the fine paved avenues and streets of Philadelphia. They had left their homes, their families and friends and a city of nearly forty thousand people to come to this.

Hannah looked over at Randolph and the children. Like the rest of the group, their expressions were somber. They had all held on to the idea of Fort Pitt as some kind of haven of rest. A return to civilization. A wonderful milestone on their journey west. But it seemed to Hannah that in some ways it was the biggest disappointment they had experienced.

When Ethan called them to start up again, they mounted up and made their way down the trail with little talking. "I thought it would be bigger," Jacob said, which fairly summed up the general feeling.

Once she got used to the sight of the meager buildings of the fort, Hannah began to concentrate on the surroundings, and these were everything she could have imagined. The fort was nestled in a beautiful valley surrounded by green hills and river bluffs on all sides. The broad, majestic Ohio flowed out to the southwest, promising rich lands beyond.

"There's the Ohio," she shouted to Peggy and Jacob.

Jacob had recovered his enthusiasm. "It's bigger than the Delaware," he said.

"Yes, indeed," Hannah answered. "And much longer, too."

"And we're going to float right on down it, aren't we, Papa?" He twisted in the saddle to look back at his father, almost toppling Peggy in the process.

"Watch out!" she cried. "Sit straight, Jacob." Her voice sounded as if she were on the verge of tears.

"We'll not be floating anywhere for a while," Randolph answered in a reassuring tone. "We'll stay to have some good food at the fort and meet some nice people. We're going to have a great time."

Hannah hoped he was correct. They all needed a little merriment before embarking on the second portion of their trip, though the journey by flatboat should not be as arduous as the riding had been.

It was twilight by the time they reached the gates of the fort. Now that they were on the same level, the structures looked more substantial than they had from above the valley. The brick blockhouse by the gate was comfortingly solid. The fort might not have Philadelphia's elegance, but it gave a reassuring impression of permanence and protection.

The exhausted travelers were greeted by a snappy-looking lieutenant who smiled and cast a quick, appreciative eye over Hannah before he walked over to Ethan and gave him a salute. "Glad to see you, Captain," he said. "I reckon you folks could stand some victuals before we get you settled in."

Ethan shook the soldier's hand warmly and smiled his thanks. Hannah tried not to pay attention to the exchange, busying herself with untying her saddlebags. From the corner of her eyes, she could see a woman running toward them across the yard. Ethan turned just as she reached him and did not look surprised when she flung her arms around his neck.

"Ethan, ye brawny boy!" she shouted. "I've missed ye."

Ethan lifted her off the ground with one arm and gave her a solid kiss on the mouth. "You can stop missing me, Polly. I'm back."

Chapter Seven

Randolph had introduced Hannah to the fort commandant as his housekeeper. They were to dine at his house their first evening to celebrate their arrival, and as they made their way across the yard, Hannah's spirits were high. For the first time she felt truly that her status had moved beyond servant. Eliza and Seth had treated her as equals from the beginning, and Nancy Trask was starting to rely on her the way Priscilla had when she had become ill. Hugh Trask was the only one of the group who had rolled his eyes when Randolph had revised her title.

They had seen nothing of Ethan since that afternoon. He had disappeared with his soldier friends and the demonstrative Polly. Hannah was relieved that he was not present at Colonel Bouquet's house when they arrived. It was difficult enough adjusting to the fact that Randolph was offering his arm to escort her into the dining room as if he were a suitor paying court. Hannah hesitated for a moment before placing her hand on him shyly.

Always sensitive to others' feelings, Eliza came up alongside the couple and took possession of his other arm. "You *did* want to escort two of the prettiest la-

dies at Fort Pitt into supper, didn't you, Randolph?''
she asked pertly. Then she leaned around the front of
Randolph and whispered, as if in a conspiracy with
Hannah, ''We have to be two of the prettiest, my dear,
since we are practically the only ones here.''

Hannah and Randolph laughed, the moment of
tension relieved. Then Seth came forward to protest
that he wasn't about to be left without a lady for himself, which more or less obliged Hugh to give an arm
to Nancy, who looked much revived by the mere fact
of having reached a temporary stopping place in their
journey.

They had left the children in the charge of the fort's
laundress, a plump, cheerful half-Indian woman who
promised the youngsters that she would tell them a
story about a real Indian princess before they went to
bed.

Colonel Bouquet proved to be a congenial host. He
introduced them to four of his officers, who joined
them for the meal. The men were obviously happy to
have visitors from the outside world. They asked
about the rumors that Parliament was going to im-
pose a tax on sugar to make up for the monies spent
on the recent conflict with the French, and they inquired about which ships had recently arrived from
home. Colonel Bouquet told them that he had a wife
and four children back in Bristol, and he hoped to be
reassigned to England soon. In spite of their good humor, the men sounded lonely, and Hannah realized
that the soldiers led even more isolated lives than the
settlers, who at least had their immediate families
around them.

They ate off wooden trenchers instead of plates and
at a table that still smelled of fresh cut pine, but the

food was abundant and delicious—roasted venison cooked with turnips and a sweet-tasting orange-colored root that the colonel called *camote*.

The evening would have been perfect for Hannah if it weren't for the presence of Trask, who looked up at her slyly every now and then from his place at the end of the table, and if she hadn't found herself glancing at the door every few minutes expecting Ethan to join them. As if reading her mind, Randolph finally asked the colonel, "Will our guide be dining with us tonight?"

Bouquet shook his head. "Ethan's had one or two better offers, I'd wager. He's a popular fellow around here."

"A woman greeted him as we rode in," Randolph observed.

"That would be Polly McCoy. Her husband was a trapper in these parts who went off with a band of Chippewa one day and never came back. Polly has just stayed on at the fort making her living as a trader. The Hudson's Bay people don't much like having her here, but she gives fair prices and the trappers like doing business with her."

"I imagine they do," Seth Baker said with a grin, then sobered when Eliza nudged him in the ribs with her elbow.

"So Captain Reed and Mrs. McCoy are friends?" Randolph asked, flicking a glance at Hannah's face.

"I guess you could say that. They seem to keep company when Ethan's around the fort."

Hannah had resolved to put Ethan out of her mind, but she could not help the little jump in her stomach as his name was mentioned. Of course she could have predicted that he would have a woman to "keep company with'' at the fort. It was just one more indication that she should stay as far away from him as possible.

In spite of the colonel's warm hospitality, none of the new arrivals cared to linger over supper. They were still recovering from the rigors of the trail, and all said that they would be better guests on the morrow. To their surprise, Colonel Bouquet suggested holding a dance in their honor. ''That is, if you approve, ladies,'' he added.

The Quaker influence in Philadelphia was still strong, and in many circles the popular pastime was frowned upon, but Eliza assured him that this particular group would join in the diversion wholeheartedly.

''Wonderful!'' the colonel exclaimed. ''We have a lieutenant by the name of Higgins who can play a reel that'll set your boots a-smoking.''

''We can make it a contest, then,'' Eliza said smugly. ''Because my husband has always claimed to be the best fiddler in the colonies.''

Seth denied her statement, but it was agreed that the following evening they would gather in the officers' mess to celebrate the arrival of the Philadelphia party. In the meantime, living quarters had been arranged. Hannah had been given a small room with one cot to share with Peggy and Jacob. When Randolph escorted her there after dinner at the colonel's, the children were already asleep, leaving only the very edge of the bed for Hannah.

''Is this going to be all right for the three of you?'' Randolph asked, looking doubtful.

''I'm so exhausted I could sleep on a board full of nails,'' she said with a tired laugh.

"Tomorrow I'll ask the quartermaster to find another cot to put in here."

"If one is available, fine. If not, we'll make do with what we have."

Randolph put one hand one the side of the doorframe just above her shoulder. "Do you ever complain about *anything,* Hannah?" he asked her with a shake of his head.

She was aware that he was standing very close to her and that he had a new, hungry look in his eyes that she had not seen before. She was also aware that his children slept not two yards away. She tried to answer lightly. "I'll probably start complaining any minute now if I don't get some sleep."

Randolph let his hand drop briefly to her shoulder, then removed it. "I expect I'll have to kiss you one of these days, Hannah Forrester," he said.

Her face flamed. "Mr. Webster!" she exclaimed.

"It's Randolph, remember," he chided. "You remembered well enough this morning when you saw that Reed was watching you."

She bent her head away from the gentle reproach in his brown eyes, but he lifted her chin up again. "It doesn't matter, Hannah. I'm patient. I know that Reed's not a man who would ever settle down with one woman, and you're smart enough to know that, too."

For the hundredth time, Hannah remembered the scene as Polly McCoy flung herself into Ethan's willing arms. She set her jaw. "Yes. I'm smart enough to know that," she agreed.

"So that's enough about that," Randolph said briskly. "Now, may I have the honor of escorting you to the dance tomorrow evening, my lady?" he asked with a little bow of his head.

Hannah could not quite get used to being pursued
by the man who had virtually ignored her for so many
months. "What about the children?" she asked.

"Oh, they'll come with us, of course. After all,
we're a family, aren't we?"

Hannah nodded, too tired to quibble with his as-
sertion. "Family" would do for tonight. In fact, it had
quite a lovely sound to it.

The bench in front of McCoy's Trading was a favorite gathering place for the civilians who called Fort
Pitt home. During the winter, the regulars moved inside to crowd around the potbellied stove. But on a
warm spring evening, the front porch and steps were
full. Ethan leaned back against the porch railing and
smiled as Beartooth Carter finished off another of his
tall tales. Nobody seemed to know where Beartooth
had come from. He claimed he'd been across the entire continent to the Pacific Ocean and back again.
And he had at least one story for each mile of the trip.

Polly had already retired to her tiny bedroom at the
back of her store. Her pretty lips had puckered in a
good-natured pout when Ethan had declined to accompany her there. Her pique was not because she was
in love with him. Polly was a woman who loved men
too much to make the mistake of falling for a particular one. But she was used to being the queen bee at
the fort and hadn't been pleased to see how Ethan's
eyes wandered time and again to one of the new settlers he'd brought in.

"You're always watching her—the skinny one,"
she'd accused. And Ethan had laughed because Polly's famous curves were a handful and becoming more

so each year. "Is she married to the tall one?" Polly had asked.

"No. She's his servant," Ethan had answered.

"Well now, that's a new name for it."

Then Ethan had said, "It's not like that." Polly had seen that he was growing annoyed, and she had wisely dropped the subject. But even with her best cajoling she had been unable to entice him into her bedroom.

One of the soldiers leaned over to Ethan and offered him some tobacco to chew, a habit they'd learned from the Indians. Ethan tore off a piece and stuffed it into his mouth. He didn't know why he did it. The damn weed tasted like hell. He didn't know why he had turned down Polly, either. He could be in her bed right now, worn-out and happy. Instead he sat listening to Beartooth's increasingly unbelievable stories, half his attention on the commandant's house across the yard where the lights were blazing and, no doubt, the guests were having a merry time. He'd seen Hannah walk there on Randolph's arm, looking each minute more like the lady of the Webster household—as he had predicted.

Hugh Trask had left the dinner party well before the others. Bouquet's liquor must not have been to his liking. He evidently preferred the Scottish whiskey that Silas Warren was pouring down him as the two sat together on the far end of the porch. That was a combination that would bear watching. Trask and Warren. The one was an irresponsible drunk whose commitment to his family seemed to diminish with each passing day, and the other was an unscrupulous trader whose specialty was making sure the Indians were not deprived of the chance to lose their health and dignity to the white man's firewater.

Ethan stood and stretched. He was ready for bed. The commandant's dinner party was still in progress, though the children had been asleep for a good while. Ethan himself had checked on them—the Trask girls and then the Websters. Peggy and Jacob were good children. They both obviously loved Hannah. And she would be a wonderful mother to them. Hell, he thought as he gave a wave to the men on the porch and started walking toward his room, she already was.

"There's no money in farming, Trask." Silas Warren leaned right up to the man next to him. "You sweat your guts out year after year and end up living like a miserable pauper begging for every crust of bread."

The old Indian trader had lost an eye in one of his earlier adventures and didn't bother to patch the fearsome-looking mess that was left behind. Trask winced and backed toward the edge of the porch. "I got two kids and one on the way and a sick, puking wife in the bargain. What am I supposed to do?"

"The best way to help out yer family is to come up with some real money."

"Right. I pick it off the bloody trees, I suppose?"

Warren offered him the bottle of whiskey they'd been sharing. "You pick it off the bloody savages," he said softly, looking over his shoulder at the group back by the steps.

Trask took the bottle. "What do you mean?"

Warren squinted his one good eye, turning his face into a demonic parody. "I'll just tell you what I mean, my friend Trask." He motioned to the whiskey. "Let's drink to our new partnership."

* * *

At the officers' mess the next evening, even Nancy Trask, her condition now obvious, was deluged with offers to dance, though she blushingly refused all comers. There were not more than a handful of women at the fort, and three new arrivals caused a stir, even if one was pregnant and one was old enough to be a grandmother. Eliza danced with one young man after another until she was breathless and red with the exertion. She laughed with them and teased good-naturedly, putting the young soldiers in mind of their own absent mothers. Only Hannah and Seth, who knew her so well, could see the layer of sadness underneath her bright eyes as she thought of the handsome young man who would never dance again—her Johnny who lay forever up on the hill back in Philadelphia.

Hannah, of course, was the most sought after. Halfway through the evening she figured that she had danced with every man in the room except one. Ethan Reed had stayed away, keeping his distance as he had promised. Not that this appeared to be a hardship. Every time Hannah turned around it seemed that Polly McCoy was in his arms. But she'd noted that he'd danced with Eliza and all three of the young girls, as well as the other four women present, all of whom were wives of men at the fort.

The music was lively and nonstop, with Seth and Lieutenant Higgins trying to outdo each other in both volume and stamina. Randolph claimed her hand without fail every fourth dance. "I suppose I have to give the others a chance," he told her, "but I find that I don't like the sight of another man's hands on you."

"It's just dancing, Randolph," she'd stammered.

"I don't like it," he'd repeated, with a smile that softened the bluntness of his statement.

After so many days on the trail without this kind of exertion, Hannah started wearing down after a particularly sprightly gavotte. "I don't think I can dance another step," she gasped.

Randolph handed her his kerchief, which she took to dab at her forehead and neck. She was flushed and smiling. Wisps of hair had escaped from her braid to frame her face with delicate, moist tendrils.

"We could walk outside and cool off for a minute," Randolph suggested.

She nodded gratefully and let him take her hand to lead her across to the door. "Where're you going, Papa?" Jacob suddenly appeared at their side. "Do we have to leave already?"

Randolph looked down at his son. "No, Jacob. We'll stay as long as you children are enjoying yourselves. Hannah and I are just going outside for a minute for a breath of air."

"Can I go with you?"

"No." Randolph's answer was unusually curt. "Stay here with your sister."

Hannah looked at Randolph in surprise, then continued the direction of her gaze to meet the eyes of Ethan, who was standing just a few feet beyond. They hadn't spoken all evening. He smiled at her sardonically and gave a little nod. She turned quickly without acknowledging his greeting. Randolph kept her hand firmly clasped in his and led her out the door.

"Sometimes children can be constraining," he said when they had stepped out into the yard. He sounded apologetic.

"I don't find them to be," she answered. She had seen the look in Jacob's eyes when his father had rebuffed him.

Randolph dropped her hand and spun around to face her. "I just wanted a minute alone with you, Hannah. I've been wanting it all evening."

Hannah crossed her arms protectively over her chest and looked up at the sky. It was becoming abundantly clear that Randolph had begun to view her as more than a servant, but it seemed to her that things had changed in a great hurry. Of course, she and Randolph had lived in the same household for two years. And his wife had been dead for some months. Perhaps it was in her own mind that the change seemed overwhelming. Her world had turned on its axis in the past few days, and she didn't quite know what to do about it.

"It's a nice dance, isn't it?" she said finally.

Randolph looked slightly exasperated at the impersonal tone of her observation, but he answered calmly enough. "I believe dancing is good for the soul."

Hannah unfolded her arms and shrugged the tenseness out of her shoulders. "I never danced until I came to Philadelphia. There was no chance in London. Though one time my mother and I passed by a great hall and she let me peek around the doorway and watch the couples swirl around the floor. I thought it was magical."

"You've learned well in so short a time, Hannah," he said, then added fondly, "as you do with everything."

"It's easy. You just go where the music takes you." They could still hear the dueling fiddles from inside the building behind them. Hannah swayed back and forth as she talked.

Randolph watched her with a smile. "They say that the French always end the gavotte with a kiss."

"They're a scandalous people, I hear."

Randolph took a step toward her. "There's nothing so scandalous about a kiss," he said, his voice husky.

Hannah stopped swaying as he gently took hold of her arms and bent down to press his lips to hers. It was over in an instant. "I guess I've been wanting that all evening, too," he said, with a little catch to his voice. "I'm sorry, Hannah. I hope I didn't startle you."

The kiss itself hadn't startled her, but she was startled and alarmed at the quick flash of memory it had evoked. Memory of Ethan and his mouth on hers that night on the beach. Not chastely and respectfully as Randolph's had been, but hot and demanding. "No, it's all right," she said, but her eyes were troubled.

"I'm sorry," Randolph said again. "I promised to take things slowly, and I'm not doing a very good job of it."

Hannah gave her head a shake, as if trying to purge it of that *other* kiss. "There's no need to apologize," she told him, mustering a smile. "But I think we should go back into the dance now. The children will be missing us."

When they walked back into the dance, Ethan was standing near the door, right where he had been when they left. Polly McCoy was across the room dancing with Colonel Bouquet. As they entered, Ethan took a step toward them. "Nice evening," he observed, his eyes on Hannah.

Randolph turned to him and said coolly, "Aye. And it appears you've been enjoying yourself, Reed. Mrs. McCoy is a handsome woman."

Ethan's eyes lit with private amusement. "Polly's a comely lass, that's for sure. But I haven't had the pleasure of a dance with Mistress Forrester yet." He made the statement into a request with a cock of his head.

"I've really had enough dancing for one night, I think," Hannah said.

Randolph gave her an inscrutable look, then said, "Well, we wouldn't want to be unfair to our trail guide, Hannah. Go ahead and dance with him."

Before she could think of a suitable excuse, Ethan had seized her arm and was leading her out on to the floor. Aware of their flagging audience, Seth and Higgins had slowed down the tempo to a stately waltz.

Ethan swung her into his arms and began to move. "I...I don't think I can dance this close up," Hannah protested.

"Haven't you ever danced a waltz?"

She shook her head.

"In Boston at the fancy dress balls this is all they dance anymore. No more circling and stomping and jumping around like so many chipmunks. Just nice and easy..." His words started keeping time to the three-four beat of the music. "Floating along with a beautiful woman in your arms."

He held her no more closely than any of the other couples, but there was a kind of heat between their bodies that was making Hannah uncomfortable. "I thought you said you would keep your distance."

"I am. I didn't come near you all night, did I?"

"What about now?"

"Ah, well, I was just checking to see that you were all right after Webster took you out in the dark for a chaste little kiss."

Hannah gave an indignant gasp, but Ethan continued unruffled. "It couldn't have been much more than that, judging from the time you were gone."

Hannah felt her neck getting warm. "Please escort me off the floor, Captain Reed. As I said, I've had enough dancing tonight."

"He did kiss you, didn't he?" He bent to look into her eyes which were spitting blue fire. "I thought so."

He twirled her twice more, then moved to the side of the room where Randolph had stood watching them for the entire dance. "Thank you for the dance, mistress," he said with a formal bow.

Hannah lifted the pink silk fan that had dangled at her wrist all evening and waved it rapidly in front of her face. Jeanne MacDougall had given it to her as a parting gift and, while Hannah had been touched by the gesture, it had occurred to her that it was not a very practical item to be taking into the frontier. Little had she imagined back in Philadelphia that she would come west to be the belle of the ball at a soldiers' dance and be kissed by two different men in less than a week. She wondered for a moment if she wouldn't be better off back in Mrs. MacDougall's big kitchen.

"You're welcome," she said to Ethan, as ungraciously as she dared without obvious rudeness.

"Would you like to leave now, Hannah?" Randolph asked quietly, taking her arm.

Ethan interrupted her answer. "Before you go, Webster. Some of the officers and I are planning a hunting expedition tomorrow. Your party is welcome to come along.''

"Does that include me?" Hannah asked, her reservations about Ethan momentarily forgotten at the thought of trying out her skills with a gun again. She had thought many times of the day they all had hunted on the trail. If the men would only give her the chance, she felt she could become quite a good shot.

Ethan answered immediately. "Certainly, Mistress Forrester. I'm sure my friends would be delighted to have you join us."

"I can't go," Randolph stated. "I've promised Colonel Bouquet that I would spend some time with him helping to straighten out the fort's account books."

Hannah looked disappointed. "I won't go either, then."

"Seth's going along. You'll be well protected," Ethan said casually.

Randolph looked from Ethan to Hannah, then across the room to where Seth was carefully putting his fiddle into its leather case. "You go ahead, Hannah, if you wish. You deserve to have a break from the children."

Hannah debated with herself. She wasn't at all sure about a day in the countryside with Ethan. But there would be a whole group with them. And if Seth was also going along... "Are you sure it's all right?" she asked Randolph.

He didn't look happy about the prospect, but he nodded his head.

"Then I guess I'll go."

Ethan's face was impassive. "Fine," he said. "We meet by the blockhouse at sunrise."

Chapter Eight

In spite of her misgivings, Hannah had to admit that she was finding the hunting expedition exhilarating. She had almost decided not to go in the morning when Seth had come up to her, a hangdog look on his face, and told her that he was not going to be able to accompany them.

"I can't leave Eliza," he told her. "She didn't sleep all night for fretting over Johnny. Sometimes I think it was a mistake to think we could leave our memories behind us."

"You're not leaving them behind, Seth," Hannah had said to comfort him. "Your wonderful memories of your son will always be with you no matter where you go. And the painful ones will fade away. Just give it time."

He had shaken his head sadly and asked, "Will you be all right without me, Hannah? I'm sure Captain Reed will take good care of you."

And that observation had been almost enough to make Hannah stay at home, but by then the five officers who were going along had arrived, all exclaiming their delight at her decision to join them. One was a boyish young major named Edgemont who had insisted on dancing with her three times the previous evening. He had a high rank for his age and an aristocratic bearing. Hannah speculated that he was probably the third or fourth son of a noble family. Back in England she wouldn't have been looked at twice by such a man. But out here he treated her as if she were a member of the royal family.

After her enthusiastic welcome by all the officers, she had felt it would be churlish to back out at the last minute. And she didn't regret her decision. It was a spectacular early summer day, sunny and warm, the very earth itself seeming to burst forth with life on every side. They rode through an emerald green meadow dotted with white columbine and bluebells, and Hannah thought she had never seen such a pretty sight.

The officers had been more than willing to serve as tutors for her lessons in marksmanship. They were polite and, with the exception of Major Edgemont, a little shy. Hannah found their attentions charming. Ethan had also been on his best behavior. There had been no suggestive remarks, no sardonic smiles. He seemed as determined as she to enjoy the day.

At midday they stopped for a lunch of cold meat pies and cider. Hannah sat surrounded by the officers and listened with a smile as they bantered back and forth.

"Say, Higgins. It's too bad that Easterner came along to show us what a *real* fiddler sounds like," Major Edgemont teased the proud little lieutenant. The men laughed, used to the major's ready humor. When she had danced with him last night Hannah had found herself laughing so hard she couldn't concentrate on the steps.

"That old man?" Higgins retorted. "I had to play most of the night with my left hand just so's I wouldn't make him feel too bad."

The men grinned and looked at Hannah for approval of their joking. "You played beautifully, Lieutenant Higgins," she said, dabbing at her mouth to wipe away the last crumbs of her pie. "I've never heard better in London Town itself."

The lieutenant beamed as Edgemont gave him a whack on the back and said, "La-di-da, Higgins. You'll be playing for King George himself before you know it."

Ethan had been mostly silent during lunch, letting his friends joke and flirt gently with Hannah. But every time she looked his direction, his eyes were on her. Hannah ignored him as much as possible, and concentrated on enjoying the attention of the others.

They had bagged several birds and one rabbit in the morning, but had not so much as caught sight of any larger game. After eating, the fervor for the hunt had diminished substantially. They talked of heading back to the fort, but the energetic Major Edgemont persuaded them to make one last attempt at tracking a bigger prize.

"I'm not about to go back empty-handed and eat salt pork for another week," he said with a grimace.

When their opportunity finally came, it was Hannah who got the chance to do something about it. They had dismounted at the edge of a small pond and Hannah had exchanged her small fowling piece for a real rifle.

"You'll have to be careful now. Stand strong or this will kick you all the way back to Philadelphia," Major Edgemont was telling her. Ethan was not too pleased at the young officer's eagerness to help her, but he stood to one side and made no comment.

Just as Edgemont was showing Hannah how to take a sight down the barrel, a graceful twelve-point buck emerged from the woods across from them, headed for the water. The animal sensed their presence immediately. For just a moment it lifted its head and froze. It was enough for Edgemont to whisper to Hannah.

"You've got him. Steady now." He had reached around her to help her hold the gun straight. "*Now,* pull!"

With his finger on hers, he helped her squeeze the trigger, which sent the gun slamming back into her shoulder. Across the pond, they all watched as the beautiful animal faltered, lurched to one side, then stumbled back into the woods.

"Damnation!" Edgemont said in Hannah's ear. Then he let go of her and recovered his manners. "Begging your pardon, mistress."

Hannah lowered the rifle with shaking arms. "What happened?" she asked.

Ethan answered, "You hit it, but didn't kill it."

Her shoulder throbbed and she felt sick at the pit of her stomach. Everything had happened so fast. "I didn't . . . I didn't even mean to shoot at it," she said in dismay.

Major Edgemont had regained his good humor. "Don't worry, mistress. You got a solid hit. It's as good as dead. We'll just have to track it a ways."

Hannah looked for confirmation to Ethan, who nodded his head. She had only seen the animal for a moment, but it had looked so majestic poised there against the trees. She couldn't believe that she had been responsible for killing it, no matter how badly Major Edgemont wanted fresh meat for his supper.

Ethan recognized her distress. It was not that unusual with a first-time kill, but it was something that Hannah would have to work through. If she was going to live on the frontier she, or at least her husband, would be killing regularly. Or they wouldn't eat.

Major Edgemont took the rifle from Hannah and put a consoling arm around her shoulders. "It's getting late," he said. "Why don't the rest of you head on back, and Mistress Forrester and I will go pick up her deer?"

Ethan looked at the young Englishman in disbelief. He had had about enough of Major Edgemont for one day, he decided. "I'll fetch the deer," he said in a tone that left no argument. "And Mistress Forrester will ride with me. We'll see you men back at the fort."

The officers looked around at each other. Finally Major Edgemont asked, "Is that satisfactory to you, Miss Forrester?"

Hannah could see Ethan bristling at the younger man's questioning of his authority. The last thing she wanted to do was ride into those woods and see the consequences of the bullet she had fired. But she also didn't want the happy day they had all spent to end in an argument. "I'll be fine with Captain Reed," she said, keeping her voice light. "Thank you all for the wonderful day. I'm not sure that I'll take up hunting on a regular basis, but I know that I won't forget how kind you all have been."

Five pairs of eyes regarded her with admiration and varying degrees of hunger. Ethan swung up on his horse, leaving it for Major Edgemont to help Hannah to mount. "Come on," he said. "If we don't hurry, we'll be traipsing after your quarry all night."

She bid the officers good-day and rode after Ethan around the edge of the pond and into the woods at the point where the deer had disappeared. The sunny day dimmed the minute they entered the trees. They had been riding through forests for days on the trail, but this place seemed different to Hannah, quieter, more sinister. She realized that her feelings were due in part to the knowledge that at any moment they might come upon the bloody carcass of the animal she had shot. She tried to concentrate on the fresh smell of the pines and the sighing sound of the wind high up in the trees.

"We're in luck," Ethan said after only a few minutes. "There it is, just up ahead."

She leaned over on her horse to peer around him, then winced as she caught sight of the deer, lying at the foot of a large, decaying log. It was utterly still, its head bent awkwardly backward due to the width of its antlers. They approached it cautiously, and Ethan jumped from his horse. "It's dead," he said.

Hannah could now see that the animal's eyes were half-open and its long tongue hung out of its mouth, touching the dirt. She shuddered. "It was so... splendid," she said.

Ethan walked over and took hold of the tip of an antler, lifting the head for her to see. "They are a noble-looking animal," he said. "And they serve a noble cause, namely, keeping us alive."

Reluctantly she slid from her horse. "I wish I hadn't shot it."

"If it will make you feel any better, your Major Edgemont actually did the shooting. He just thought it was a good excuse to hold you in his arms while he did it."

Hannah did not want to be responsible for the animal's death, but she also did not want her efforts at learning to use a gun to be belittled. "I held the gun. I pulled the trigger. And it's my shoulder that feels like it was stepped on by a bull."

Ethan frowned and dropped the deer's head. "Are you hurting, Hannah?" he asked, suddenly solicitous.

She bit her lip to keep it from quivering. "I guess I'm not as much of a frontierswoman as I thought."

He came over to her and took her chin in his hand. "Don't you believe it," he said. "Not one woman in twenty out West can fire a rifle. Back in Philadelphia, not one woman in a thousand, I'd wager."

"I'm not sure that I'll be firing one again soon." Her eyes went once again to the dead deer.

"Judging from the way Webster was shooting the other day, I'd say you might have to."

She looked up sharply. All at once she was reminded of their encounter at the dance last night when he had accurately surmised that Randolph had kissed her. In her distress over the deer, she had forgotten for a moment that she had determined to stay away from Ethan. Had forgotten that he engendered feelings in her that were dangerous to her peace of mind...and to her future. Standing steps away from the animal whose life she had ended, she was reminded that the things one does in life have consequences. Sometimes grave ones.

She took a step backward. "I would rather not discuss Mr. Webster with you, Captain. Not his hunting ability or any other aspect of his life. Or mine, either, for that matter."

He gave her one of those infuriating smiles. "There, I've made you angry. Now at least you're not going to be crying over a dead deer."

She glared at him. "What do we do with it?" she asked.

Ethan's eyes were still on her, not the deer. "We'll field-dress it, then tie it over your horse."

Hannah looked at the carcass with distaste. "I have to ride with it?"

"No." Ethan walked away to pull some rope from the back of his saddle. "You'll ride with me."

She stood as if riveted to the ground while Ethan tied the rope around the deer's hind legs. "I could use some help to hang it," he said. "If you're going to be a frontierswoman, you might as well start now."

Reluctantly Hannah moved to his side. "What do you have to do?"

"We'll hang it over that limb," he said, motioning to a nearby tree.

Hannah bent to help him drag the deer underneath the tree and hold it as he tossed one end of the rope over the limb. The deer's hair felt warm and smooth under her fingers. Together they pulled on the rope until the deer hung high enough so that its antlers cleared the ground. Then Hannah stepped back quickly as Ethan slit the throat to let its blood drain out in a thick red pool. She felt a sick taste in her throat.

"You don't have to watch," Ethan said.

"No, you're right. If I'm going to be a frontierswoman, I might as well start now."

"Good girl." Ethan nodded his approval. After a few minutes, he swung the animal around and gave it a final shake, then lowered it to cut out the viscera. Hannah viewed the entire process without flinching.

Ethan worked as quickly as he could. Hannah had grown pale. She'd held up pretty well, but dressing a deer was not the prettiest of sights. He didn't want to end up with a swooning woman on his hands. "Bring your horse," he said, trying to distract her.

He dragged the deer a few steps away from the mess he had made. "I'll tie it on," he told her. "You just hold her steady."

She looked white and fragile, more like a frightened child than the stalwart young woman he had come to know. He finished his task, then he tied both horses to a young ash tree. "There's a stream yonder," he told her. "We can wash up before we start back."

Without speaking, she followed him through the darkening woods toward the sound of rushing water. The late afternoon sun was throwing curious patterns through the trees to the soft forest floor. Hannah took a deep breath. She felt as if she'd learned her first lesson about survival in this land. The first of how many yet to learn? she wondered.

Together they crouched by the stream and washed their hands. "So now you've shot and dressed your first deer," Ethan said, glancing at her. She had pushed up her sleeves. Her arms were white and slender. Deceptively fragile, like the rest of her. On the trail he had seen her carry armloads of wood and stretch a tent rope taut. Today she had pulled her weight as they had hoisted the deer. And she had shot a rifle that would bowl over some soldiers he knew.

"You dressed the deer," she reminded him. "And I thought you said that Major Edgemont was the one who really shot it."

Ethan grinned at her. "I was just trying to make you feel better. You looked like you were about to pass out on me."

She turned toward him indignantly. "I've never fainted in my life, Captain Reed, and I don't intend to start now."

Ethan sat back on the bank, watching as she reached carefully under her skirt to dry her hands on one of her petticoats. He caught just a flash of trim ankles and felt an unsettling in his middle. "Since I've kissed you, not once but twice, don't you think you could call me Ethan—at least when we're alone?" he asked softly.

"I hadn't intended to be alone with you, *Captain*. And I do not intend that it shall happen again." There was anger in her eyes as she answered him, and there was something else, too. Alarm? Was she afraid of him or of herself? Either way, he should get to his feet and leave it alone. To all appearances Webster had finally discovered her. It shouldn't take long now for him to put a claim on her. Which meant that Ethan should be staying the hell away from her. But some unmanageable part of him kept him from moving.

"We had a rather thorough kiss the other night, if I remember. And I *do* remember, Hannah."

Hannah hugged her knees close to her chest. "What do you want from me, Captain? Can't you go to your... friend, Mrs. McCoy, for this kind of thing?"

The anger had won out over the alarm. Ethan smiled and felt a perverse stab of pleasure. His relationship with the fort's buxom female trader obviously did not sit well with her.

"Polly and I have been friends for years," he said casually.

"*Good* friends," Hannah added.

"Yes, *good* friends."

"So go bother her with your talk of kissing, Captain, and let me alone."

There was no doubt about it. He knew the signs. Hannah was in the throes of that miserable, nasty, gut-gnawing feeling called jealousy. The same kind of feeling he had had last night after she had come in from kissing Webster outside the dance. The kind of feeling he had right now just remembering it. Suddenly he lost the urge to bait her. "In case you're interested, Polly and I have decided we can't be anything more than friends."

Her eyes betrayed her with a quick flash of interest before she said nonchalantly, "I'm sure I couldn't care less what you and Mrs. McCoy have decided."

Ethan gave a rueful chuckle. He didn't blame her for not owning up to the truth. Hannah was smart enough to see that there was no future in letting herself be attracted to a rover like himself. "It's Randolph you're interested in now, is that it?"

Hannah ignored the question and pushed herself to her feet. "Can we go back to the fort?" she asked.

Ethan stood beside her, unable to resist one last comment. He leaned close and whispered in her ear, "I *will* remember that kiss, Hannah. And if Webster doesn't make you melt in his arms, the way you did in mine that night, then, mark my words, you'll find yourself remembering it, too."

* * *

"Does this mean you'll be scratching at my door trying to beg your way back into my bed?" Polly McCoy gave Ethan a good-natured shove that almost toppled him backward off the bench. They were sitting at her table, and over two pints of ale he had just finished recounting his day in the woods, including the final encounter with Hannah. He righted himself on the bench and grinned. Rough horseplay seemed to come naturally to Polly. Outside of the bedroom, she sometimes seemed more like a man than a woman. Though a blind man could see that she was most definitely female.

"One thing has nothing to do with the other," he explained impatiently. "I had no illusions about forming a liaison with Mistress Forrester. We just had a couple of weak moments when we were thrown together in such close proximity on the trail."

"Uh-huh." Polly raised her thick, rusty-colored eyebrows. "Did ya ever notice how you start to talk fancy and Boston-like when you get riled about something?"

"I'm not riled."

"Well, you sure act riled every time you talk about her. I'm beginning to think you've gone soft in the head, Ethan Reed."

"She's an attractive woman, that's all. And she has a lot of spirit. But there'll never be anything between us."

"She's an attractive woman, he says," Polly mimicked. "And she's got that long blond hair and that long skinny body that has half the rummies in the fort with their tongues on the floor."

"Are you jealous, Polly?" Ethan teased.

"Not on your account, you lout."

They shared a comfortable smile. After Polly's initial pretense of hurt, deciding to switch their status from lovers to friends had been a mutual decision, one which they both admitted was overdue. They had met each other's needs over the past few years, but it had been some time since their lovemaking had inspired much passion.

"So you're just going to give her up to that weak-kneed bookkeeper?"

"Webster's not a bad fellow. Though I'll admit I have my reservations about leaving him on his own out in the wilderness."

"He's handsome enough, that's for sure. And he's a real gentleman toward the ladies."

Ethan frowned. "You think he's handsome?"

Polly gave him another whack with the side of her hand. "So *now* who's the jealous one, mate?"

Ethan stood up and paced over to the fireplace. "Let's change the subject, all right? You said that Silas Warren was asking around for some cheap guns?"

She nodded. "And cheap liquor. Which is a bad combination in anyone's book."

"For the Indians, you think?"

"I'd put money on it."

He rubbed his hand along the smooth wood mantel. "But you don't know which tribe he's planning to contact?"

"All I know is that the rumor is he's gathering more merchandise than he could possibly handle by himself."

"So he must be working with someone?"

Polly shrugged. "It would take a damn fool to work with slime like Warren, but then I guess there are enough of those in this world."

"I'll do some poking around and see what I can find out."

"But you and your party will be leaving soon, won't you?"

He nodded. "Unless Bouquet frightens them out of the whole idea with his talk of bloody war parties."

Polly shook her head sadly. "Do you suppose we'll ever find a peaceful way to live together out here?"

Hannah, Eliza and Nancy ambled along arm in arm, talking and laughing like schoolgirls. "I feel as if I were back in Philadelphia heading down Front Street for an afternoon's shopping," Eliza said happily.

"I don't think the trading post is going to look much like Front Street," Hannah observed.

"As long as they have soap," Nancy said longingly. "I can't believe that we've already used all of ours. I guess I didn't plan very well."

"You should have known better, Nancy," Eliza said sarcastically. "After all, don't you pack up and move your family halfway across the country every month or two?"

Both the younger women smiled. "I guess we all have to learn as we go along," Nancy said.

They had decided on the expedition the night before when the men had returned with the supplies they had purchased to take to the new settlement. There were traps and tanning knives and powder horns, bars of lead to melt into bullets and various types of farming equipment, but none of the little amenities that the women had been hoping to add to the meager stores they had brought from home.

Hannah had wanted some lengths of worsted to make the trousers Jacob would need to keep up with his growing legs. Eliza had declared that she needed to replenish her stock of teas and herbs. And Nancy had shyly mentioned that she and her daughters needed soap. So the men had agreed that the women should themselves visit the cluster of trading huts that were beginning to form into a little town at the north end of the fort.

Randolph had given Hannah what seemed an immense amount of money to spend. The money, along with the new feeling of acceptance and equality with her two friends, had Hannah feeling almost giddy. Though she hadn't thought of herself as a lonely child, she'd never really had girlfriends when she was growing up, and she was finding the experience delightful.

It had meant a lot to her when Eliza and Nancy had exclaimed over her prowess when she and Ethan had returned yesterday afternoon with the deer. Randolph had not said a word about her trophy, and Ethan had left the horses and deer carcass in the care of a corporal and had stalked off to his quarters. But her two new friends and the children had been enthusiastic with their praise.

"You'll have to do the bargaining for us, Hannah," Nancy teased. "Those lonely traders will give you a better price than they will Eliza or me."

"Don't be silly, Nancy," she replied with an easy smile. "They'll hardly look at me when they see that pretty face of yours."

Nancy grimaced. "Not when it's on top of *this* body."

"Pooh," Eliza said. "You both had those officers drooling in their beer at the dance the other night."

"I didn't see that you were lacking for partners yourself, Eliza," Hannah said, giving her friend a little nudge.

They all laughed and continued on out the back gates of the fort and down the dusty street to the Hudson's Bay outfit, the largest of the traders. The big building had a wooden sidewalk entrance and real glass windows. They went inside, pausing a moment for their eyes to adjust to the dimly lit interior. What they saw was a fantastic jumble of merchandise, easily rivaling any trading dock back in Philadelphia.

"I think they'll have soap," Hannah whispered to Nancy, and they both giggled.

They dropped their linked arms and walked into the store, marveling at the trappings of civilization that they had not even realized they missed—perfumes and hair ribbons, china and beeswax candles, silk slippers and lace collars. But who was going to wear silk and lace on the frontier? Hannah wondered.

Tucked at the end of one counter Hannah saw a box of marzipan, the kind her mother had sometimes bought her for a very special treat. She thought of Ethan and his "sweet tooth," but pushed the memory out of her mind and moved on.

Suddenly the loud, unpleasant voice of Hugh Trask sounded in the doorway. "It's the ladies' shopping day," he said mockingly.

Hannah's good mood disintegrated. She couldn't think of anyone who could spoil a day more effectively. Hugh was with another man, a frightful-looking fellow with dirty clothes and a nasty scar across one missing eye.

The two men moved into the store. "What are you spending my money on, woman?" Hugh said to Nancy. The light had gone out of her face.

"I won't buy much, Hugh," she said in a low voice. "Just a few personal things for the girls."

"See that you don't," he said gruffly, then turned to his companion. "Of course, Mistress Hannah, here, will be able to buy whatever she pleases the way she's got Webster panting after her."

The scarred man gave a gurgling chuckle that made Hannah feel sick. Skirting around a table full of iron kettles so that she wouldn't have to pass the two men, Hannah went to Nancy's side. "Let's go down the road and see what else there is before we decide on anything."

Gratefully Nancy let Hannah lead her out of the trading post. Hugh and his friend watched them with smirking faces. If she wasn't a servant, Hannah thought fiercely, she'd slap that smirk right off Hugh Trask's face.

"I just want you folks to be aware of the risks." Colonel Bouquet stood at the head of a long table covered with maps in the post headquarters. "Pontiac is trying to convince the tribes that the British settlers aren't going to be as easy to deal with as the French trappers were. It appears that a good many of them are listening to him."

"What do you have to say about it, Reed?" Seth Baker asked their guide.

Ethan looked around at the circle of faces. When they reached their destination, the Philadelphia party would be on their own. With the withdrawal of Amos Crawford, there were only three men left. Baker was old. Trask drank too much. And that left Webster, who couldn't hit the broad side of a barn with his eyes open. Not a very promising first line of defense against a war party.

"It has to be your decision," he said. "But it's the British army that's responsible for the safety of the settlers arriving here. So I think you'd better listen to what Colonel Bouquet has to say."

"Are you telling us that we've come all this way and now we have to turn back?" Randolph asked, smacking his hand down on the table.

"I'm sure as hell not going back," Hugh Trask said.

Colonel Bouquet picked a map off the table. "I'm not forbidding you to go on with your plans. I'm just recommending that you don't go too many days away from the fort. There are plenty of good sites for settlement without leaving British protection."

"What do you think about that, Captain Reed?" Seth asked. "You know the area."

Ethan walked around the table to stand next to the colonel. He avoided looking down the table to where Hannah sat next to Webster. He had not spoken with her in the two days since they had come back from the hunt with Hannah's deer.

"As a matter of fact," he said, "I know just the place. It's not more than a week's travel downriver."

"What do you have in mind, Reed?" Colonel Bouquet asked.

Ethan took the map from him and spread it out on the table. His finger stabbed into the map. "It's right here—prettiest darn spot in the territory. It's called Destiny River."

Chapter Nine

The three Philadelphia families had contracted for two flatboats that would carry them and as many belongings as they could fit down the broad Ohio to the point where it was joined by the tiny Destiny River. Ethan had assured them that it was one of the most beautiful areas he had explored. The Destiny was the perfect size to provide them with water and transport without exposing them to hostile parties that might be traveling up and down the Ohio.

"Does this mean we won't meet any Indians after all?" Jacob asked two evenings before their departure as he sat with the three girls and Ethan in the officers' dining room.

Ethan had made the boy a present of the fowling piece he had lent him the day they all went hunting, and he had been showing him how to clean it and take care of it. "We're going to *hope* we don't meet any, Jacob," he said.

"But I wanted to see what they were like," Jacob said glumly.

Ethan put the gun to one side and put an arm around the boy. "Some of the Indians around here aren't too friendly right now. They think the English people are coming to take over lands that belong to them.''

''Do they hate us?'' Though Jacob was asking the questions, Ethan could see that Peggy and the Trask girls were listening intently.

''Some of them hate us. Not most. But if one of their chiefs says they should fight the English, then they likely are going to do what he says. Just like you'd fight if your pa told you to.''

''Or Hannah,'' Jacob added solemnly.

''Or Hannah.'' Ethan nodded. The children obviously had taken to Hannah as a replacement for their mother. Webster was lucky he'd had someone at hand who could step into his wife's place so competently. He wondered briefly how long it would be before Hannah would be taking Priscilla Webster's place in every respect. He hoped it wouldn't be until after he had settled these people down on the Destiny and was himself leagues away.

Jacob reached for his gun. ''I'll put this away now. Do you want me to put away the Sure Shot?''

''No. I'll take care of it. A good woodsman always looks after his own weapon.''

Jacob started out of the room but turned back. ''Captain Reed?''

''Yes, son.''

''I still wish I could see some Indians.''

Ethan smiled at his youthful persistence. ''You will someday, Jacob. One of these days we're all going to have to learn to live in peace in this territory.''

''Maybe then some of them will even be our friends.''

''I wouldn't be surprised.''

The hinges on the log door squeaked and Randolph walked into the room. "It's time for you children to be in bed. We have a busy day for everyone tomorrow, and then the commandant's party tomorrow night before we leave."

Jacob handed Ethan the rag they'd been using to polish his gun and turned obediently toward the door. "Look at it, Papa. The barrel's gleaming." He held the fowling piece out for his father's inspection.

Randolph smiled at his son absently. "Off to bed with you, now. You too, girls."

Both men were silent as the children reluctantly got to their feet and headed outside. "It was kind of you to give the boy the gun," Randolph said stiffly after the door had banged shut behind them. He was trying to tamp down the unreasonable annoyance he felt when he saw Ethan Reed teaching his son about the frontier.

Ethan stood and answered, "My pleasure. He's a fine boy, eager to learn. He'll do well in the wilderness."

Unlike his father, Randolph thought with some resentment. He faced Reed directly. The two men were of similar heights, but the captain's body was much more filled out, stronger. Randolph stayed with the subject of his son. "He's a bit overeager at times, I'm afraid. You've been very patient with him."

Ethan made a move to leave. "Both your children are fine young people, Webster. You're lucky to have them. And I think you and ... Mistress Forrester will make a splendid pioneer family."

"Thank you." Randolph was not about to confirm or deny his plans as far as Hannah was concerned to Reed. It was none of the man's affair. He'd seen the way Reed looked at her, and he was not entirely sure that Hannah did not return the interest. After all, Reed was an adventurer, an exciting kind of character. And a ladies' man to boot, with those spellbinding dark eyes. He would be relieved when Ethan Reed's job with them was finished and he had ridden off over the horizon, the way men of his type always did.

As much as she was looking forward to reaching their destination, Hannah was feeling sad to leave the fort. For the first time in her life she had been able to enjoy herself with a group of young people. The fact that they were mostly men—men who put her at the center of attention—amazed and delighted her. Not even her disturbed feelings about Ethan Reed could dampen her enjoyment. When they left tomorrow, it would be months before she would see anyone outside of the small circle that would make up the Destiny River settlement. She was lucky to have such a good friend in Eliza. And now it appeared that she and Nancy Trask, too, would be able to form a bond. As to her relationship with Randolph...well, it would be easier to have a clear head about Randolph once Ethan Reed was gone from their lives. And that couldn't happen too soon for Hannah.

Peggy and Janie were also showing reluctance to leave the fort. Both girls hovered on the edge of that leap that would take them into womanhood. Much to their giggling delight, the soldiers had teased them and flirted with them outrageously, though none had crossed the boundaries of propriety. Bridgett, who at nine was still firmly locked into childhood, had been embarrassed by the attention and had been spending more time with Jacob.

Most of the new friends they had made were present at the farewell dinner that Colonel Bouquet was giving for them at the officers' dining room. Major Edgemont, whose courting of Hannah had become more and more audacious, had been at her side all evening, tolerated by Randolph only because he knew they would be leaving the fort behind in the morning.

Hannah shrugged off the boisterous major's more suggestive remarks and dedicated herself to enjoying her last evening in this congenial company. It annoyed her that she found herself cranking her head every now and then in search of Ethan. It seemed unusual that he would not be present for their farewell dinner. She had also noticed that Polly McCoy was not in attendance. But Ethan had told her that he and Polly were no more than friends.

"I've been up the Destiny," a portly British major named Blanchard was telling them. "It rolls out of the prettiest little valley you'd ever want to see. Puts me in mind of the lake country back home."

The children had gotten tired of the adult conversation and were over at the fire roasting ears of corn. Randolph and Seth Baker were trying to get every piece of information they could about the place they would be settling, while Nancy, Eliza and Hannah listened mostly in silence. Hugh Trask was also missing from the gathering. He probably wanted to take advantage of the fort's stores of liquor on his last night, Hannah thought, giving Nancy a sympathetic look.

Nancy was looking healthier after a few days' rest at the fort, but it seemed that every day she got bigger under the shawl she wore constantly to cover herself.

Eliza had discussed the upcoming birth with the fort's doctor, trying to learn as much as she could. He had given her a tincture to put on the baby's stomach when it was born and a willow bark tea to ease the mother. Hannah had trouble believing that the event would really happen and that she and Eliza would be solely responsible for the well-being of their friend and her baby.

Her thoughts were interrupted by the mention of Ethan's name.

"Reed said he'd be here..." Colonel Bouquet was saying.

"He must have changed his mind," Major Edgemont interrupted. "We saw him heading toward Polly's, and he hollered at us that he wouldn't be able to make the dinner."

Bouquet gave a suggestive laugh. "I guess we all know what that sailor's looking for his last night in port, so to speak. Begging the ladies' pardon," he said belatedly, nodding to the bench where Hannah sat with Eliza and Nancy.

Hannah saw Randolph studying her intently. She was sure her face showed no emotion, but inside she felt a wave of hurt and anger. While it was true that Ethan's affairs should have nothing to do with her, she couldn't help a feeling of betrayal. He had lied to her about Polly. Her mother had always told her that men would tell any kind of lies to get their way with a woman, but this was the first time she had experienced it. All her life she had fought to maintain her optimism and trust in people in the wake of her mother's bitterness, but as she remembered Ethan's words out in the woods, she had to wonder if her mother's assessment of the world had been more correct than Hannah had ever wanted to believe.

As the other men tossed out a few more ribald comments about Ethan and Mrs. McCoy, Major Edgemont approached Hannah. "Would you do me the honor of walking with me, Mistress Forrester?" he said with a bow. "We can exchange this smoky room and unpleasant conversation for a little bit of cool night air."

Edgemont was a handsome man and obviously was aware of the fact. He exuded confidence, and his smile said that any request he made was bound to be granted. Hannah had found his longish blond hair and merry blue eyes attractive, but as she looked at him now, she saw only another man trying to deceive her with sweet words for his own devices.

"No thank you, Major. I'd like to stay here with everyone else for our last evening together."

Edgemont was surprised but undaunted at her refusal. "Perhaps we'll not let you go in the morning, mistress. The fort has been a fairer place since you arrived. Since *all* you ladies arrived," he amended, including Nancy and Eliza with a nod.

"If I were a single woman again, I'd be swept off my feet by that one," Nancy said with a little sigh as the major sauntered away. "But it's you he's had his eye on, Hannah, ever since we came here."

"I can guess just exactly what Major Edgemont wants," Hannah snapped. "All these other soldiers, too."

Eliza looked at her friend in surprise. "Why, Hannah. What bee has gotten into your bonnet? These men have been perfect gentlemen."

Hannah looked down at the floor. She had never told Eliza about her less-than-gentlemanly episodes with Ethan Reed. She'd told no one, nor did she intend to. "I suppose I'm jumpy tonight, thinking about leaving tomorrow." She turned to Nancy. "I'm sorry if I spoke sharply."

Nancy reached out and took her hand. "We're all jumpy, Hannah. Don't worry about it. I'm just happy that when we do head out into the wilderness, I'll be with two such good friends."

Hannah gave her hand a squeeze in return. Then Eliza reached around her and placed her hand on top of the two of theirs. "We'll take care of each other," she said. "Thank the Lord for friendship."

With some discouragement Ethan opened the second bottle he had brought with him to the gathering at Polly's to try to loosen tongues. Tonight was his last chance to find out what Silas Warren was involved in and who was helping him. Ethan had not wanted to miss the farewell dinner for his group, but it was more important to get the information he needed. Unfortunately, the first bottle had been passed around and finished off in short measure without anyone getting overly loquacious.

He decided on a more direct approach. "I guess the army would be pretty interested to know what Silas Warren is up to these days," he said loudly.

A sergeant major whom Ethan knew casually gave a snort of disgust. "Whatever that vermin's up to, you can bet it's no good."

"I heard he's been making some heavy purchases of guns," Ethan said, watching the faces of the men in the circle. There was no reaction from most of them, but a young private who was close to being cashiered for falling asleep one too many times at his post looked guiltily in another direction.

"He could make a fortune right now," the sergeant major observed, "as badly as the Indians want guns these days. Of course, he could well lose his no-good scalp in the bargain."

"If he's selling guns to the tribes, I reckon the army might be willing to pay for information that might help stop him," Ethan said loudly.

None of the men spoke, but the nervous private cast a furtive glance in the direction of the blockhouse. Ethan waited for a minute, then stood. "I'm taking my party south tomorrow, and I sure as hell would like to know if someone's going to be out there arming the tribes right where we're heading. If any of you men know something, I'd appreciate it if you'd see me privately. I'll make sure you're rewarded."

He gave a last glance around the circle, then headed in the direction of the blockhouse. He had developed keen instincts during his years with the Rangers. He couldn't be sure that the private knew anything, but something told him that it might be worth checking out. Sure enough, as he reached the distinctive square redoubt, he heard Silas Warren's voice. Quietly he walked toward the wall of the building and sidled along it until he was near the door.

"I'll let you know when it's time," he heard Warren say. "Just be ready."

The reply was muffled. Ethan realized the men were at the end of their conversation and could get away before he could find out the identity of Warren's partner. He stepped into the doorway in plain view and said, "Evening, gentlemen."

Warren spun around toward him, but the other man sank quickly back into the shadows and darted out the door on the other side of the building. Ethan took off after him, but when he reached the door, the man had disappeared into the darkness. Frustrated, Ethan turned back to Warren. "Your friend's not very sociable."

Warren grunted. "Ain't no law that says a person's got to be sociable."

The interior of the blockhouse was almost black. Ethan walked toward Warren and loomed over him menacingly. "No, but there *is* a law against selling guns to Indians. Spirits, too. You do know about that law, don't you, Silas?"

Warren stood his ground. "What's it to you, Reed? You're not even in the damned army."

Ethan leaned close enough to see the glint of white from the man's one good eye. "It's not a matter of armies anymore, Silas. There are women and children heading out to settle these parts nowadays. And if the Indians come after them with British guns, it's scum like you who will be responsible for their deaths."

"You ain't got no proof against me, Reed. So go on and leave me alone."

Ethan took a step back and forced his voice to sound calm. "I don't need proof, Silas. If I hear that one of the tribes has gotten a new shipment of guns, I'm coming after you. And when I'm finished with you, you'll be sorry the Indians didn't kill you first."

They had divided the supplies and the animals evenly between the two flatboats. Hannah was relieved to discover that Ethan and the four Trasks would ride on one, while she would be on the other with the Bakers and the Websters. Each family had been allowed to keep two horses or mules, which, with Ethan's horse, put three animals on one boat and four on the other. In addition, a double pen had been built on the Trasks' boat to house five squealing piglets and a dozen chickens.

Nancy Trask had wanted to bring along a cow, in case her milk was not enough for the baby, but there were none available for purchase at the fort. Anyway, Hannah thought as she viewed the impossibly full deck, she didn't see how a cow could have been squeezed onto either of these boats. There was barely room for the people who would have to make the vessels their home for the next few days.

In the center of each boat was a small cabin to provide shelter in case of bad weather. At the front and back were two long, attached oars that the boatmen at the Fort Pitt landing called sweeps. The vessels looked ungainly and inefficient next to the sleek bateaux of the fort traders, but they held an amazing amount of supplies. Hugh Trask in particular had piled dozens of crates and bundles on his boat, saying that he needed more supplies with a new baby on the way. Perhaps, in spite of how he had acted at the Hudson's Bay post the other day, he was finally becoming more responsible about equipping his family.

Hannah watched from on board as the men made the preparations to cast off. The farewells had mostly been said last night, though Major Edgemont had come down to the docks this morning to say goodbye to Hannah and present her with a little bouquet of spring wildflowers. They lay wilting and forgotten in her lap as she sat perched on a barrel of salt, one of the more precious of the supplies they carried. Without salt they'd have no way to cure meat for the winter.

Suddenly there was a shout from Peggy at the front of the boat. "Hannah, Jacob's going to fall right over the edge."

Hannah sighed and pushed herself off the barrel. The children had been up since before dawn, excited about the adventure ahead. "Tell him to be careful," she hollered back. She climbed over crates, plow parts, kettles, Eliza's spinning wheel and other assorted clutter and made her way around the animals to the flat-nosed front of the boat. The gunwale surrounding the four sides of the boat was low. It would be easy for even a small child to tumble over it. Jacob was on his hands and knees hanging over the wooden lip to touch the water.

"Get back, Jacob. They're about to launch and there's going to be a jerk that could toss you right overboard," she told him.

"I told you so," Peggy said smugly.

Jacob crawled backward and turned to Hannah with an apologetic expression. "I just wanted to feel the water, Hannah."

She reached the boy's side and knelt beside him. "There'll be plenty of chances to do that, Jacob. But right now you have to stay back." She put her arm around him. "I'm counting on you to use good sense on this trip. Can you promise me that you'll do that?"

"I promise," he said solemnly.

"You stay away from the side of the boat unless you're with me or your papa, all right?" she added.

He nodded, his eyes on the fast-moving water. There was a sudden lurch of the deck and the boat began to float away from shore into the center of the current.

"We're off!" Randolph shouted from somewhere in back. It was good to hear excitement in his voice again. He had seemed to be getting more and more discouraged as the trip progressed. Perhaps now that they were on the last leg of their journey, he would regain some of his enthusiasm. Ethan had predicted a week's travel time if the trip went smoothly. It was hard to believe that in just a week they would be seeing the land they had come so far to claim.

Randolph appeared around the corner of the tiny cabin. "Can you believe it?" he asked them. His tone was more boyish than she had ever heard it. At the fort he had purchased a buckskin jacket, completely unlike his typical clothes. His usually tidy hair was loose and blowing in the river breezes. Hannah smiled at him and thought that his friends back in Philadelphia would hardly recognize him as the Randolph Webster they had known.

"It's the final stretch," she said, buoyed by his good spirits.

The children were watching the river churning around them, Jacob carefully staying back from the edge. They seemed to catch their elders' good mood. Jacob did a little dance of excitement, and Peggy climbed over a crate to give her father a hug.

Suddenly they heard yelling from the other boat. Hannah looked up to see Ethan waving his arms and shouting angrily. "You'd better man those oars, Webster, or you'll end up with a pile of firewood instead of a flatboat."

Randolph's smile died. He pulled Peggy's arms from around his middle and turned to make his way to the front sweep while Seth took over at the rear.

Hannah, Peggy and Jacob looked after him soberly.

Finally Jacob said softly, "I don't think Papa knows how to run a boat, Hannah."

Hannah gave his head a pat. "He'll learn, Jacob. We'll all learn."

After the frantic beginning when Randolph and Seth had lost complete control and had almost sent their boat careening into shore, the journey had gone peacefully, and Hannah, for one, found the travel much more pleasant than the trip by horseback. The broad river stretched out before them like a smooth silver highway. By the second day everyone in the two boats except Nancy had had a turn at the sweeps, and the men were becoming adept at keeping the vessels calm and steady in the midst of the current.

When they had stopped at the end of the first long day they had not even made a campsite. Exhausted from learning to manage the boats and from the emotional goodbyes at the fort, they had built their fires right on board in the small sandboxes built for that purpose in the sterns. Then there had been a haphazard assignment of every possible sleeping space. On the Websters' boat, Peggy and Eliza slept inside the cabin, while Hannah, Randolph, Seth and Jacob found places outside on the deck. Hannah was squeezed between two piles of boxes, but when she looked up from her narrow bed she could see an expanse of star-spangled sky that took her breath away. The gentle rocking and the lapping of the water against the sides of the boat lulled her into a dreamless sleep.

The second night they decided to make a camp and stretch out their cramped limbs. They were not as fatigued as they had been the nights on the trail, however, and the supper turned into something of a party.

When they had tied up that afternoon, Ethan had showed Jacob how to cut an alder pole and tie a hook and line to it. The two had then disappeared upriver, and in what seemed like no time at all were back with a string of four trout, still flopping.

While Ethan and Jacob skewered the fish with sticks through their mouths and began to roast them, Eliza and Hannah set out the last of the freshly baked food they had brought from the fort—corn johnnycakes and raisin tarts. They would make a feast of the meal, they decided, since it would be awhile before they would have the like again.

After supper the group sat contentedly around the fire, listening to the lullaby of the river's rush and the symphony of insects in the thick woods surrounding them. Seth turned down a request to play his fiddle, saying there couldn't be a sweeter sound than a peaceful spring evening.

"Aye, peaceful, that's the key. Are we safe in these parts, Reed?" Randolph asked. "Do you think we need to cover the boats?"

Ethan shook his head. "We're not likely to come across hostiles while we're still this close to the fort. The only Indians we should encounter in this area are the Wyandots, and they're friendly."

"There are Indians here, right where we're camping?" Jacob asked, instantly attentive.

"Somewhere hereabouts."

Jacob craned his neck to look around at the dark trees. "Can we see them?"

Ethan laughed. "I wouldn't be surprised if they could see us, but I doubt that we'll see them. They keep to themselves mostly."

"Could I talk to them if some came here?" Jacob persisted.

"That might be a problem. I think you would find that only a few speak English. A few speak some French."

"But mostly they talk Indian?"

Ethan answered the boy's questions patiently. "There are lots of different tribes of Indians, and they each speak their own language."

"So they can't talk even to each other?"

"Well, the Indians seem to be better than we white folk are at communicating with each other even without all the right words. They use hand signals, and somehow they just manage to understand."

By now all four children had gathered around Ethan. "Like magic, almost," Bridgett piped in.

"Kind of like magic, I guess," Ethan agreed, smiling at the youngest Trask girl.

As usual when the children seemed to be getting too fascinated with Ethan's frontier lore, Randolph had begun to look impatient. "I think that's enough talk about Indians," he said, getting to his feet.

Ethan stood, also. "That's probably enough talk, period. Tonight you can all get a good sleep on solid ground."

"Can't I stay on the boat like last night?" Jacob asked. "I liked going up and down with the water." He turned to Hannah for an answer.

"Your papa already set up our tent..." she began doubtfully, looking at Randolph.

As though he were trying to make up for cutting off his son's discussion with Ethan, Randolph gave a tolerant smile. "I don't see why you can't sleep on deck. If you get scared during the night, just climb ashore and go into the tent with Hannah and Peggy."

"I won't get scared," Jacob said.

"Can I, too, Mama?" Bridgett asked her mother. "It's so hot and stuffy inside the tent. And there's not room for all of us anymore."

No one made a comment on this obvious reference to the increasing size of Nancy's girth. "You want to sleep out in the open?" Nancy asked without much energy.

Bridgett nodded vigorously. "Under the stars. Didn't you see the sky last night? It looked like a black quilt sewn with sparkles." Both the Trask girls had medium brown hair and rather plain little faces, but when her eyes shone with enthusiasm, Bridgett took on some of her mother's beauty.

Nancy looked over at her husband, who shrugged. "All right," she said. "But you sleep over on Jacob's boat, so the two of you are together."

Bridgett and Jacob looked at each other shyly. After a moment Jacob said, "Well, come on then. I'll show you where you can put your blankets smack in the front. You can see the *whole* sky from there."

There was a general busyness as everyone made their arrangements for the night. Hannah had a prick of uneasiness over the children's plan to sleep by themselves, but she shook it off. The boat was just a few yards away from where she and Peggy would be in the tent. If anything should happen, Jacob could cry out and they would be by his side in seconds.

Chapter Ten

Someone's shout had awakened her, but Hannah was still groggy when she felt Randolph's hand shaking her shoulder. He had never before come into their tent when she was sleeping, and she sat up in surprise, pulling the blankets around her neck. His face was drawn and something in his expression reminded Hannah of the day Priscilla had died. "What is it?" she asked, her speech thick.

"Jacob's gone! Bridgett, too. We can't find them."

Hannah's stomach plunged. "What do you mean, gone?" She scrambled out of the covers and sat on her knees. "They've probably just gone off to...you know, morning things."

Randolph ran both hands back through his disheveled hair. "We've looked up and down the banks. Trask's out hollering for them now."

In the distance Hannah could hear Hugh Trask's angry shouts. "I'll go. I'll find them," she said, trying to sound calm. But inside, her panic was rising. How could they be *missing*? What could have happened to them? And how would they ever find them in the middle of this vast wilderness?

She followed Randolph out of the tent and was immediately confronted by a nearly hysterical Nancy. "My baby, Hannah! Bridgett's my little baby."

Hannah looked at the pregnant woman in alarm. Her eyes had a wild, haunted look. She was without her ever-present shawl, and her stomach looked painfully big for the rest of her fragile form. Hannah took her arm. "We'll find her, Nancy. You have to stay calm or you'll hurt your other wee one."

Randolph came up to them, running. "We've looked everywhere. They're just not here. Reed says we may have to consider the possibility that they were taken off the boat in the night by the savages."

Nancy gave a moan of anguish and sagged against Hannah. "Help me with her, Randolph," Hannah said sharply.

For the first time, Randolph took a good look at Nancy's face. "Dear Lord," he said, then bent forward and lifted the pregnant woman in his arms. In spite of her extra weight, he carried her easily over to a mossy section of the riverbank. "Fetch some blankets, Hannah," he said to her.

Hannah brought a bedroll to lay her against and blankets to cover her. Randolph stepped down to the edge of the river and shouted for her husband. Trask came quickly, looking worried, but it appeared that his concern was only for Bridgett, not his wife.

"Why'd you let the foolish child sleep all by herself out on that boat?" he yelled at Nancy, who cowered at the anger in his voice.

Randolph put a hand on Trask's chest and pushed him backward, almost causing him to stumble into the water. "Can't you see she's distraught, man? Do you intend to kill your own baby before it's even come into the world?''

Trask took a step toward Randolph, his fists raised. Hannah stepped between them. "Stop it, both of you! We should be thinking about Jacob and Bridgett. What are we going to do?''

Ethan came up behind Hannah. "I haven't been able to find any tracks.''

Randolph turned on him. "What kind of a guide are you, anyway? How could a bunch of Indians have sneaked up on us during the night and carried off two children?''

Ethan shook his head in bewilderment. "It doesn't make a lot of sense to me. But if it was Indians, they most likely wouldn't leave any trace. They know how to move without leaving a trail.''

Peggy and Janie were sitting on the edge of the boat, holding each other, tears running down their faces. Randolph, his chest heaving, was glaring at Ethan as if he wanted to start up a fight with him, too.

Hannah took a deep breath and sent a look of appeal to Seth Baker, who stood with Eliza at the rear of the group. Seth stepped forward. "It appears to me we better get a search organized. We know the youngsters aren't in the vicinity. We've looked everywhere.''

Ethan moved back, out of range of Randolph, and let Seth's calm voice soothe tempers. "Eliza will stay in camp with Mrs. Trask, here, and the girls. The rest of us can move out and start looking.''

Ethan nodded his approval. "We should form two parties. I'll go inland with Seth and try to pick up some tracks. Webster and Trask, you should follow the river downstream.''

"Why downstream?" Trask asked.

Ethan gazed at Nancy, who was lying on the bank looking very pale. "Let's go discuss this down by the boats," he said.

Nancy sat up. "No! I want to hear what you have to say."

Ethan hesitated for a moment, then said awkwardly, "Whoever took them might be traveling downriver, but the other possibility is that they somehow…" He glanced at Nancy, then Randolph. "They might have fallen into the water, been taken by the current." He bit his lip and looked down at the ground.

"Oh, my poor baby." Nancy began swaying back and forth and moaning. Hannah dropped to her side and put her arms around her. "We'll find them, Nancy. You just calm yourself and take care, because we're going to go out and bring them back."

Eliza joined them, bringing another blanket to wrap around her. "You go, Hannah," she said, giving her hand a pat. "I'll take care of things here."

"Come on, Hannah," Randolph said. "Let's get started."

"Hannah will come with me," Ethan interrupted.

"The hell she will." Randolph bristled with anger.

Ethan turned to walk toward the boat. "Don't be a fool, Webster. Think of your boy. Whoever finds him, he's going to scared and upset. He'll want to see either you or Hannah."

"You said it's likely they went downriver."

Ethan stood by the side of the boat with his back to them, making up a pack of his cartouche box, powder horn and various other supplies. "We don't know who will find them," he said.

Hannah hesitated, then walked down the bank to Randolph and put her hand gently on his chest. "He's probably right, Randolph. You go ahead with Mr. Trask, and I'll go with Seth and the captain."

The strain, worry and anger were all evident in the tight pull of Randolph's face. "Please," she said. "We have to think about Jacob."

Randolph braced his shoulders and roughly brushed her hand away. "Do whatever you damn well please," he said. Then he snatched his rifle from the ground and started off down the river.

Ethan had discovered a trail heading west that he thought would be the most likely path for anyone leaving the river. Without talking, Ethan, Seth and Hannah started out on it. Now that they were away from Nancy's hysteria and Randolph's belligerence, Hannah began to feel calmer. Perhaps it was the cathedral effect of the trees towering above them, or watching Ethan's skilled, methodic search for signs of tracks, but for some reason she was more confident. They were going to find Jacob and Bridgett, she told herself, and they were going to be just fine.

"Someone or something has definitely been through this way," Ethan said, after studying an area along the badly overgrown trail.

"Do you think it could be the youngsters?" Seth asked, bending over the broken branches that Ethan was indicating.

"It could be nothing more than a deer, but deer don't usually follow trails. Whatever came through, it was not long ago."

They continued walking up the trail, Ethan stopping now and then to observe what he called "signs."

Hannah had just about come to the conclusion that her optimism at the beginning of their search had been premature, when Ethan made an exclamation. Ahead of them right in the middle of the path lay the small musket that Ethan had given Jacob.

Hannah pushed around Ethan and started running toward the gun, but he grabbed her arm and pulled her back. "Let me take a look first before you mess up any tracks."

They approached the spot carefully, and Ethan squatted down to survey the ground. "Something went on here," he said. The dirt is pushed around. It's too hard for footprints, but you can tell that there were definitely a number of people here, milling about."

"A number of people?" Hannah asked, the fear creeping back into her voice.

Ethan nodded grimly. "In moccasins."

"Lord-a-mercy," Seth said under his breath.

Ethan straightened up, his expression speculative. "If this were a war party, they'd have attacked all of us and taken our weapons. They're not interested in two children."

"And what if they're the friendly Indians you were talking about last night?" Hannah rubbed together her hands, which had started to sweat as she thought about how terrified Jacob and Bridgett must be at this very moment, if, indeed, they were still alive.

"I can't think why friendly Indians would want two children, either. It doesn't make sense."

"Can you track where they're headed?" Seth asked.

Ethan nodded. "It doesn't look as if they're trying to cover up their trail."

"Should we go back and get Webster and Trask?"

Ethan shook his head. "They'll be a good piece downriver already. By the time we find them and get back here, we may have lost our chance." He retrieved Jacob's gun and motioned for Seth and Hannah to follow him.

Hannah's heart was pounding, and she found the walking more difficult than before, but in less than half an hour they emerged from the woods into a meadow, much like the one they had hunted in the other day. It sloped to a little stream in the center, and there, relaxing in the bright midday sun, was a band of eight or nine Indian braves. They looked just as Hannah would have imagined—brown skinned, starkly black hair and handsome, strong faces. They were gathered around two small figures. Jacob and Bridgett sat cross-legged, smiling, looking up at the Indians with total fascination.

"Thank God." Hannah held a hand over her heart.

"They're not Wyandot after all," Ethan said. "They look like Potawatomi."

"Are they friendly?" Hannah asked in a low voice.

"I don't know." He pointed his rifle at the ground, held up his hand, palm outward, and shouted a word that Hannah did not understand.

Two of the Indians had already gotten up and were coming toward them. One was an older man. He had strains of gray showing in his black hair, which was pulled back in a knot on the side of his head except for a fringe of short bangs covering his forehead. A single eagle feather hung alongside his face. He answered with the same word Ethan had used.

"Do you speak their language?" Hannah asked with amazement.

"A few words, here and there."

By now Jacob and Bridgett had seen them and jumped to their feet. "Hannah!" Jacob called, waving his hand excitedly.

Bridgett didn't join in his enthusiastic welcome. She looked guiltily down at the grass as if she knew that she had done something wrong.

"Can I go to them?" Hannah asked Ethan.

Ethan had kept his hand in the air as the two braves approached. "Wait just a minute," he said. "They're obviously all right. We'll just be sure that these men don't misinterpret our arrival."

The two Potawatomi men stopped a few feet from them. Ethan pointed to himself and then to the children. The Indians nodded, and one of them began speaking. When he stopped, Hannah asked, "Could you understand what he was telling you?"

Ethan continued looking at the Indians but said to her, "Not very much. But I think they were telling me that they found the children along the trail and were watching over them until their people came for them."

Hannah let out a deep breath. "So they didn't kidnap them?"

"I don't think so." He set his rifle on the ground, then reached behind his shoulder to pull off his pack. Digging inside, he pulled out a leather pouch full of tobacco. Taking a step forward, he offered it to the older man with a half bow and a few halting words.

"What are you doing?" Hannah asked.

"I'm thanking them for caring for our children."

The older brave took the pouch and answered Ethan with another flood of strange words. The other Indian had his eyes fixed on Hannah.

Ethan was nodding to the older man and both were smiling. "You don't usually see Potawatomi this far east,'' Ethan said quietly to Hannah and Seth. ''But they seem peaceful enough.''

The braves wore clothes made of some kind of skin—breechclouts over tubular leggings and loose shirts painted with bright designs. The older man had a pattern of colored porcupine quills around the neck of his shirt. The younger had parallel blue stripes painted on his cheeks, making him look fiercer and more alien. Suddenly he looked at Hannah, stepped back and held out his arm, as if telling her to go to the children. She walked between the two men, her eyes avoiding the painted brave, who continued to stare at her, and quickly made her way toward Jacob and Bridgett.

They ran to meet her as she approached, and she caught one up in each arm, hugging them to her side. ''Are you all right?'' she asked, her voice shaky. ''You're not hurt?''

Bridgett had started to cry. ''We were awfully scared, Hannah. I thought we weren't going to find you again.''

Hannah blinked back the tears that threatened in her own eyes and eased her hold on them. ''What happened to you?'' she asked.

Bridgett looked at Jacob, who looked away, his face red.

''Did these men take you off the boat?'' Hannah asked.

Jacob shook his head vigorously. ''They didn't do anything bad, Hannah. They're nice, and they talked to us with their hands, just like Captain Reed said.''

Hannah looked around in confusion. ''But how did you get here?''

Jacob lowered his head and mumbled, "I wanted to see them. I wanted to see the Indians."

Bridgett took over the story. "We woke up real early, Hannah, and Jacob said we could go into the woods and see if there were any Indians. He said we'd be back before anyone else got up. But then we didn't know which way it was back to the river."

Now the girl's tears came in earnest, and Hannah gave her another hug, resting her chin on her shiny brown hair. "Oh, sweetheart," Hannah said. "Your mother was so worried about you. We all were."

"I didn't mean to make Mama worry," the girl gasped through hiccuping sobs.

The men by the river were watching them with curiosity. Hannah tried to smile at them as she rocked Bridgett back and forth, comforting her.

"My pa's going to whip me," Bridgett said, her sobs finally subsiding.

Jacob's eyes grew round. "He wouldn't do that, would he?"

Bridgett nodded.

"I'll talk to him," Hannah said soothingly. "No one's going to get whipped. But you children made a bad mistake going off by yourselves." She put her hand on Jacob's head. "Remember we talked just a couple days ago about having to be responsible out here on the frontier?"

Jacob nodded and looked ashamed. "I wanted to see the Indians," he said mournfully.

"I know. Well, now you've seen them. And the rest of the trip I expect you to stay within a stick's throw of me or your papa. Is that understood?"

Both children nodded vigorously. Hannah let them loose just as Ethan and Seth came up behind her, followed by the two Indians.

"They're fine," she said to Ethan. "They left early this morning to go exploring and got lost."

"We're damn lucky that these men are in a amicable frame of mind," Ethan said soberly.

"They're really friendly, Captain," Jacob said with a tentative smile that indicated he knew he was in the wrong.

Ethan looked at him sternly and handed him the gun he had picked up off the trail. "Not all Indians are friendly, Jacob. And a good woodsman never leaves behind his gun."

Jacob took the musket. "I...I dropped it. We were pretty scared at first when the men came out of the woods. We didn't even hear them coming. Suddenly they were just there."

Ethan nodded. "As I said, you two were lucky. But it will be a good lesson for you."

The younger Indian said something to the older one. Ethan turned around to face them again, then shook his head as the older one spoke.

"What's he asking?" Hannah asked. The young brave was still watching her.

"They want to know if you're my woman."

Hannah gave a little jerk of surprise and felt her cheeks grow warm.

Seth looked from Ethan to Hannah. "What did you tell them?" he asked with a grin.

"I told them not yet."

By now all of the braves were standing and some had moved close to Hannah and the children. Some of the others had the odd-looking stripes across their faces. The young brave who had come out to meet them reached behind Hannah and lifted her thick blond braid for the others to see. He said something and the other men laughed.

She pulled away. "What did he say?" She was starting to feel uncomfortable as the men circled around her.

"I didn't understand," Ethan said with a frown. "But I think it would be a good idea if we got on our way."

He turned back to the older man and spoke, motioning toward the woods in the direction from which they had come. Hannah listened intently, as though she might be able to understand some of the words, but all she could tell was that they seemed to be taking a long time for a simple goodbye.

Ethan began motioning with his hands. Hannah could tell he was not happy, but he kept his demeanor calm. She turned to Seth, who raised his eyebrows and shrugged.

Finally Ethan took her arm and drew her away from the children and the crowding Indians. Seth followed them. "They want us to stay for a meal."

Hannah looked around for signs of a fire. "How long would that take?"

"It could be hours, even days, if they felt like making it that long. Indians have a different sense of time than we do."

Hannah was shaking her head before he had finished his statement. "We have to get back to tell Nancy that Bridgett is safe. It's dangerous for her to be worrying so long."

"Do we all have to stay?" Seth asked. "Someone could go back and let them know that we're all right."

Ethan glanced at Hannah. "They especially want the woman with sunshine hair to stay."

"Sunshine hair?" Hannah asked with a smile. She thought the reference was rather pretty.

Neither Ethan nor Seth appeared to share her pleasure at the term as they exchanged a significant look. "What happens if we just try to leave?" Seth asked.

"I don't know."

The noon sun was hot, but Hannah felt a sudden chill. "I'll stay, then," she said. "Ethan, you take the children back to the camp."

"No," Seth said firmly. "I'll go back and tell Mrs. Trask that the children are well. By now Randolph and Hugh should have returned, and we'll all come for you."

Ethan shook his head. "If they see more white men, they might start to get less friendly." He thought for a moment. "Seth, do you think you can follow the trail back to the boats?"

"Of course."

"What about the children?" Hannah asked.

Ethan looked at her soberly. "I'd feel better if they went back with Seth."

Seth nodded his agreement. "But are you sure you don't want us to return for you? What if you have trouble getting away?" He lifted an eyebrow and tipped his head in Hannah's direction.

Ethan looked over at the group of braves. Most were looking back at them. "I think there'd be more chance of trouble if they saw you all coming for us," he said slowly.

"And you don't know how long you'll be here?"

"You just keep everyone at the camp. We'll be there as soon as we can get away."

Finally, saying that Ethan knew best, Seth shrugged and agreed to the plan. The children did not want to leave Hannah and voiced their protests, clinging to Hannah's skirt.

"Mr. Baker will take you right back to the river, and your mother will be waiting," Hannah assured Bridgett.

"But what's going to happen to you, Hannah?"

"Nothing. We're just going to stay here and talk with these men for a while. Then we'll be following you back."

"Talk with your hands?" Jacob asked.

"I suppose so," Hannah said with a smile. "Now you stay right with Mr. Baker and don't give him any trouble. Promise?"

Ethan had been communicating with the older Indian, who seemed to be the leader of the group. They were looking at Seth and Hannah and then the children. Finally the brave nodded and made a motion of dismissal with his hand. "It's all right for you to leave," Ethan said, nodding to Seth, who looked uncertain. "Go on quickly before he changes his mind."

Seth hung his rifle over his shoulder and took a child's hand in each of his. "You young'uns will have to help me follow the trail back to the river. You think you can do that?"

They followed along with him, their heads turning back toward Hannah. "We'll see you in a little while, then," Jacob said anxiously.

Hannah smiled and waved. "We'll be back with you soon," she agreed. She kept the smile on her face until the little group had disappeared into the trees, then she turned to Ethan. "We will, won't we?"

Ethan had been right about the different ideas of time. It was late afternoon and the midday meal was still underway. After Seth had left with the children, the Indians had gathered around Ethan and Hannah once again, motioning toward Hannah and pointing at her hair. The young brave who had first greeted them had finally addressed Ethan directly and, emphasizing his words with hand movements, had told him to tell Hannah to take her hair out of its braid. Ethan had asked her if she would be willing to comply with his request. It seemed a small enough thing, so, with the nine Indians watching her intently, she had unbraided her hair and shaken it out around her shoulders. There had been murmurs of approval from the men, but when several of them had pushed forward to touch it, Ethan had stood in front of her and barked a couple Indian words. Fortunately, no one had objected to either the words or his tone. They had maintained their distance while Ethan and the old Indian began to speak.

The older man was a *sachem,* or chief, of his particular clan, which was called the Turtle clan. Ethan had not understood the word for turtle, and the chief had bent over to indicate a shell and moved his head comically back and forth. They all had laughed, and it gave Hannah a curious satisfaction to realize that she could be sharing a joke with people who were so different from her.

The laughter had set a jovial tone for the rest of the afternoon. Ethan and Hannah had sat alongside the stream and watched as the Indians gathered wood, built a fire and began roasting wild potatoes wrapped in corn husks.

They had brought out smoked meat, parched corn sweetened with honey and a kind of berry that Hannah had never seen before. She was completely full, but the hours went by and the food continued to appear.

The young brave who seemed to be so interested in Hannah urged her with signals to eat more. She smiled at him and shook her head. When he persisted, she put her hand over her stomach and puffed out her cheeks. Finally he laughed with her, imitating her gesture, and threw aside the piece of meat he'd been holding. His name was Skabewis, they'd determined, and it seemed that the others in the group had ceded him interest in their pretty female guest.

As the others cleaned up the remainders of the meal, he went over to one of their packs and took out a small wooden object, then presented it to Hannah. It was a carved needle case with several finely carved bone needles inside. Skabewis watched her intently as she examined it, evidently waiting for some kind of reaction. Hannah looked at Ethan for advice on what she should do.

"It's a fine gift," he said. "Just nod and say thank you. He'll understand the sentiment if not the words."

She did as Ethan suggested, but the gleam in the young Indian's eye was making her increasingly uncomfortable. "When do you think we can leave?" she asked Ethan.

"They seem to be drawing this meal out extra long," he said. "I think they like looking at you." He grinned. "Can't say that I blame them."

"I just keep thinking that they'll all be worried back at the boats until we get there. In spite of what you told Seth, Randolph might insist on coming after us."

Ethan nodded. "I'll see what I can do." He turned to the chief and started to talk. The chief listened politely to Ethan, then turned to Skabewis, who spoke for a very long time. Hannah could tell that Ethan was making an effort to stay calm. When the young brave stopped talking, Ethan spoke in cool tone of voice, but with emphasis, punctuating the words with chopping hand signals.

"What's happened?" Hannah asked, mystified.

Ethan waved her to silence as the debate went on for several more minutes. Skabewis kept looking over at Hannah, and she was certain that the discussion was somehow about her. Too impatient to wait, she asked Ethan again, "What does he want?"

He stood up and paced down to the stream, then came back and let out another torrent of the strange words. The chief's sentences seemed to grow calmer as Ethan's grew more agitated.

Finally Hannah could take no more. She stood and grabbed Ethan's arm. "Tell me what you're talking about," she demanded.

He looked down at her. "Skabewis wants to buy you," he said stiffly.

Chapter Eleven

"To *buy* me?"

"Yes."

"Is this some kind of joke?"

"No, it's no joke. They have a cache of furs near here, and he's offering them for you."

Like every other colonist, Hannah had heard the tales of white women who were carried off to live for years with the Indians. What if these men actually insisted on taking her? Even with his rifle, what could Ethan do against nine of them? Hannah glanced over at Skabewis's stoic face. He nodded at her and she looked quickly away. "What did you tell them?"

Ethan saw the fright in her eyes. They reflected the fear that had started uncoiling in his gut the minute he had seen the young brave's eyes on Hannah, fascinated and hungry. Ethan knew the look. He'd looked at her that way himself. There was a chance that when they realized he would not accept their offer, things could start to get difficult. But he needed Hannah to be strong and keep her wits about her.

"I'm negotiating," Ethan said, a glint of humor turning up his mouth. "Holding out for a better offer."

Hannah did not return the smile. "They can't... they can't *make* you give me to them, can they?"

"Not while I'm still alive," he answered calmly.

"What are we going to do?"

He looked over at the trees, gauging the distance. "I want you to start walking toward the trail we came out on. Do you think you could find your way back to the river by yourself?"

"By myself? But—"

He interrupted her. "You won't have to. But just in case, remember that the river is due east of us here. Watch where the sun is setting yonder and go the opposite direction, as quickly as you can."

"I'm not leaving you—"

This time his interruption was more effective. He pulled her toward him and gave her a hard, short kiss that stopped the words dead in her mouth. "Just go. Do what I tell you. I should be following along behind you any minute."

He gave her a little push and she started to walk. Over her shoulder she saw that the Indians were watching her. Two of them made a move to go after her, but Ethan stepped in front of them and started speaking. She made her way quickly to the edge of the trees. Ethan and Skabewis were face-to-face, talking heatedly.

Once she was within the shelter of the woods, she stopped. She couldn't decide if she should wait there for Ethan or go on as he had directed. The sun was already low in the sky. Soon it would be dark. This time the cathedral of trees seemed more sinister than peaceful.

If she had a gun, she would stay and try her new skill to help Ethan. But she had no weapon. The best thing would probably be for her to get to the boats as soon as possible and come back for Ethan with the other men. She set out, following what she hoped was the right trail, but she stopped frequently, miserable with worry and indecision. Perhaps she *should* go back to Ethan. There may be a way she could help after all. If all else failed, she could agree to stay with the Indians until Ethan could come for her with a rescue party. The very thought made her shudder. But what if by the time she came back to the little meadow with reinforcements, Ethan was dead? How would she feel?

Her steps grew slower and slower. Finally she turned around and started retracing her steps back to Ethan and the Indians. She couldn't leave him. If she couldn't help him, at least she would be by his side for whatever happened.

The sun was no longer in sight above the trees. The dim twilight left the forest floor completely dark. She picked her way, trying to put all her focus on the trail, as she had seen Ethan do earlier that day. Shouldn't she be back at the meadow by now? Her heart started beating faster as she realized how easy it would be to become lost. Perhaps she was lost already. She looked around her in sudden confusion. Was it over *those* trees that the sun had sunk just minutes ago? Where was the lighter sky? Through the dark trees, it all looked the same.

"You're going the wrong way," a voice said behind her.

She whirled around, relief washing over her. "Ethan!"

Without thinking, she flung her arms around his neck. He laughed and stumbled a little, but returned the embrace, drawing her close against him. "Where did you think you were heading?" he asked.

"I was coming back to help you," she said. She joined in his laughter, but inside she felt weepy.

Ethan wrapped his arms around her waist and rested his chin against her hair. She could feel him shaking his head. "My brave, foolish Hannah. If you had reappeared I might never have been able to settle this thing."

Becoming aware all at once of the closeness of their bodies, she pulled back. "How *did* you settle it?"

He shrugged. "I just kept talking. Wore them down, I guess."

She took a good look at him. Something was missing. "Where's your pack?"

"I decided to leave that with the Indians."

That wasn't all. "Ethan, your rifle!"

"I made them a present of that, too."

"Not your rifle?" she cried in dismay.

He grinned at her in the gathering dusk. "I guess you're worth the price, Mistress Forrester."

"Oh, no." Tears stung her eyes.

He seized her back up in his arms. "Don't worry about it. I've another gun back at the boat."

"But not the Sure Shot."

"Not the Sure Shot," he agreed.

She looked up into his face. He hadn't shaved since they left Fort Pitt, and what had been stubble was turning into a dark beard that emphasized the strong features of his face. His hair hung in glossy waves to his shoulders. He looked like every picture she had had of a rugged frontiersman, yet his eyes on her were tender. "I'm sorry," she whispered.

A single tear escaped down her cheek. Unexpectedly Ethan bent and kissed the wet trail. "Don't cry, sweetheart," he answered, his voice thick. "The only thing that's important is that you're all right. When I saw that randy young brave touching you, I could hardly stop myself from strangling him."

"You looked calm enough."

He gave a shaky laugh. "I was anything but calm. If they had decided to make trouble, we would have been lost. Even with the rifle, I could only have gotten a couple of them, maybe another one or two with my knife. That would have left five to take their revenge on you."

Hannah swallowed a wave of sickness and glanced down at his belt where Ethan's wicked-looking hunting knife usually hung. "They took that, too," he said with a rueful smile.

She looked down the trail in the direction of the meadow. "They won't come back for us now?"

"No. They headed out the same time I did, traveling west."

"They were nice to the children," Hannah said, trying to get out of her mind a picture of the pretty little meadow filled with bodies—the Indians' and Ethan's. She preferred to think about the way they had cared for Jacob and Bridgett and the companionship and laughter they had shared earlier that afternoon.

"Yes. The Potawatomi don't make war on children. But if we hadn't come, they would have taken them back to their own tribe."

"And we may never have found them."

The dark look in his eyes was answer enough. "It's important to make everyone realize that the frontier is still a very dangerous place."

"I think this will be a good lesson for us all, especially Jacob," Hannah said.

"The boy has a little too much curiosity for his own safety, but I have a hard time faulting him for it."

Hannah smiled. "I would suspect that young Ethan Reed was a curious little scamp himself."

"Still is," he agreed with a grin.

For a moment they just smiled at each other, sharing the knowledge that they had faced a perilous situation and come out of it safely. Then the expression in Ethan's eyes changed subtly. Hannah had seen that look before, and as it had before, it produced an odd, yearning feeling through her middle. She took a step backward and said, "Ah . . . I suppose we should start back."

Ethan nodded, still watching her. "We can start, but I don't know how far we'll get."

"What do you mean?"

"I have no supplies, no flint, no way to make a torch. There's not enough of a trail to see our way once it gets completely dark."

The unsettling inside returned, mixed with a touch of fear. "You mean we'll be out here all night?"

Finally he took his eyes from her face and looked upward. "I can't see enough of the sky through the trees to even tell a direction. We don't want to risk getting ourselves lost."

"No, of course not. I just hope they aren't too worried about us." But her thoughts were not really on the people back in the boat. They were on the long hours ahead, alone with Ethan.

"We'll get as far as we can," he said, sounding unconcerned at the prospect of a night by themselves in the middle of the forest.

They set out, but in only a few minutes Ethan straightened up from studying the ground and shook his head. "It's no use. I'm going to mark this spot for us to start from tomorrow. Then we'd better look around for the most comfortable place to sleep."

Just a few yards away they found a small clearing where the ground sloped upward to a half circle of pine trees. The soft ground was covered with pine needles. "This will do," Ethan said, taking her hand.

"Right here in the open?"

"We're not likely to find an inn in these parts, sweetheart."

It was the second time he had used the endearment. The first she had attributed to the emotion of the moment when they had found each other after their scare. But this time his use of the word seemed deliberate. And Hannah knew that it was a mistake for her to feel such pleasure in hearing it.

She made no acknowledgment of the term. "Not an inn, but a...I don't know...cave or something. Where does one sleep in the wilderness?"

"You're looking at it," he answered with a sweep of his hand. "The forest floor for a mattress, the sky overhead for a roof, and the wind in the pines to sing you to sleep."

"It sounds more poetic than it looks. We don't even have a blanket."

"If I weren't a gentleman, this would be the opportunity for me to say that I could help keep you warm."

"You're *not* a gentleman." She giggled at nothing in particular. She was starting to feel giddy. It had been a long, stressful day, topped off by the horrible moments when she had thought that Ethan might be killed for her sake.

He had walked up to the circle of pines and was using one foot to scrape the pine needles into a pile. "You'd better hope I'm a gentleman, Hannah Forrester, because it's going to be one hell of a long night."

Something in his voice told her that he was not teasing. She walked timidly toward him and began to push the needles from the other side of the "bed."

"So are you or aren't you?" she asked softly.

"A gentleman?"

She nodded.

He squinted to see her better in the dark. He spoke slowly. "I...don't think so." Then he took a giant step over the piled-up needles and seized both her arms. She could hardly see his face, but she felt his lips, and then the rest of his body hard against her. Her eyes closed, and she felt as if she couldn't move as his lips skillfully worked against her mouth, opening it to entwine his tongue with hers in a liquid mating. He made a low sound in the back of his throat that sent a chill of excitement racing along her skin.

His arms moved around her and pushed against her waist, bringing her against the heat of his lower body. Her own softness responded, and Hannah found herself moving back and forth in a rhythm that seemed familiar, though it was completely new. His mouth never stopped as her lips and chin grew tender from his beard, her breasts grew hard and her arms weak.

Finally, after endless moments, he pulled back his head and took a ragged breath. "There! I had to do that, lass. I'm sorry."

He released her and stepped backward, scattering pine needles every which way. "I'm no gentleman, but neither am I a scoundrel. Lie down and go to sleep. If you get too cold, wake me. We'll try to share each other's warmth without sharing anything else."

Hannah had felt cold the moment he stepped away. She supposed she should be grateful that he had not taken their embrace further. Her mother had always told her that once men were excited by a woman, they would stop at nothing until they had had their evil way with her. But Ethan had stopped. And Hannah didn't know whether to feel ashamed or angry at the fact that she hadn't wanted him to.

Ethan sat with his back against a big maple tree, a few feet from Hannah's prone form. He had watched her for what seemed like hours. Watched as she had turned and rolled and changed positions until finally she had curled up like a kitten and grown still. His eyes had become accustomed to the dark, and he could plainly see the soft curve of her hip and the gentle movement of her back as she breathed in deep slumber.

He had no desire for sleep himself. He was used to taking his rest in brief snatches and often didn't need any more than that. Though at times he would arrive at a wilderness station or other safe haven and sleep through a day and a night or more. This night his thoughts were too confused for resting. He had been a long time without a woman. Too long. And he wished he could blame his feelings about Hannah solely on that fact. But he knew what that kind of wanting felt like, and this was something beyond that.

He wanted Hannah. Hell, he *wanted* her. But the wanting was coiled up with a whole lot of other feelings. Feelings like admiration, protectiveness, tenderness, respect. That last one was the troublemaker. He hadn't wanted *and* respected a woman at the same time since he was twenty years old. He'd been young and foolish. The Boston society queen had not been worthy of either his respect or his desire. He had the feeling that Hannah was deserving of both. What she *wasn't* deserving of was his interference with the very nice life she would have with Randolph Webster.

He sighed and stood a moment to stretch out his muscles. The moon had risen. It was close to midnight, he reckoned. A long time till morning. Days ago on the way to Fort Pitt he had sworn to keep his distance from Hannah, he remembered as he slid back down against the trunk of the tree. But he hadn't reckoned on spending a night alone with her—a long, empty night looking at the soft curtain of her blond hair spread out over the pine needles, almost close enough for him to touch.

Hannah had no idea of the time. It was still the middle of the night, she was sure, though the moon had risen and the little clearing looked almost bright. Something had awakened her. She was lying on the bed of pine needles that she and Ethan had made, but he wasn't at her side. A look around showed him sitting, propped against a tree, evidently asleep. The sound she had heard must have awakened him, too, because he lifted his head and slowly pushed himself against the tree trunk until he was upright.

"I think I heard something," she said softly.

He motioned her to silence as they both strained to listen. All they heard were the night sounds of the woods. Without a sound Ethan got to his feet.

"I don't know what it could have been. Something woke me." She spoke in a low voice. "You don't think it's the Indians, do you?"

He walked over and dropped to his knee beside her. Now they could both distinctly hear a rustling in the woods to their left. Ethan made a reflexive move toward his belt, looking for his absent knife.

"If the Indians had wanted to come back after us, they wouldn't make any noise," he told her. "It must be an animal."

"Wolves?" Hannah thought back to the wild animals Randolph had described when he had first told them about the Ohio River valley. Jacob had been fascinated by the wolf packs and had invented elaborate tales concerning them until his father had forbidden him from frightening his sister.

Ethan's head was lifted to listen. "I don't think so. They come in groups, and I only hear one thing out there. It could be a bear, though."

All thought of sleep had fled from Hannah's mind. She edged closer to Ethan. "Should we try to climb a tree or something?"

Ethan laughed. "If it's hungry enough, a tree wouldn't help us."

"Do you imagine it's hungry?"

He put his arm around her shoulders and pulled her against him. She looked up at him, her eyes wide. For a moment the animal was forgotten as he gave in to the impulse he had had earlier and ran his hand slowly along her hair. It was as soft as rabbit fur against his roughened fingers. He swallowed. "Probably not.

Most of the time bears are more afraid of us than we are of them. But if they decide to come after you . . ."

He stopped. Her blond eyelashes flipped back the moonlight as she looked up at him, trusting, frightened. She was nestled against him, the side of her breast brushing his chest. The bear may or may not be hungry, but Ethan sure as hell was.

All at once the rustling became louder. Hannah drew in a breath and clutched his chest. They both looked over toward the sound. At the edge of the trees a dark shape emerged into the clearing, round and furry, but most definitely not a bear.

"It's a coon," Ethan said with a little laugh of relief. "A big fat ol' coon."

The animal stopped at the sound of his voice. In the moonlight Hannah could see the stripes across its face and the beady little eyes that looked at them warily.

"Do they bite?" she asked.

"Yes. They can be nasty little critters when they want to be." He made a noise that sounded like "whoosh," and the raccoon skittered around and back into the forest. "He won't bother us. He's just looking around for a bit of dinner, and, thanks to the Indians, we don't have a morsel of food with us."

Hannah pulled herself out of his arms and flopped back down onto the ground. "I wouldn't mind a bit of dinner myself," she said.

Ethan leaned on one arm and looked down at her. "I seem to remember that after all that food with the Indians today you said you didn't care if you ever ate again."

"The way the day ended up, we both came a little too close to never eating again, if you ask me," she said fervently.

He smiled at her and touched her hair again. "I wouldn't have let them hurt you."

"But as you said before, it was one against nine. You may not have been able to do anything about it."

He continued to stroke her hair and she made no protest. "Well, at least I was able to save you from that ferocious coon," he said with a grin.

"You've protected me more than once now, Ethan, and I'm grateful to you." She tried to sit up again, but he pushed her gently back down again.

"Stay there," he said. "I like watching you lie there in the moonlight."

She smiled and looked around her at the moonlit trees. "I've decided your wilderness bedroom is not so bad after all," she said.

"I told you so." Watching her, touching her, Ethan's insides were turning to knots, and his resolutions were crumbling.

"Are you going to go back to sleep?" she asked. The smile faded from her voice.

He shook his head slowly. His hand moved from her hair to the tiny jet buttons at her neck. "Not yet," he answered, his voice roughened.

She reached up to stop his movements, then after a moment she released his hand and let it continue along toward her thudding heart. The night air felt cool on her hot skin as the dress opened. He unbuttoned with one hand, while the other made circles on her cheek, her neck, then lower on her chest, reaching soft sensitive places where no man had ever touched.

She gave a little gasp as his warm palm covered a nipple. Then her dress was open to the waist and he said in a barely audible voice, "You're so beautiful, sweetheart."

He kissed her then, gently, just on the lips, soft touches again and again until she wanted him to deepen the caress as he had earlier that night. She opened her mouth, but he pulled away and moved lower to lavish the same restrained kisses on her breasts.

He lay almost on top of her, one of his legs between the two of hers, and an ache had centered there where his hard thigh rubbed against her. She arched her back and moaned.

"Shh, sweetheart," he murmured. Molding her right breast with his hands, he brought her peaking nipple to his mouth.

Hannah felt a spike of heat through her middle. So this was desire, she thought dazedly. She looked down at Ethan's dark head as he moved against her breast. Her fingers moved into the waves of his hair. He lifted his head.

"I've been fighting this since the day I saw you bending over your candles in Philadelphia," he told her. "But there's something between us that won't go away."

"I don't want it to go away," she said.

He slid up to her mouth, and this time made his kiss as deep as she wanted. It lasted for several minutes, while her bare breasts chafed against his linen shirt.

The line had been crossed. All his doubts and arguments aside, Ethan knew he had to have her, but he wanted to make it good, and he wanted to be sure that there would be no regrets. He rolled to one side, leaning on his elbow, his other hand still covering one of her breasts.

"You've not done this before, Hannah," he said gravely.

It was a statement, not a question, but Hannah answered with a shake of her head.

"I want to make love to you, but you know that I...you know that I'm not a settling-down kind of man. This may not be the wisest move for your future."

Hannah found it hard to listen to his words when all her being was centered on the feeling of his hand on her breast. She knew that she was making a momentous decision. She knew that she should appreciate the control it took for Ethan to have pulled away to remind her of what she was doing. But she felt only impatience at the interruption. He had been fighting this since Philadelphia, he'd said. In a way, she realized, *she* had been fighting it all her life. Not fighting Ethan, of course, but fighting the idea that she couldn't be a woman and enjoy the natural feelings and pleasures of her womanhood. Her mother had tried to tell her that those feelings were wicked. But what she felt with Ethan was not wicked. It was extraordinary and beautiful. And she wanted more.

"I thought frontiersmen were supposed to be strong and silent," she chided him gently. "Do you want to talk or do you want to make love?"

It was all the permission he needed.

Chapter Twelve

Ethan made a bed of their clothes. Hannah marveled at how natural it seemed to be naked with him, to have him run his hands over her lithe body. And after just a touch of shyness, to do the same to him. From the beginning he urged her participation, helping her learn the feel of the hard muscles and rough hair of his thighs, the silkier, longer hair of his chest, the smoothness of his belly, hard and flat, not soft and gently rounded like hers. When he began to move her hand lower on himself she pulled it out from under his. He instantly let her go and moved back over her to touch her swollen mouth with his, time and again, until she felt she would drown in kisses.

And then as she sank farther beneath the waves of sensation, his hand touched her between her legs, just the softest of touches, but it jolted her like the touch from a burning brand. There was a certain place he massaged with his fingers, and Hannah hissed cold air into her mouth as an explosion of feeling radiated upward. Her limbs grew stiff, then melted, feeling trembly and odd.

Ethan was watching her, his eyes different, hooded. "You're quick to passion," he said with a sensual smile.

Hannah closed her eyes, trying to come to terms with what had happened to her. There were no terms, she decided. Ethan was gently nibbling at her breasts.

She opened her eyes and reached for him. "Now let's try it together," he said, taking her lips in a demanding kiss that swirled her back into a fever of waiting, wanting. And then he was inside her, with one inexorable thrust that made her gasp in pain.

"It's all right, my love," he murmured between kisses. And soon, his words were true. The pain subsided and in its place was the buildup of feeling, as before, but this time reaching so deep inside her that she wanted to cry out in wonder. She clung to him and let him move, strong and slow, until suddenly his breathing deepened and he began a series of frantic thrusts. This time the explosion was not just hers. It was his and theirs, a fusing of flesh and a melding of spirit.

His arms had tightened around her so that the skin now felt tender where they had pressed. Yet she had not felt confined, indeed, she had more of a sensation of flying free like the hawk they had seen over the river yesterday. Their bodies were moist. His head fell heavily on her chest and she put a weak hand on his soft hair. Neither spoke for a very long time.

"Are you all right?" he asked finally, without raising his head.

She gave a watery laugh. "I have no idea."

He lifted his head with a look of concern. "I didn't mean to be so. . . I lost control," he admitted with a frown. He reached up to her cheek to wipe away tears she didn't know she had shed. "I'm sorry."

The chills were subsiding and strength was coming back into her limbs. She stretched underneath him, relishing his heaviness on top of her.

"Don't you dare be sorry." She lifted her head to give him a quick kiss on the mouth, then lay back down again and smiled at him.

His frown turned into a relieved grin. "You liked it, then?"

"That's a rather mild word for it, wouldn't you say?"

Ethan's heart seemed to expand inside his chest as he looked down at her. Her expression was one of sheer elation, relaxed and uninhibited. There was not the least hint of reproach. No timidity, no posturing to keep some of her feelings to herself. Here was a woman who, in spite of her inexperience, was able to indulge her own passion in full measure and share it with him without reservation. Ethan felt as if he'd just conquered a continent.

"I rather enjoyed it myself," he said nonchalantly.

She pounded lightly on his arm. "Only 'rather'?"

He laughed, feeling carefree and young. "I don't know if I've ever enjoyed anything quite so much. Is that better?"

"Much," she said with a happy nod.

He pulled himself up and nestled her in his arms.

"I can't believe I'm lying stark naked in the middle of a forest," Hannah said dreamily.

"Like Adam and Eve."

Hannah giggled. "Isn't that blasphemy, Captain?"

Ethan rubbed his hand along the smooth curve of her side. "I figure...the Lord's the one who gave us this equipment. He probably meant for us to use it."

"So this is our own Garden of Eden?"

"Complete with delicious apples," he said with a mischievous grin as he ran his palms once again over her full breasts.

Hannah laughed and hid her blushing face in his neck. How could it be so *easy?* she wondered with amazement. And so much fun? How could she be glorying in this act that she had been warned against so sternly all her life? Lovemaking was *wonderful.* Life was wonderful.

She put her hand on top of Ethan's. "What about the serpent?" she asked with a silly grin.

Ethan looked down the length of his body and shook his head with a smile. "The serpent's all tuckered out, I'm afraid. For another minute or two anyway." He nibbled at her ear and whispered, "You could probably wake him up, though, if you wanted to."

"I'd never dare awaken a serpent," she said with an impish smile.

He moved himself above her again and looked up and down her white, moonlit form. His expression grew serious. "I'm afraid, Hannah Forrester, that you already have."

They slept in a jumbled mixture of his clothes and hers, some underneath and some on top, but in between, their bodies stayed entwined throughout the night. Hannah awoke once just before dawn and smiled dreamily to find herself still wrapped in his arms, then she drifted back to sleep.

The morning already had a good head start when she finally came fully awake. Ethan was gone. His buckskin jacket still covered her and his shirt lay on the ground beneath her, but the rest of his clothes were gone, too. She sat up just as he appeared through the trees carrying a makeshift basket of leaves with two hands. His chest was bare, and for the first time she saw in the daylight the sculptured strength of his body—strong, wide shoulders and chest tapering to a narrow waist, cinched by a broad leather belt.

"Good morning," he said softly, not bothering to hide the fact that his eyes were also roaming freely over her half-naked body.

She pulled his jacket around her and tucked her long legs up under it before she answered, "Good morning."

"Don't cover up on my account," he said with a grin. "You're as beautiful in the sun as you were by the light of the moon."

"But it's...daytime. And we're out-of-doors. Out..." She looked around her.

"I thought we were in Eden," he said, walking over to kneel next to her. "Or at least, you sure had me convinced last night."

He balanced his leaf basket in one hand and reached out the other to stroke her cheek and draw her near for a brief, sweet kiss. "Perhaps we were there," she said wistfully. "A moonlit Eden."

"But one that disappears in the harsh light of day, is that it?" His hand held her chin and his compelling eyes questioned her.

She looked away. "I don't know," she murmured.

He sat back on his heels with a sigh. "I warned you about regrets."

"Oh no. I'm not regretting anything, Ethan. I'm just . . . a little confused, I guess."

He ran a finger down her neck and along the slope of her shoulder where it was bare above the jacket she held clutched around her. "I like to hear you say my name."

Hannah shivered. The slow trail of a single finger was enough to bring the night's memories flooding through her. "I'm cold, I think," she said lamely.

He drew back from her. "I suppose I'll have to let you get dressed, though they didn't wear clothes in paradise, you know."

Hannah bit her lip. She didn't know if the sound that wanted to come out of her mouth was a laugh or a sob. She had told Ethan the truth. She didn't regret her action of the previous evening. She would never forget the incredible things she had learned about physical love and about herself. But it was also true that in the daylight things did not appear as simple as they did under the spell of the moon. She now had to go back to the boats and face everyone. Face the children and, dear God, face Randolph. Would they know? Would Randolph somehow immediately know that she had spent the night in Ethan's arms?

"I've brought us breakfast," Ethan said lightly. "Berries." He indicated the leaves full of dark red fruit. He did not seem any different this morning. But then, he had made love to many women. The night had not been momentous to him as it had been to her. It didn't seem fair, and a little worm of anger gnawed at her.

"Hadn't we better get started back?"

Ethan noted the lack of warmth in her voice. He had anticipated her remorse, but he was surprised by the degree of regret it caused him. He had experienced something with her last night that he had not thought was possible with any woman. It had been a dimension beyond normal physical pleasures. He didn't know what it all meant, but now, as he had said, in the harsh light of day, it didn't seem that he would have the chance to find out. He and Hannah must leave their little Eden behind and return to their real worlds. And those two worlds did not coincide beyond the span of this short trip down the Ohio. Then he would leave her to her new life. A life in which all that sensual energy, that natural zest for loving, would someday be Randolph Webster's possession, not his.

He reached over and put the basket of fruit in her lap. "I'll leave you alone to get dressed," he said. "Try to eat something to give yourself strength for the trail."

"Hannah! Thank God!" Randolph was the first person they saw as they neared the campsite. It appeared that he had been waiting for them to appear. When he saw her, he sprang forward and took both her hands in his. He looked, Hannah thought guiltily, as though he had not slept all night.

There was not time to say anything before they were joined by all four children, running. Jacob scooted around his father and threw his arms around Hannah's legs. She bent to hug him. Behind them Seth appeared with Eliza.

"You made it back all right, I see," Ethan said to Seth.

"I'll make a woodsman yet," the older man said proudly.

Ethan stepped past Hannah to pat Seth on the back. "That you will, my friend," he told him warmly.

"We were so worried, Hannah," Peggy told her. "Why didn't you come back last night?"

Hannah felt that all eyes were on her as they awaited the answer to her question. She hoped her cheeks did not look as red as they felt. "The Indians didn't want to let us go," she said, unsure of how much of the story she should tell.

Ethan had no qualms about revealing that part of their ordeal. "They wanted to buy Hannah," he said flatly. "Made me a good offer of mink and otter furs."

"To buy you!" the three young girls chorused.

Hannah nodded. "Captain Reed had to bargain so that they would let me go. He gave them his pack and his rifle."

"Not the Sure Shot?" Jacob asked in dismay.

Ethan squatted down next to him. "The very one," he said lightly. "So I reckon I'll just have to name my other gun Sure Shot, too."

"Sure Shot Two, I get it." Jacob's round face regained its normal cheerfulness. "Anyway, I reckon it's the person that makes the shot sure, not the gun."

Ethan grinned at him. "You're a wise boy, Jacob Webster."

He straightened up and addressed the rest of the group. "The Indians seemed satisfied with their loot. I don't think they had any intention of circling back to trouble us, but just in case, I would suggest that we get back out on the river immediately."

Randolph cleared his throat. "Reed, I reckon I owe you a load of thanks for finding my boy, here, and taking care of Hannah."

Hannah watched the two men shake hands. It didn't appear to be a comfortable exchange for either one of them. Ethan uncharacteristically avoided looking Randolph in the eye.

"I'm not sure we can leave immediately," Eliza said from the back of the group. Her kind, wrinkly face was drawn with worry.

"Why not?" Ethan asked.

"It's Nancy. She's not doing well. It was a terrible strain on her when Bridgett was lost all those hours."

Ethan rubbed his growing beard and thought for a moment while the others awaited his decision. This time no one was likely to question his authority. "I imagine her condition would be even worse if we suddenly were confronted by a bunch of hostiles. Let's try to arrange a bed for her on one of the boats."

Randolph and Seth nodded their agreement, and without further discussion, everyone turned back to camp to prepare to pack up.

Randolph took Hannah's arm as she passed. "You can't imagine how awful it was when I wasn't sure if you would ever make it back, Hannah."

She tried to make her smile normal and reassuring. "Well, I'm back now, so we don't have to think about it anymore."

He shook his head. "I did nothing but think about it, think about *you,* all night long. I'd like to share some of those thoughts with you, Hannah."

Hannah felt all the ups and downs of the past twenty-four hours crowding in on her at once. "We have to board the boats," she said, almost in a panic.

"Aye. But later... tonight, promise me we'll find some time to talk alone."

"All right," she agreed, a sinking feeling in her stomach. "I promise. Tonight we'll talk."

If Hannah had never had the chance to be courted like other girls, that day on the river at least gave her a taste of what she had missed. Randolph was rarely far from her side. When she wanted to stand up, his hand was there to help her rise. When she wanted to sit down, he was behind her plumping a sack of flour to make her a comfortable seat. At the midday meal, he filled her plate and cup, refusing to let her do so herself or to help the children "after her ordeal."

Her mother had begun her bouts of sickness when Hannah was only eleven, and since that time she had not had anyone caring for her, caring about her. Priscilla had tried, briefly, but she had succumbed too soon to the exigencies of her own illness. The kind of solicitous attention Randolph was lavishing on her was new, and it was a heady sensation. She only wished it weren't tainted by a sense of guilt that increased as the day went on.

She was glad that Ethan had taken his place in the other boat. She didn't want to talk with him or even see him. He had made it clear this morning that the night she had found so magical had been simply a physical pleasure for him. He'd been detached and distracted on the trail back to the river, and had immediately stepped back and let Randolph take charge of her the minute they arrived. He'd not said another word to her before they all boarded the boats.

She'd wanted what he had offered her last night. She wouldn't pretend that she had put conditions on her participation. Ethan had, in fact, tried to warn her to think about the consequences of what they were doing. She had been the one who had let the emotions and the feelings and the moonlight overcome her good sense. So be it. She couldn't change what had happened, but she could make sure that she acted with more wisdom in the future. And that meant staying away from Ethan.

Seth was taking a turn at steering the boat when Randolph came to sit beside her. The section of river they were passing fulfilled all the expectations Randolph's descriptions back in Philadelphia had created. The Indians had named it O-hi-o, Beautiful River, and with its sloping forests and bright green meadows and hills, it truly lived up to its name. Here and there redbud and dogwood dotted the vista like bright splotches of paint dripped from an artist's brush. Birds in brilliant colors fluttered suddenly out of the trees—cardinals, blue jays, green and yellow parakeets. In spite of all the turmoil of the past two days, Hannah found that floating along and watching the passing landscape filled her with peace and contentment.

"You don't look any the worse for wear after your scare yesterday," Randolph told her, looking intently at her face.

She smiled at him. "It was probably harder on you than it was on me. First the worry over Jacob and then our tardy arrival back."

"I'm afraid I spoke harshly yesterday morning when we were forming the search parties." His eyes were remorseful.

"It doesn't matter. We all were under a strain."

"I just didn't want you to think that I was angry with you. It was Reed who was causing the trouble, really."

Hannah turned her face to study the shoreline. "Let's not talk about it, Randolph. It's over. We're all safe, so let's just enjoy this beautiful day."

Randolph followed the direction of her gaze. "It's not quite so beautiful out there when you consider that hostile Indians might be lurking behind those trees," he said soberly. "When I think of Jacob in their hands..."

Hannah turned back to him. "I believe the Indians who had Jacob were friendly. They treated him well, and they treated me well, too. It's just that one particular brave was...a little too interested, I guess." She ended with a half laugh.

Randolph did not join in her levity. "I couldn't really blame any man for wanting you, Hannah. But when I think of one of them putting his hands on you, touching your hair..." He was watching her with much the same possessive look she had seen on Ethan's face when he had left the Indians yesterday. And Randolph must have gotten some of the details of the encounter from Ethan, because she hadn't talked about how the braves had touched her.

Suddenly she felt tired. She was, of course, glad that she wasn't in the hands of the Indians, but it seemed that her own people felt the same kind of need to possess her that Skabewis had. The young Indian had been respectful and admiring and, according to Ethan, had offered a good price for her. Was his offer so much different than the indenture through which Randolph had purchased her three years ago?

Late in the afternoon they had reached a spot where the river took a great sweep west, and just at the bend the shoreline had parted to form a pretty little island.

Ethan had motioned for them to pull over to it. Though it was early to stop, Ethan pointed out that the island would provide them with some added protection. Besides, they were all worn-out after the previous day's adventures. Nancy was in particularly bad shape. She had been having cramps all day and could find no comfortable position to rest on the crowded boat.

There was not a lot of conversation as they prepared their camp and the evening meal. The children were unusually subdued, still chastened by what had happened to Jacob and Bridgett.

Hannah was glad when the meal was finished and everyone agreed that there would be no gathering around the camp fire that night. Peggy and Jacob had already retired to their tent, and she was about to do so herself when Randolph stopped her. "We said we would talk this evening," he reminded her.

"But...we've been talking all day. You said you were sorry about being gruff yesterday, and I told you not to worry about it. Surely it's not still on your mind?"

He took her hand and pulled it through the crook of his arm, as she'd seen the gents do with their ladies back in London. "Just walk with me a spell," he said. "Let's go across the island and look out at the river."

She had no other graceful choice but to accompany him. And after the initial reluctance, she found that the stroll felt good. The sounds of the night were peaceful, and she started to relax.

"What did you want to talk about?" she asked as they came out of the trees to the rocky river side of the island.

Randolph pointed to a couple of large stones. "Let's sit down."

Hannah perched on a rock just above the running water, pulling up her boots so that they would not be splashed. Randolph sat slightly above her. His long legs stretched so that his boots were in the water, but he didn't seem to notice. "I've not asked you your opinion of the West, Hannah," he began.

She twisted her neck to look at him. He'd asked her opinion of very little in the two years she had known him, but it seemed now that would change along with all the other things that were changing in their relationship.

"It's beautiful," she said. "Wild and . . . fascinating." Her voice became almost reverent, and for the first time she realized how the land was taking hold on her.

Randolph sounded surprised at the intensity of her answer. "You're not fearful of it, even after yesterday?"

She thought for a moment, then shook her head. "There's danger, of course, but then isn't there everywhere? I'm as likely to be knocked over by a runaway carriage in the crowded streets back home as I am to run into a hungry bear out here." Or a big ol' coon, she thought, pushing away the sudden, unwanted memory.

"I knew from the first minute I saw you, Hannah, at the indenture block, that you had a valiant spirit."

Hannah was startled by his comment. Randolph had seemed to regard her as no more than a workhorse for his wife during those first years. Perhaps his memory was faulty and he was now remembering the beginning of their relationship with the coloring of everything that had gone on since.

"That's a day I'll not forget in this lifetime," she said. "But I never got the impression that you thought much about me one way or the other."

He gave a harsh laugh. "If you could but see yourself with a man's eyes, Hannah, you would realize how ridiculous a statement that is. It's true that I didn't come to appreciate the full depth of your spirit for a long time, but you intrigued me from the very first."

"You never said anything—"

"Of course not!" he interrupted. "What kind of man do you think I am? I had the most wonderful wife in the world and two beautiful children. I certainly was not going to let myself get involved with a fascinating, beautiful young woman and see the people I loved most destroyed by my actions."

His voice trembled and his hands tightened on the edge of the rock beneath them. "But there were times, my dear Hannah, when I was hard put not to damn them all and myself, too, to claim you."

Hannah was dumbstruck. She had never so much as suspected, for all that time. Randolph's devotion to his wife had not wavered, not once. Even through the most terrible times of her illness. She turned around to see his face better in the dim light. "I never knew..."

He took a ragged breath. "Nor did Priscilla, Lord rest her saintly soul. I made sure of that, no matter what it cost me."

Hannah's feet slipped on the rock and she pulled herself up to sit more on Randolph's level. "Why are you telling me this now, Randolph?" she asked.

"Perhaps it's unfair. It was my burden, and I carried it gladly those years. Priscilla deserved no less of me. But yesterday when I thought I may never see you again, I decided that I couldn't go any longer without letting you know how I feel."

Hannah's mind was spinning. What a truly good man Randolph was, moral and caring about the people in his life. And how different he was from Ethan Reed, who would sleep with Polly McCoy when it suited his fancy and then days later do the same with her. But she didn't know how to respond to Randolph's declaration. She didn't know if he even wanted a response. After all, she already belonged to him. For many employers of indentured servants, that would be enough to lay any kind of claim they chose.

"I'm contracted to you for another three years..." she began carefully.

But again he interrupted impatiently. "Forget the damn indenture, Hannah. I'll dig out the papers and burn them tonight, if you want. And then you'd be free to go."

He put his hands along each side of her neck and ran his thumbs gently along the lines of her jaw. The moonlight caught the glint of tears in his eyes. "Only... don't go, Hannah," he pleaded. "Stay with me. I've already lost the love of my youth, but now you're the one I want to build a life with—to grow old together."

Her own eyes filled with tears at his declaration. She was about to reply when there was the crackling sound behind them of someone walking through the woods.

Randolph dropped his hands and they both turned to see who it was. He didn't emerge into the light, but Ethan's powerful figure was unmistakable.

Randolph gave an exasperated, angry laugh. "What the *hell* do you want, Reed?"

Hannah could not see Ethan's expression. His voice was even as he said, "Mrs. Baker sent me to fetch you, Hannah. Nancy Trask is having her baby."

Chapter Thirteen

Hannah rubbed her stinging eyes. It had been a day and a half since she had slept, and that sleep had been the eventful night she had spent with Ethan. It seemed a lifetime ago.

Eliza had said that they would take turns sitting up with Nancy, and Hannah had urged the older woman to leave the sick woman's side for periods of rest. But she herself could not leave. She had sat this way with her mother and then Priscilla. She knew how suddenly and easily the fragile soul could slip away to the other side, and she did not intend to let that happen to Nancy. At least not without a fight.

All during the long night and the longer day she had watched Nancy slide in and out of consciousness. She had wiped the sweat from her face and held her hand when the pains came strong and hard.

Nancy's own husband was not available to comfort his wife. Last night he'd appeared once at the entryway of the makeshift lean-to they'd built for the birthing. He was stumbling and reeking of liquor, and Eliza had told him sharply that he'd better be sober before he bothered them again.

Nancy had not asked for him. She seemed content to have Eliza and Hannah by her side. She smiled at Randolph on one of several visits he made to inquire about her progress. And she murmured a weary "bless you" to Ethan, who came by to tell them that he had occupied the children in building a rough raft and was now going to take them downriver on a fishing expedition.

Hannah had not met his eyes when he had ducked his head under the deerskin canopy of their little shelter. But she, too, was grateful for his thoughtfulness, for now Nancy was not able to restrain her cries as the pains became more fierce.

"What can we do, Eliza?" Hannah asked, feeling her own stomach wrenched with each one of Nancy's outbursts.

Eliza's normally sunny face was taut with worry. "I don't know. It should have come by now, if you ask me. Maybe it's not going to come out right because it's coming so early."

"Do we have any of the willow bark tea left?"

Eliza shook her head. "It's gone. And I don't think it eased her much, anyway."

Hannah watched as Nancy moaned and thrashed back and forth on the soft bed they had made for her atop a pile of furs. "I don't think she can take much more."

"She's out of her head now," Eliza said. "She'll remember none of this, I wager. You usually don't, you know, once you have the baby in your arms. The pain is forgotten."

"I hope Nancy forgets," Hannah said fervently.

"I just hope she ends up with a baby in her arms," Eliza added. "The little mite's going to be a wee one, coming this early."

Hannah stood up to ease the tension in her back. She peered out the doorway. "The children and Ethan should be back by now," she said.

Eliza gave her a shrewd look. "Who are you worried about—the children or Ethan?"

Hannah turned sharply. "What do you mean by that?"

Eliza gave her one of her gentle, wise smiles. "Don't bristle at me, girl. You may be able to fool the rest of the folks here, but I know you too well. I've watched you mooning over our handsome captain since we started this trip. And when you both came back from the woods yesterday, I'd swear that you were a woman with a secret. A troubling secret, the kind that involves a man."

Hannah walked back to Nancy's side and sank down on a deerskin. "It doesn't matter," she said, her voice dull.

"Hogwash. Of course it matters. I don't have any criticism of your eyesight, my dear girl. The man's bonny enough to make even an old heart like mine skip a beat every now and then. But it's your brains I'm aworrying about. Captain Reed's not the kind of man who's going to settle down to make a home for a woman and a family."

"I know that, Eliza. I haven't lost my mind completely."

"Just partially, is that it?"

Hannah gave her a rueful smile.

"It's Randolph Webster you should be setting your cap for, my dear. Now there's a man who could make a woman happy."

"I'm not setting my cap for anyone, Eliza. After all, I'm still an indentured servant..."

Eliza held up her hand. "You fold those papers around yourself like a shield, my friend. But I don't think it will work out here on the frontier. Randolph would no longer hold you if you asked to leave. You know that as well as I do. But you think that if you are still bound as a servant, you don't have to face the real decisions of life the way the rest of us do."

Was her friend some kind of sorceress? Hannah wondered. There was no way Eliza could know of the discussion she and Randolph had had last night by the river, yet she seemed to be reading inside Hannah's very soul.

There was a wail from the bed and both women turned their attention back to their patient. She had opened her eyes. "Am I going to die?" she asked, her raspy voice barely intelligible.

Hannah came back to her side and leaned over her, taking hold of her shoulders. "Absolutely not, Nancy. We're not going to let you die. Not you, or the babe."

Eliza put her hands soothingly on Nancy's distended stomach. Then she lifted the fur covering and looked between the pregnant woman's legs. "Just hang on a little while more, Nancy dear. I think that little one is finally going to make its appearance."

"Is it coming?" Hannah asked, clutching at Nancy with a swift wave of fear mixed with exhilaration.

Eliza looked up with a smile. "Black hair and all, just like its mama."

Nancy gave a tremendous gasp as the pains gripped her. Her face screwed into a grimace of agony. "It *is* coming, I think," she panted.

"Is there something we should do?" Hannah asked, feeling her own stomach clench with her friend's effort.

"I think the rest is up to her," Eliza said, sounding relieved.

There was another loud cry from their patient, and Randolph came to the door of the lean-to. "What's happening?" he asked. He sounded anguished.

"The baby's finally arriving," Hannah said. "We can see the head."

"Thank God!" Randolph said fervently. He hesitated a moment, then said, "Should I fetch Hugh?"

"If he's sober enough to know what's going on," Eliza said curtly. "Which I doubt."

"But this is his child being born," Hannah argued. "He should at least be informed."

"I'll tell him," Randolph said.

"What about the children?" Hannah asked.

"They came back with Reed a few minutes ago. They're fine. You just worry about Mrs. Trask."

The minutes crawled by as Nancy's spasms grew more violent. Hannah felt sweat trickle down her sides underneath her arms. But finally, after one final, violent push, Eliza cried, "I've got it!" and Hannah looked down to see a bloody, tiny creature in the older woman's two hands. "It's a boy. Nancy, you have a beautiful little boy."

Nancy made an attempt to raise her head, then fell back against the furs with another moan. Hannah wiped her wet face as Eliza cut the baby's cord with a hunting knife and tied it with thread. She had stopped exclaiming over the child and something in her silence made Hannah look up sharply. Eliza looked meaningfully over at Nancy, then picked up the baby in a piece of soft deerskin and walked toward the door, motioning for Hannah to follow her.

"Something's wrong," she said, keeping her voice low.

The baby was lying still in Eliza's arms and was not making a sound. Underneath the smears of blood, the tiny body was bluish. "I don't think he's breathing," Eliza whispered.

Hannah felt a surge of anger. She knew firsthand the callous injustice of death, but she couldn't believe that Nancy had labored so hard to bring this little being into the world only to have him die before their eyes.

"Trask's still drunk," Randolph's voice reached them from out in the darkness. He came nearer and stopped when he spotted the deerskin-wrapped child. "Is it born, then?" he said with a little cry of joy.

Eliza was bouncing the little bundle up and down in her arms. "The lad's not breathing, Randolph," she said, beginning to sound panicky.

"We have to do something," Hannah said fiercely. "We're not going to let him die."

"We sure as hell are not," Randolph agreed, seizing the child. He knelt on the ground with the baby cradled in his arms. "It's got to breathe. Somehow we've got to make it breathe." He bent over it and, to Hannah's surprise, began to blow right into the baby's minute mouth.

"What are you doing?" she started to ask, but before he could say anything there was the slightest movement of the tiny chest, then a larger one and the little creature gave something like a cough. Randolph pulled back as the baby began to take tiny gasps and make a mewling sound.

Hannah thought she had never heard anything so beautiful. "He's breathing. You did it!" she said to Randolph.

They both watched as the tiny breaths turned into larger ones and the blue skin began to change to pink.

Randolph's eyes were shining. He stood up, holding the baby tenderly in front of him, then walked over to Nancy's side. "Here's your son, Mrs. Trask," he said. "He's a beautiful, healthy boy."

Nancy opened her eyes and gave Randolph a tired, grateful smile. "Bless you," she said. "Bless you all." She fell back and her head lolled to one side. For a horrible moment Hannah thought that they had saved the child only to lose the mother, but Eliza did not appear concerned.

"She's fainted," the older woman said. "Probably the best thing for her now. I'll tend to her while you get the baby cleaned up and ready to meet his sisters."

Randolph reverently handed the child to Hannah. "I'll go tell the others," he said. "It's a miraculous thing, isn't it?" His voice was full of awe.

Hannah met his eyes over the squirming infant in her arms. Their smiles reflected shared wonder.

"Well, get on with it, Randolph," Eliza said. "I can't get Nancy fixed up with you hovering here."

Randolph grinned and said, "Yes, ma'am."

And suddenly all three were grinning at each other and laughing. In some ways this had been their first real test of life in the wilderness, and they had passed.

* * *

The new baby was so small that they had made a bed for it in a cartridge box no bigger than Hannah's boot. But after those first anxious moments, it appeared to be thriving. The ominous blue color was almost gone and the pitiful mewling sounds were changing to tiny, hungry cries.

Nancy had still not awakened, but Eliza assured Hannah that her color was good and her breathing peaceful. She and Randolph were trying to convince Hannah to go for some sleep herself. Randolph had been back and forth to the little shelter all evening, picking up the baby, rocking it, crooning a little wordless tune.

It was almost midnight. Everyone in the party had been duly paraded in and out to see the new arrival. Trask had been the last to arrive. He had refused to hold the child when Hannah had offered it, but had said with a possessive gleam in his eye, "Finally she sees fit to give me a son. It'll be another Hugh after his pa." Then, without inquiring about his wife's health, he'd left.

Randolph shook his head as he watched Trask leave. "I don't understand the man," he said in disgust. "How can he not be affected by such an event? The birth of his own son."

In her position as a servant, Hannah had never felt it her place to voice her opinion about Trask, but as Ethan had once predicted, the farther they got into the wilderness, the less she felt like a servant. "He's not worthy of such a wonderful family."

Eliza had laid her head on some of the furs alongside Nancy and appeared to be dozing off. Randolph spoke softly. "Did Priscilla ever talk to you about the child we lost, Hannah?"

"No. It was one subject that we never shared."

"When we found out that we were going to have another child, we were so pleased, though I worried because even then the sickness was tightening its grip on her."

Hannah watched as the painful memories flickered across his face. He looked over at the baby in the little box. It was quiet now, sleeping. "It wasn't meant to be," he said after a moment.

"She never spoke of it."

"No. But I think it nearly broke her heart."

"I'm so sorry." Hannah wished she had more comforting words, but she had gone too many hours without sleep to think clearly.

Randolph gave a little shiver. "I don't know. Sometimes I think these things are best left to nature, or God, or whatever it is that controls our fates. Perhaps if the babe had been born, we wouldn't have had those final two years with Priscilla."

"They were precious years."

"Aye. They gave Jacob the chance to be able to remember his mother. And they gave the children time to learn to love you, so that you would be able to soften their loss."

Hannah felt her heart swelling as she listened to Randolph tell her again of her importance in their family. Could a person ask for greater happiness than to be able to make life better for three such wonderful people as Randolph and his children? "I'm glad I was there," she said.

He reached to take her hand. "I'm glad you're *here,*" he corrected gently. "It means more than I can say to have you with us."

Hannah felt the uncomfortable closeness of the walls of the little shelter. Her head was really not working well, she decided. She needed sleep, as they had said. "Well," she said, pulling her hands away. "It certainly meant a lot to have *you* here tonight. I believe you saved that baby's life."

"You and Eliza were the ones who did all the nursing hour after hour."

Hannah gave a little laugh. "And I suppose we should give Nancy herself a little credit for the results."

Randolph looked over at the sleeping woman. "She's a brave lady. And she doesn't deserve the lot she's been given in this life."

"But at least she has a wonderful new son, thanks to you."

Randolph picked up the baby, which had begun to move about again in its tiny cradle. A measure of pride slipped into his voice as he said, "He's a bonny lad, isn't he?"

"Aye, he's *bonny,*" Hannah said, gently teasing. All the Websters had touches of the MacDougalls' Scottish speech. Hannah was glad that they seemed to be able to retain this bit of heritage from Priscilla without painful memories.

Randolph put the infant on his knees and moved them back and forth. The baby's whimpers stopped and for the first time his gluey eyelids opened a crack to peer up at the big man bending over him. "He's opening his eyes," Randolph exclaimed.

His voice awakened Eliza, who pulled herself groggily upright. "What are you still doing here, Hannah?" she scolded. "You're supposed to be sleeping."

When Randolph added his urging to Eliza's, Hannah finally got to her feet and started to leave the shelter where she had kept watch for a day and a half. She was, she decided, grateful for the excuse to retire. Her conversation with Randolph had again drifted into serious subjects. And sitting with him sharing the excitement of the new baby, she found herself projecting a picture of the future, a family of her own. It was an enticing thought, one that should make her happy instead of melancholy. The problem, she admitted as she ducked into her little tent, was that in her visions of the future, her baby, absurdly and impossibly, had the dark, compelling eyes of Ethan Reed.

They stayed on the pretty little island three more days to give Nancy and the baby a chance to grow stronger. The child had been named Hugh Wallace Trask, using Nancy's maiden name for its middle name. Eliza, Hannah and Randolph had taken to calling it "Wally," using the excuse that "Hugh" was too adult sounding for such a little mite. No one voiced the thought that the father seemed each day less worthy of such a miraculous namesake. Unlike Randolph, who spent hours sitting inside the little shelter and had even changed the infant's wet linens, Hugh came rarely and stayed for a few brief moments. He had not yet held his son in his arms.

The children had all taken turns rocking little Wally. Bridgett and Janie were fascinated with their new brother and would have been underfoot all day if Eliza had not told them that their mother needed to rest.

Ethan put in brief appearances. He also declined an invitation to hold the child, saying that he did not want to get the little thing dirty. The second afternoon, he came when Nancy was sleeping and Hannah was alone by her side.

"Mother and babe are doing well?" he asked, his voice sounding formal and restrained.

"Everything seems to be fine," Hannah answered, the words sticking in her throat. It was the first time they had been alone since their night on the trail.

"And you have rested?"

She nodded, her eyes on Nancy, not on him.

"We've not talked..." he started, but she held up her hand to interrupt him.

"There's no need," she said simply.

"What happened out there that night..."

"I said there's no need to discuss it."

Ethan sighed. "So you're having the regrets I warned you about, after all."

Hannah stood and walked away from Nancy's bed. It would probably be easier for both Ethan and herself if she admitted regret. But could she honestly say that she regretted that night? "I think it would be best if we didn't mention what happened between us."

He walked over to stand close enough to touch her but made no move to do so. "You think not mentioning it will make you forget it?"

Her answer was brittle. "I have to forget it."

"Because you've had a better offer?" Ethan's voice, too, was unusually hard.

"What's that supposed to mean?"

"Webster's finally come to his senses and discovered he wants you in his bed himself."

Hannah felt as if he had slapped her. "Of all the vulgar..."

Ethan took a step back. "I'm sorry. That was unfair. Webster's in love with you. Any fool can see it every time he looks at you."

Hannah's swift surge of anger died immediately, replaced by the vague sadness she had been feeling since the baby's birth. She'd tried to attribute it to the loss of sleep over those two long days.

"Are you going to marry him?"

Hannah wished she could get out of the stuffy lean-to, but she didn't want Ethan continuing his conversation where everyone could see them. "He hasn't asked me," she snapped.

"I thought that's what he was doing—the other night by the river."

"No."

A little of the tightness left his voice. "He will, though. Webster's an honorable man."

"Unlike some men I know," Hannah couldn't resist saying.

Ethan shook his head in exasperation. "I gave you fair warning. The life I lead doesn't allow room for a wife and family. Did you suppose that night would change that?"

For the first time, she looked straight into his dark eyes, the ones she had been imagining in her own child. "I didn't suppose anything, Captain. I was... how do they put it in the love sonnets?...*swept away* by your ardor."

"And now you blame me for it," he said grimly.

She held his gaze for several moments, then said calmly. "No. I mean it when I say I have no regrets. But I also mean it when I say we are not going to talk

of this again. It's time I started thinking of what kind
of life I'm going to create for myself.''

Ethan's expression was admiring. ''Ah, Hannah.
You're a woman in a thousand.''

A devilish impulse made her retort, ''Or in your
case, Captain Reed, one of thousands.''

A reluctant smile twisted Ethan's lips. ''You're
wrong, but perhaps it's best after all if that's how you
think of me.''

''Once we're all settled on Destiny River, Captain,
I don't intend to think of you at all.''

The river was somber under a dark sky when they
finally loaded up the boats and pushed out into the
current. There was little talking and the settlers' moods
seemed to match the weather. Ethan had taken his
customary place on the front boat with Hugh Trask
and his children, but they had switched Nancy and the
baby to the little cabin on the Websters' boat so that
she could be near Hannah and Eliza.

By the second day, the sun came out to light the
river with sparkles and the travelers had regained some
of their spark, as well. The terrain was changing,
showing the promise of the rich land they had come so
far to find. Although there were still miles of forbidding dark forests, more and more often they floated
along past plains waving with bluegrass and wild rye.
Meadows dotted with clover and wildflowers tapered
off into rolling green hills. Then farther south still,
they encountered marshy canebrakes lined with great
willows bending toward them in graceful obeisance.

On the ninth day out of Fort Pitt they rounded a
bend to discover an Indian village stretched out on the
eastern bank. The Indians crowded curiously at the

edge of the river as they passed, the mostly naked children making signals to get their attention. Jacob and Peggy laughed and waved from the side of the boat.

"Reed didn't say anything about an Indian village," Randolph said with a frown. He was manning the big oar at the back of the boat.

Seth looked up from a fishing net he was mending. "They look friendly enough. I'm sure the captain would have shouted to us if there were a problem."

Hannah had felt little flutters in her stomach at the sight of the Indian braves, some of whom had horizontal lines painted across their cheeks the way Skabewis had. But the people on shore just seemed to be politely interested in the settlers. If she was going to live in this land, Hannah told herself, she would have to learn to live with the Indians. She remembered the good humor of the old chief. They were people, just like the English. There's room in this great land for all of us, she said firmly. Then she moved to the side of the boat to join Jacob and Peggy in waving to the friendly faces along the river.

Chapter Fourteen

It was their last night. It seemed almost unbelievable after all the days of hard travel—the aching muscles of those first days on horseback, the endless winding paths through the wooded hills of central Pennsylvania, the long days of vigilance keeping their boats floating smoothly along the bends and eddies of the great river. Tomorrow, Ethan had told them, they would arrive at Destiny River.

They had made good time. In spite of little Wally's birth and Nancy's weakness, they would be reaching their new home early in the summer, early enough to plant the bags of seed corn weighing down the back of the Trask boat. Early enough to build sturdy log cabins to provide shelter and warmth for their first long winter on the frontier.

There was an air of anticipation that night around the camp fire. Seth had taken out his fiddle to play some celebratory music in honor of the occasion. Trask had tapped yet another of the kegs of rum that occupied an inordinate amount of the space allotted to his family.

Randolph was elated. He had regained something of the original fervor that had made him plan this expedition in the first place.

"How far up the Destiny do we have to go?" he asked Ethan.

Their guide shrugged his broad shoulders. "The territory's open here. You could stake your claim at the mouth, right on the Ohio if you want. But if you go upriver just a piece, you'll be out of the way of any of the river activity you don't want to mess with."

"That makes good sense to me," Seth said, and the others nodded agreement.

Ethan continued, "We'll pull up and make a little camp at the mouth of the Destiny. Then you can go up and down both sides of the river and pick out the best spot for building cabins and clearing fields."

Hannah felt a little chill of excitement as she realized that as of tomorrow, their dream would turn into a reality. She only wished that her excitement was not mixed with the uncertainties that had plagued her over the past few days. Exactly what would her new little home on the Destiny River be like? Since they had left the island where Wally had been born, Randolph had not spoken to her again in the serious vein he had begun as they had sat with Nancy after the birth. She did not particularly expect him to. There was little chance for them to be alone with each other, and everyone had a lot on their minds. But she couldn't help wondering what kind of cabin they would build. Would she sleep in a traditional servant's room, attached on the back of the structure? Or would there be a loft for the children that she would also use?

And then there was Ethan. He would be leaving them soon. Would she be able to forget him and the lovemaking they had shared, as she had told him she would? Or would she be moving into Randolph Webster's cabin and perhaps his bed with images of Ethan's naked body bending over her in the moonlight, his lips at her breast?

"A penny for your thoughts, mistress," Ethan's low voice said into her ear.

Heat rose to her cheeks. She looked quickly across the camp fire to see that Randolph and Seth were engrossed in conversation. Ethan had come up behind her quietly. No one else was paying any attention to them. "I'm just thinking about tomorrow," she told him. "I can't believe we're here at last."

"You won't be disappointed," Ethan said. As usual, when he was describing his beloved wilderness, his voice took on a warm, rich tone. "I've picked out my favorite spot on the whole river for you folks. The Destiny flows out of one of the prettiest little valleys you'd ever want to see, but the hills flatten out into rich bottomlands that will grow you up crops faster than you can plant the seeds."

"None of us have much experience. . . ." Her voice trailed off doubtfully.

"You'll do just fine," he said, leaning back on his hands and studying her. "You, especially, Hannah. You've the spirit it takes to open up a new land—the persistence and the strength."

Hannah was thankful that the darkness hid the quick flush of pleasure that came at his compliment. "You overestimate me, I think. Remember how frightened I was that day with the Indians?"

"I remember that you were trying to find your way back to save me, without weapons or reinforcements," he said with a fond smile. "And I remember that you pulled Mrs. Trask through when she might have given up on us all and died.''

"Eliza was the one who knew more about the birthing," she protested. "And Randolph was the one who breathed life into the baby."

"But you were the one who breathed willpower into Nancy. You wouldn't *allow* her to die. I heard you telling her so."

His strong shoulder was almost touching hers. Hannah had a perverse wish to lean against it. "We've already been through a lot," she said pensively. "I wonder how much more we'll have to go through before we can consider this venture a success?"

"However much it is, you'll be up to it."

Whatever they'd have to face now, they would do it without Ethan. He'd be leaving soon, and Hannah felt bereft at the thought. "Thank you for your confidence," she said, trying to keep her voice normal. "I . . . I don't suppose we'll see much of you once you get us established."

Ethan moved around to put himself between her and the fire so no one could see his face but her. "As I've told you before, I don't stay around the same place for very long. But I'll come back and see how you're doing." His grave eyes studied her, not just her face, but along the length of her. Suddenly he gave a forced smile and said lightly, "Perhaps you'll invite me to your wedding."

Hannah gave a huff of exasperation. The man had the most infuriating way of making her feel exhilarated, then weepy, then angry all in rapid succession. "Perhaps I will, Captain," she said, rising to her feet. "For now, I'll bid you good-night."

"Good night," he said softly, still watching her with intense eyes.

One thing was certain, Hannah told herself as she made her way to her tent for the last time out on the trail. Her life would be much more tranquil when Ethan Reed was no longer a part of it.

Ethan felt a pang of regret as the Destiny came into sight around noon the next day. He didn't know what impulse had made him choose this site for the Philadelphia settlers. It was one of his favorite spots on the whole Ohio, which he had explored all the way down to its meeting with that other mighty western highway, the Mississippi. It had always seemed to him that the land around the Destiny was special—the fields richer, the hills bluer, the trees more noble. It had even occurred to him that if the time ever came someday for him to want his own little cabin to return to through the long winters, he would build it on the banks of the Destiny.

Now there would be people here ahead of him—thanks to his own planning. At least it would help to think of Hannah making a life for herself here in a place he loved. He was having a hard time shaking the hold she had placed on his head. On his body, too, for that matter, and, if he was being honest, he might as well throw his heart into the formula.

Everything about her captivated him. Her voice, the way she moved, the little thrust of her lower lip when she was tackling a new problem. She handled the four children as if she'd been a mother for years. Every night when Eliza's years showed in the tired hunch of her back and Nancy's weakness forced her to rest, it was Hannah who took charge, assigning the tasks of setting up camp, planning the night's sleeping arrangements, organizing the supper. All without a cross word for anyone, even Hugh Trask, whose lewd glances and suggestive remarks sometimes made Ethan want to shove his face into a tree trunk.

Randolph was getting himself a prize, he thought darkly. She could even shoot a gun, and she was stronger than most women, in spite of her slender, long body. He knew exactly how strong. The vivid, erotic memories of the night they had spent together came often and hard. Sometimes at the worst moments. Like now, as he watched her help unload her boat at the mouth of the river. The flatboats would not go up current, so they would have to use the animals to take the supplies to the final site they chose for their settlement.

He watched the long curve of her back as she strained to lift crates many men would be loath to try. Willing his unruly body to calm its unwelcome arousal, he stepped off the Trask boat and walked back to the Websters'.

"Don't hurt yourself," he warned her, taking the other side of a trunk she was struggling to lift.

"I won't." Her smile was pure sunshine, without any of the reservation he had seen in her eyes since their night together. It made his heart soar.

"So what do you think of Destiny River?" he asked, his mood matching hers.

"It's beautiful. It's everything you said." She stopped lifting for a moment to gaze at a row of ash trees blowing in the light wind. In the distance behind them, gentle hills made a graceful silhouette against the blue summer sky.

"There's a place about a mile up at the edge of a rich meadow that would be perfect for building cabins. I've camped there myself."

They moved down the gangplank with the heavy trunk, Ethan walking backward. "Thank you for helping," Hannah said, meaning with the trunk, but then she broadened the statement. "Thank you for leading us to this place. Thank you for everything."

Ethan couldn't resist the urge. He leaned close to her and asked, "For everything?"

She met his gaze, refusing to be daunted. "Aye. For everything." She dropped her end of the trunk, making him stumble forward, then she gave him a bright smile and waltzed away.

Ethan had agreed to stay for a couple of weeks to help with the cabins. Everyone in the group except for little Wally and Nancy, who was having trouble regaining her strength, worked from dawn to sunset trying to establish their foothold on the wilderness. They chose the site Ethan had mentioned where a broad meadow stretched out for half a mile from the banks of the river to the hills behind. The open area would mean that they would not have to clear land for the houses and the crops, but even so, the work was backbreaking.

Trask and Seth were in charge of breaking up enough of the meadowland to plant a small crop. By next year they would have their farms fully organized, but this year they would have only the essentials. Near the riverbank where they had discovered a dark, loamy soil, they would plant the burlap-wrapped seedlings of peach and apple trees they had brought from Fort Pitt. Hannah herself walked up and down the rows Seth and Trask had dug, carefully depositing the precious plants. There would be no fruit for some years yet, but it gave her a little thrill to think that the tiny trees would grow along with their settlement, each year sturdier and more prosperous.

Randolph and Ethan were in charge of dismantling the boats and transporting the lumber upstream, dragging it behind the horses in trip after endless trip. The long-hewn boards would make stout frames for the little homes they would build.

Hannah, Eliza and the children helped wherever they were needed, though Eliza tired quickly in the hot summer sun.

"I'm not as strong as I thought I could be," she confessed to Hannah one day as they rested along the bank.

"You're more than doing your part," Hannah assured her. "Just think what Nancy would have done without you and your nursing."

Eliza shook her head sadly. "It's not the same as when Seth and I started the brickyard thirty years ago. We had so much energy and enthusiasm...." Her voice trailed off.

"You're both working very hard," Hannah said firmly. "You have nothing to feel bad about."

"It's not that we don't like it here ... it's a beautiful place. If only Johnny were here to help out his father, we'd be so happy."

Tears filled her soft eyes. Hannah put an arm around her shoulders. "Just give it time, Eliza. It's like everything else. Everything gets better with time."

Hannah herself was feeling the effects of the hard work. Each day her troublesome back ached more from all the unloading and carrying and dragging. She tried to cover up her discomfort, but she had seen Ethan watching her as if he could see through her pretensions.

A week after their arrival at their new home, the pain was more than just a bother. They were still using the tents they had used on the trail, and she made an effort not to awaken Peggy and Jacob as she tossed restlessly, trying to find a comfortable position. Finally she gave up and crawled out of the tent. As usual, Ethan was still awake, sitting alone by the camp fire.

"Can't sleep?" he asked her softly.

Hannah walked over to the fire, surreptitiously stretching out her back. "It's all the excitement, I suppose."

"Or that back of yours that you've been nursing all week long," he said dryly.

She didn't answer, but sat down at the fire across from him. "It *is* your back, isn't it?" he persisted.

She shrugged. "It's a problem I've had since I was a girl. It gives me trouble every now and then. I'm used to it."

Ethan gave a snort of disgust. "It would give you less trouble if you didn't insist on hauling around the heaviest loads available as if you were working the London docks."

Hannah smiled. "You're the one who talks about how important it is to work hard on the frontier."

"Work hard, not kill yourself."

"I'll be all right." She stared into the fire.

"Doesn't Eliza have any willow tea left?"

"I think we used it all for Nancy. Don't worry about it. It's just a nuisance, that's all."

Ethan gave a sigh, then stood up and disappeared into the darkness. In moments he was back, holding up a small round jar. "Liniment," he explained.

Hannah looked at the jar in surprise. "Oh. Thank you. Er...tomorrow I'll ask Eliza to help me put some on."

"And in the meantime you'll stay awake all night with the pain," he said dryly. "That doesn't make a lot of sense, now does it?"

The words had suddenly fled her throat. She shook her head.

"I'll put it on you," he said. His voice was very even, detached.

She swallowed to put some moisture back into her mouth. "But I don't see how..."

He gave an impatient wave of his hand. "Use some common sense, girl. There's no reason for you to suffer just because you don't want me to catch a glimpse of something that I've already given what, I assure you, was a thorough study."

Hannah's face flamed. "It wouldn't be proper..."

Before she could frame her answer, he seized her hand and pulled her after him toward the riverbank. "We'll go over here where it's dark," he said, then added mockingly, "to protect your sensibilities."

Hannah looked back at the sleeping camp. There was no sound from any of the tents. It was well past midnight. Perhaps Ethan was right. If the lotion could relieve some of the pain, she'd be able to get some sleep for another busy day of work. He stood beside her, waiting.

"Just give me a minute," she said, ducking into a clump of bushes. With fingers grown icy, she unlaced the bodice that she wore over a cotton shift that tucked underneath her full skirt. Carefully she put the bodice to one side and pulled the shift up around her waist. She was still decently covered from neck to ankle. Ethan would just have to reach under her shift to apply the liniment. That wouldn't be so bad. She stepped out of the bushes.

Ethan had known from the minute he had seen Hannah crawling out of her tent that he was going to make a mistake. It was as if all the good intentions he had mustered and resolutions he had formed throughout the past few weeks had exploded in one heart-stopping second. From then on the results had been inevitable. The liniment was just fate giving him a hand.

He motioned for her to sit at a place where moss covered the sloping bank. She sank to the ground and turned her back to him, timidly reaching behind her to lift the hem of her shift. "Just the upper part of my back would be fine, down to the waist," she stipulated carefully.

Ethan grinned and dropped down behind her. He set the jar aside for a moment and gripped her shoulders over the thin cotton. "You'll have to relax if this is going to work," he said in the same even tone.

His hands felt miraculous on her tightened neck and back. Involuntarily she moaned as his big hands gently manipulated her, his thumbs pushing upward with just the right amount of pressure. "I think I'm relaxing," she said with a nervous little laugh.

"Good." His hands moved along her side and down to her waist, massaging gently on top of her shift.

"When are you going to put the liniment on?" she asked. The strange melting had begun again inside her, and all at once she didn't know if it was a very good idea to be once again alone with Ethan in the middle of the night. In fact, she decided as his hands never stopped moving, she could be pretty sure that it was *not* a good idea.

"Just lie on the bank, facedown," he ordered. He lifted gently under her arms and helped her to spread out on the mossy grass. Her body followed his lead, as though it were entirely detached from her head.

Then he pulled up her shift and she felt the cool night air on her bare back. "I need to loosen your skirt and petticoats so I can reach your waist," he said smoothly.

His hands skillfully undid the fastenings at her waist. Hannah made no protest.

Ethan was trying to keep his senses leashed, but as the moonlight shone on her bare skin—the hollows just below her waist and the beginning of the round swell of her neat little rear—he felt the first surge of urgency in the lower portion of his body. He didn't even bother to argue with himself that he was acting disgracefully, that Hannah was as good as engaged to a fine, decent man who would make her a wonderful husband. The argument was already lost.

He covered his fingers with the oily cream. It smelled faintly of pine. He did not want to startle her, so he reached first well up underneath her shift to the top part of her back. Making small, rhythmic circles he worked his way down to her waist, then below, to that soft white skin he was itching to touch. Hannah gave a little jump when he touched her there. He moved upward again, kneading her waist, then stroking outward toward her sides, almost reaching the tender outer skin of her breasts.

Hannah had never felt anything so sensual. Without kisses, without love words, Ethan was seducing her. And she wanted nothing more than to be seduced. Her back pain had disappeared, only to be replaced by a more demanding, spectacular ache right through the center of her body. She was still inexperienced, but in one night Ethan had instructed her well enough to know exactly what that ache meant and how to relieve it.

Passive and dreamy, she let him pull her shift over her head, leaving her naked from the waist up. His massage of her back continued until she felt the slight tingle of the liniment all over her skin. Then his fingers reached lower and covered her bottom, stroking gently, methodically.

Suddenly he turned her around and lifted her in his arms. His mouth sought hers in a desperate mating, hot and hungry. "I need you, Hannah," he whispered.

Her bare breasts swelled under his fingertips. She moaned and arched her back. In one swift movement he swept off the rest of her garments. She lay naked against his fully clothed body.

Ethan had always prided himself on his control. It pleased him to be able to make a woman delirious with desire before he himself took his pleasure. But for the first time he wasn't sure if he could wait. Not even long enough to remove his clothes. Hannah's round bottom moved against his stiff arousal and she gave a little whimper. Without conscious thought, he tore open his pants and lifted her hips to position her over him. She clutched at his shoulders and fastened her lips on his neck as he carefully entered her. All the feeling in his body seemed to drain into his loins as they moved together, exquisitely slow at first and then in an increasing frenzy that ended in total oblivion.

Little by little the world came back into focus around them. Still joined, he pulled her closer in his arms. He kissed her hair, then her forehead, her eyes, her lips. "How's your back?" he muttered.

Hannah gave a helpless laugh. She had not said a word, not made a move to stop him. Though she had abandoned coherent thought some time ago, she was fairly certain that she had had no desire to stop him. She was her mother's daughter all right. And with her mother's taste in men, evidently, since she, too, had chosen to fall in love with a man who would disappear once the lovemaking was over. But that didn't mean that she had to throw away the rest of her life the way her mother had.

Calmness seeped back into her bones and coolness into her damp skin. Slowly she pushed herself away from him and stretched to retrieve her abandoned shift. "I do believe my back is cured, Captain Reed," she said, with as much dignity as she could muster in her totally naked condition. "Thank you."

He let her go. If her voice hadn't been so aloof he would have pulled her back into his arms. Instead he just watched in some confusion as she gathered her clothes and walked behind the bushes to get dressed. She hadn't ranted at him as she had every right to do. The euphoria of just a few minutes ago dissipated as he fastened up his trousers, feeling like a randy schoolboy who'd been caught behind the corncrib.

She hadn't ranted at him, but she hadn't smiled, either. As he stood and stared out at the tranquil Destiny, he realized that he'd give half his soul right now if she would just do either one.

* * *

Far from feeling guilty over giving in to her feelings with Ethan, Hannah felt that their passionate encounter had somehow liberated her. She had admitted to herself that she had all the sexual desires that her mother had warned her about, and she had decided that she was still the same person and, most important, that she was still in control of her own future. And her best chance for that future lay with Randolph Webster and his children. Even Ethan had conceded that fact.

And every day she was more certain that Randolph intended to make her his wife. He saw to her every need and was rarely far from her side. He was building their cabin with a loft for the children and two separate bedrooms for the two of them, but he had explained with some embarrassment that soon Peggy would want her own bedroom, and perhaps by that time Hannah would be ready to move.

She briefly debated over whether it would be necessary someday to tell Randolph that she had been intimate with Ethan. But she concluded that very few female indentured servants ended up intact by the end of their ordeal. Randolph could think what he wished of her past experiences. He was too much of a gentleman to inquire.

He did seem increasingly hostile toward Ethan, as though he sensed that there was something between them. When a day after their middle-of-the-night meeting Ethan had inquired a little too politely about her back, hoping no doubt to rile her, Randolph had flashed him an angry look. Then he had turned on her. If she was hurt, he'd insisted, she should be telling him about it, not some hired hand. After his initial flare of anger, he had apologized for his abrupt manner and had insisted that she should lift absolutely nothing until she felt better. For the next week if she had so much as a sack of cornmeal in her hands, it was plucked from her with a gentle scolding.

Ethan stayed out of her way, working hard as the first crude structures of the cabins started to take place. Once the three frames were up, he would be leaving. And Hannah awaited the day with a mixture of impatience and sadness. As she watched his brawny form working on the cabins, listened to his ready laugh and smiled at his tall tales by the camp fire, she realized that she might never in her lifetime meet anyone quite like him. She also might never again feel what she had felt in two short nights with him. But she would work side by side with Randolph in this beautiful new land. She would build a home for him and his family. And only during the long winter nights when her family was tucked safely and snugly in their little cabin, would she close her eyes and let herself remember.

Chapter Fifteen

September 1763

The summer had raced by. Beyond the meadow where they had planted their first crops, the beech groves had turned russet and the hickories were burnished with gold in the early autumn sun. In the two months since Ethan Reed had left the Destiny River settlement, the three cabins had been finished. A neat little pen kept the pigs from wandering as they had that first chaotic week. A corral housed the horses. Adjoining it, the frame was in place for a communal barn, which would provide winter shelter for the animals.

Artichokes, peas, pole beans, squash and turnips shared the vegetable garden while several acres of corn stretched out behind. For a time corn would serve multiple needs. It would be ground for flour and pressed for oil. The plumpest ears would be shelled for eating and the husks would be fed to the pigs. As Ethan had promised, the tall green stalks seemed to grow like magic and now towered over their heads, even with the late planting they'd had.

To Hannah, her little cabin was starting to feel like home. The Webster and Baker cabins had been built in a flat, clear area at the edge of several feet of sloping riverbank. The Trasks had positioned their house a short distance away, downriver, where a grove of trees gave them the privacy that Hugh had insisted upon.

The Bakers' house was the smallest. They had somewhat sadly declared that they didn't need much room, and that the wood should be used for those who still had families to shelter. The Webster and Trask cabins were nearly identical, though Hannah had found time to fix hers up in a way that Nancy couldn't do, having the new baby to care for. She had never completely recovered her strength from the difficult birth, and Hannah felt sorry for her. But when she had offered to make an extra set of the yellow dimity curtains she had made for the Webster cabin, Nancy had politely refused, saying that she would be able to decorate her own home when she was feeling herself again.

Nancy's burden wasn't helped any by the fact that Hugh had ridden off on several "hunting forays," returning sometimes days later with very little to show for the time gone. His absences were causing dissension between him and Randolph and Seth. For one thing, he wasn't doing his part in working on the crops, and for another, his wife was in no condition to be left to care for the family by herself.

Randolph had discussed the matter with Hannah, as he seemed to do with everything these days. They agreed that in the interests of trying to maintain harmony through the first winter of the settlement, they would do nothing for the time being. But Hannah noticed that Randolph visited the Trask cabin more and more regularly as Trask's disappearances became longer. He doted on little Wally, as they all did, and many days Hannah would see her normally serious employer on his hands and knees bent over the baby's blanket making funny faces and communicating in nonsense sounds.

Hannah herself had settled into a tranquil routine of frontier life. She loved her little house. She loved walking along the beautiful Destiny, picking wildflowers and stopping to watch the birds, the squirrels and the rabbits. When they had a yearning for fresh meat, she and Seth would hunt in the woods to the south of their meadow. It had become something of a joke among the group that Hannah was the hunter in the Webster household. Randolph had yet to show that he could hit a moving target, and since they were concerned about the diminishing supplies of gunpowder, he agreed to let Hannah bring home their supper.

With the success of their venture so far and the promise of rich crops for the winter, there was a feeling of well-being and a great deal of merriment in the Webster cabin. Hannah was growing closer each day to Peggy and Jacob as the memory of Priscilla became a little dimmer. If it wasn't for a vague sense of longing, which she did not dare define even to herself, she would say that these were the happiest days of her life.

The longing seemed to sharpen each time Randolph suggested one of their private evening walks. They would stroll along the river in the long summer twilight, and he would talk about his plans for this place. How one day a town would grow up in the Destiny valley, with shops and banks and hospitals and an actual government with real courts of law. Hannah found it difficult to share his vision. Cities and courts had not been especially kind to her. She loved the freedom of the West and secretly cherished the idea that the pretty little valley belonged just to them and no one else.

Randolph held her hand on their walks, and when the twilight turned to darkness, sometimes he would lean toward her and kiss her on the lips, gently, never demanding. The first time he had done so, she had pulled back in surprise and he had said gravely, "Don't worry, Hannah. I'll not hurry you. Just because we have left civilization doesn't mean that I have become uncivilized. I know you need time to grow accustomed, and the children, too. I have every intention of giving Priscilla the year of mourning she deserves."

Hannah told herself she was grateful for his gentility and his thoughtfulness. She let him kiss her, and she kissed him back. Sometimes she felt a flicker of those feelings Ethan had taught her. She would stop and let the night air cool her face. And she would wonder if she wasn't just a little bit wicked after all.

They'd promised the children a husking party complete with music and dancing. They had butchered their first hog to have fresh bacon and chitlins for the occasion. Jacob had asked to be part of the butchering team, but he had come running back to the cabin halfway through with his face a sick shade of green, and Peggy had teased him the rest of the day.

It was still light late enough into the evening to put in almost a full day's work in the fields and have plenty of time for the festivities afterward. Hannah and Eliza had gone back to the cabins in the midafternoon to work with Nancy in preparing the corn cakes they would have with the last of the maple syrup they had brought from Fort Pitt.

"Why don't you take a walk down to the river and pick us some berries, Nancy?" Eliza suggested as she and Hannah entered the Trask house. "We'll watch Wally for a while." Hugh had been gone for days, and Nancy had hardly been out of her house except to fetch water and wood.

With a grateful smile she grabbed a basket and started toward the door. "I've just fed him," she said, nodding at the tiny boy who had finally graduated from his cartouche box into a real wooden cradle. "He shouldn't be any trouble."

"Just go," Hannah said, giving her friend a little push. "Get some fresh air."

"I think I'll skin that Hugh Trask alive when he finally decides to show his face around here," Eliza said vehemently, after Nancy had disappeared down the path.

Hannah nodded agreement. "I'll help you. And Randolph will, too. He thinks it's disgraceful the way that man treats Nancy."

Eliza looked down at the peas she was shelling. "I've noticed that Randolph has been spending a lot of time over here."

"Aye, he tries to help out as much as he can, and of course he's extremely fond of Wally."

Eliza continued watching her peas. "But...it doesn't bother you?"

Hannah furrowed her forehead in confusion. "Bother me? Why would it bother me?"

"Oh, never mind. I'm just a meddling old lady, my dear. I don't want anyone to get hurt."

Hannah was still not completely sure she understood what Eliza was saying. "Are you implying that Randolph and Nancy...?"

"Well, a few years back Nancy was one of the most sought after girls in town. And the years have not ruined her looks entirely."

Hannah laughed. "Eliza, Randolph has asked me to marry him. Well, not in so many words...he wants to wait out his year of mourning for Priscilla. But he talks of it regularly."

Eliza gave a sigh of relief. "Well, that's enough of that, then. Randolph's too honorable to be courting two ladies at the same time."

"What an idea! Why, Nancy's a married woman."

"If Hugh keeps traipsing off like he's been doing, she won't be any more married than that Polly McCoy woman back at the fort. And she's got all kinds of men after her."

Including Ethan Reed, Hannah thought sourly. "There's no way Randolph would be involved with a married woman. I'm positive about that."

"I guess you're right," Eliza agreed. "You know him better than any of us. And I'm happy that the two of you are going to be together. He's a good man. And those children love you like they did their mama."

"I'll never replace Priscilla, but we do get along well, and I love them both dearly."

Their conversation drifted to other subjects. By the time Nancy returned with the berries, Hannah had almost forgotten Eliza's odd remarks. But later that evening, as they sat around a big table that the men had built in the center of their clearing, she watched Randolph sitting on the bench next to Nancy. The two were cooing together over Wally just like an old married couple. She told herself that the notion was ridiculous. She should be pleased to see Randolph's delight in the child. It just served to show what a good father he would make for the children they would someday have together, God willing.

The children had been playing "deer and stalker" while they waited for the adults to finish eating and start the music. Jacob came running over to Hannah and pulled on her hands with surprising strength for his age. "Come on and be the stalker, Hannah," he begged.

"I'm far too full of corn cakes," she protested. But then Peggy, Bridgett and Janie gathered around and added their pleas to Jacob's. "All right," Hannah conceded, laughing as they pulled her into a circle. "But just one game."

She let them tie a kerchief around her eyes and whirl her in a circle so that she would make a disoriented hunter while they cavorted around as "deer." It was growing dark and even looking down along the edge of the blindfold, she could see nothing. The children's shouts seemed to come from all sides at once. She lunged in what seemed a likely direction, only to be met with an armful of air.

After several more attempts at capturing one of her targets, she could no longer sense where she was or even if she was still within the circle of the cabins. The laughter seemed farther away, and she began to be a little afraid that any minute she would go stumbling down the bank and into the river. She stopped and tried to keep her head from spinning. "Where are my deer?" she demanded loudly.

From behind her there was a shuffling sound, then the cracking of a branch. She whirled around and grabbed for her quarry. The quarry grabbed her back, then held her off the ground against a solid wall of chest. With a gasp of fright she tore away the kerchief and looked up into the dark, laughing eyes of Ethan Reed.

Hannah's back ached. The past week they had all spent hours in the field harvesting the vegetables and the corn. But she would sooner bite her tongue off than let anyone know her problem. Especially Ethan. She had been horrified at the immediate and violent response of her treacherous body when he had held her against him earlier this evening. As soon as she had realized who was holding her, she had jumped back as if she had been scalded. But her heartbeat and flushed face gave her away, and from the look in Ethan's eye, she could tell that he knew exactly what effect he had had on her.

She only hoped no one else had noticed. Randolph had left Nancy's side immediately at Ethan's appearance and had walked swiftly across the camp to stand next to Hannah.

"This is a surprise, Reed," he'd said in a calm, not-too-pleased tone.

But all overtones of hostility had disappeared when they had heard Reed's mission in visiting them. Pontiac had finally succeeded in allying the tribes to march against the English, Ethan told them. They'd taken a number of British forts, and Colonel Bouquet had been forced to meet them in battle at a place called Bushy Run, just twenty miles from Fort Pitt. Bouquet's men had won the battle, but the British were urging all settlers in the area to return to the safety of the fort at once.

The music and dancing were forgotten, and the remains of the supper lay uncollected on the trestle table as the settlers soberly discussed their options.

"It sounds to me like we have no choice," Seth said. "We certainly have no way of putting up any defenses here."

Ethan pounded his hand on the table with impatience. "I don't know why you're even discussing it. You're not going to risk the lives of your women and children staying out here on your own surrounded by a dozen tribes on the warpath."

"How long would we have to stay up at the fort?" Randolph asked.

Ethan shrugged. "The winter, for sure. You'll not be back here this season."

"We've not finished the harvest..." Randolph started to protest.

"Forget the crops!" Ethan interrupted. "They won't do you much good if you're massacred in your sleep."

"We have to think of the children," Hannah said gently, laying her hand on Randolph's arm. She understood his resistance. The thought of leaving their little settlement on the Destiny, of abandoning their cozy little cabin, was hard for them all. But she knew that Ethan would not be urging them to do so unless the situation were grave.

"We've worked so hard..." Randolph swung his legs over the end of the bench and stood up. His frustration was evident in every muscle. "I'll do whatever the group decides," he said. Then he stalked off toward his cabin.

The others were silent for a few moments. Then Seth said, "So that's it. We'll pack up in the morning."

"It will be a more difficult trip upriver on horseback than it was floating down her," Ethan reminded them. "Try to get all the rest you can."

They nodded at each other and quietly began moving toward their own places. No one bothered to clean up the rest of the food. They would have to leave almost all their belongings and supplies behind, and there was no guarantee they would ever see any of them again.

Randolph finished banking the fire. The fall nights were beginning to grow cool, and it was good to have the embers still burning in the morning when they woke up to the cabin's chill. Hannah couldn't believe that they were sleeping in their new home for what might be the last time. The children had already climbed up to their loft. Neither one had had much to say. Randolph, too, had been mostly silent since the party had broken up and everyone had retired to their own homes to deal with the shattering news Ethan had brought them.

Ethan would be spending the night in the Trask cabin, a measure of protection in Hugh's absence, though everyone knew that if a war party happened upon their little Destiny River site, there would be little they could do to defend themselves.

Hannah looked around at the room that served as a living room, dining room and kitchen. Every piece of furniture, every dish, every pot, she had placed there. It had been the first house that she had ever felt belonged to her. But she regretted the turn of events even more for Randolph's sake than her own. After all, she had moved many times with her mother during her childhood, and she would survive if she had to pull up her roots yet one more time.

She could see the weight of Randolph's defeat in the slumping of his shoulders, the lack of energy in his walk. She went to stand behind him as he gazed down into the fire. In a rare gesture, she put both her hands on his shoulders and squeezed. "We'll be back," she said with more confidence than she was feeling. "We'll just tuck everything nicely away tomorrow morning, and it will all be right here waiting for us next spring."

"Aye. We'll come back to a fine settlement of rotted crops and dead animals and, most likely, burned-out houses."

"We'll bring new animals and plant new crops, and, if need be, we'll build new houses, too."

Randolph turned around and took her in his arms. She went willingly, sensing that he was seeking comfort, not passion. "Do you never get despondent, my valiant Hannah?" he asked, his face turned against her hair.

"There's only one kind of loss that can't be replaced—the loss of someone you love. My mother. Priscilla. But we're all still alive and healthy. We have our whole lives ahead of us and the strength and energy to make of them what we will."

He held her for several minutes while neither spoke. Finally he said, "Of course, the most important thing is for us to stay safe and well. If that means returning to the fort, then that's what we'll do. As usual, Hannah, you help me see the world more clearly."

Hannah could almost feel the bitterness seeping away from him as he held her, and it gave her a sense of deep satisfaction to know that she could make that happen. She offered her mouth gladly as he turned her face up for a kiss.

"I beg your pardon," said a mellow voice. They both looked over to find Ethan filling the doorway. "The...er...latchstring was still out," he said without sounding particularly apologetic.

Hannah and Randolph took a step apart. "What do you want, Reed?" Randolph asked curtly.

Ethan took a step into the room. "I need to talk with you about Trask." His eyes were on Randolph, which allowed Hannah a moment to compose herself. She had no reason to be embarrassed at being seen in Randolph's embrace. After all, Ethan himself had said that it was inevitable that she and Randolph would marry someday.

Randolph moved away from the fire and sat at one side of their table, motioning for Ethan to take a seat across from him. He did not offer him food or drink. Hannah quietly took a seat on the bench next to Randolph.

"I've just been talking to Mrs. Trask," Ethan continued. "She says Trask's been disappearing for days at a time."

"The man's a drunk," Randolph said with a snort of disgust.

"Maybe so. But drunks don't need crates of muskets in order to go on a bender."

"Muskets!"

"I just found a box of them hidden away in the corner of their cabin. I asked Mrs. Trask about them, but she didn't want to tell me anything. I think she's afraid I'm going to arrest her husband."

"Arrest him for what?"

"For selling arms to the Indians. I suspect that he's in partnership with a seedy, one-eyed character by the name of Silas Warren."

"I saw Trask with that man when we were at Fort Pitt," Hannah said with dismay.

"Could you tell what they were talking about?" Ethan asked her.

"No. They...ah...they made some unwelcome comments and I got away as soon as I could."

Randolph turned to her with an expression of concern. "What kind of comments? You never told me about anything like that, Hannah."

Ethan waved his hand impatiently. "Never mind that now. The important thing is to find out if it's true that Trask is dealing with the Indians. Colonel Bouquet should have that information."

"Could you really arrest Hugh?" Randolph asked.

Ethan nodded. "I'm working for the army again temporarily. I'm supposed to be meeting with a group of Potawatomi right now, trying to convince them to abandon Pontiac's alliance. But I told them at the fort that I wouldn't go until I had you folks safely back there.''

"That was good of you, Reed. We may all owe you our lives.'' Randolph looked straight at Ethan, as if acknowledging that their current situation superseded any rivalry the two might have felt in the past.

Ethan accepted the concession with a nod. "We're not out of danger yet, and if Trask is handing out rifles to the hostiles as we're sitting here, we may be in deeper trouble than we know.''

Randolph considered for a moment, then stood. "I'll go talk to Nancy and find out what information she has. She trusts me, and I think I can convince her to talk to me.''

Ethan pushed back his stool. "Fine. Give it a try. She seems to be scared to death of me. I'll just wait here until you get back.''

Randolph looked from Ethan over to Hannah, who sat without moving. "I'll be right back,'' he said, then left the room.

Hannah turned around on the bench and looked at the fire, but she could feel Ethan's eyes on her. "Would you like some ale?'' she asked after several moments.

"No.''

Surprised by the abrupt answer, she turned to face him.

"I see Randolph has finally discovered your many charms,'' he said. His smile was not quite normal.

"He has asked me to be his wife, and I have accepted,'' she said stiffly.

"Ah." Unlike the last time she had seen him, he was clean-shaven. His hair was tied back in a queue. His eyes lingered on her lips. "There's a preacher at Fort Pitt. You can be married as soon as we get there."

Hannah's heart had started to pound. She felt a chill in spite of the fire at her back. She stood up to put another log on the hearth. "We intend to wait until the end of Randolph's year of mourning."

Ethan looked at her in disbelief. "Whose idea was that?"

"Well, Randolph's. But of course it's... the civilized thing to do."

She stood with her back to the fire and warmed her hands behind her. Ethan kicked away his stool and came toward her. He walked like a real deer stalker, no children's game this time.

She couldn't move backward as he approached or her skirt would catch in the fire. He stepped close to her and put his arms against the wooden mantel, trapping her. "So it's to be a *civilized* marriage, is it?"

Hannah tried to push through his arm on one side but it held like an iron door. "I'd rather not discuss my marriage with you, Captain. Could you please step aside?"

There was a shaky plea in her voice, and part of him wanted to respond to it. He could step aside, leave her alone. They all had enough on their minds right now without adding problems. When he had told Bouquet that he would go himself for the Destiny River settlers, he had had no intention of interfering in the life Hannah was building for herself. He had thought that he could accomplish his mission and walk away from her, just as he had earlier in the summer. But the minute he had felt her against him tonight he had known that he'd been deceiving himself. There had not been a night through the long, sultry summer that he had not dreamed of having her in his arms again. He had spent four dreary weeks at Fort Pitt in strategy sessions with the British officers. And there had not been a minute of it that he had not wished to hear her laugh again. Polly had mocked him and called him lovesick. He had not denied it. He was in love with Hannah. It was a simple fact. The not-so-simple part was that he had absolutely no idea what he was going to do about it.

"Please, Ethan," she said again, drawing in a ragged breath.

He moved his arm. Hannah slipped out and went to the other side of the room. He made no move toward her, but his expression made her insides churn. "There'd be nothing civilized about it if you were mine," he said, his voice low. "It would be riotous and untamed and . . . magnificent."

"For how long? For a night? A week?"

"For as long as we both wanted," he answered simply.

She had backed up against the rough wall of the cabin. She and Randolph had planned to smooth the logs with mud from the riverbank. Now there would not be time. She dashed a hand angrily across her eyes. She would *not* cry.

Ethan finally turned his head away from her. "I'm sorry," he said. "I didn't come here to cause you pain. Randolph's a good man, and I wish you both well."

Hannah nodded, not trusting herself to speak.

"I'll head back to the Trasks' now and see if he's been able to get her to talk."

Hannah kept herself flat against the wall as he crossed the room. At the door he stopped and looked back at her, but at her continued silence, he turned and walked out into the night.

Chapter Sixteen

A misty rain dimmed the vibrant fall colors, adding to the gloomy atmosphere around the settlement. Ethan had agreed to postpone the departure until the rest of the hogs could be butchered and hung in a makeshift smokehouse they had quickly thrown together. He looked as if he thought their efforts were futile—that there would be little if anything left of the settlement by the time they came back next spring. But he made no comment other than an offer of help. The women stayed in their respective homes, packing the few things they could take back, their doors shut against the dreadful cacophony of squeals and shrieks.

Hannah, Peggy and Jacob had finished their bundles when Eliza appeared at the door, her face puffy from recent tears.

Hannah walked over to her friend and slipped an arm around her. She took a quick look out the door. "The rain's letting up. Do you children think you could start tying these on the horses?" she asked.

They nodded and, grabbing up some packs, detoured around Eliza and Hannah, Peggy murmuring a polite "Morning, Miz Baker" over her shoulder.

"It's a sad day," Hannah said, drawing her friend into the room.

Eliza seemed older this morning, her walk more stooped. "The saddest day since my Johnny left us," she said, her lip trembling.

Hannah went to put an arm around her. "But we'll come back next spring. Everything's going to be all right."

Eliza shook her head. "No. Seth and I've been talking all night long. We've decided that we're not coming back."

"Not coming back!"

"In some ways, Hannah, it hasn't been right from the beginning. We were trying to run away from Johnny's death, and the truth is, it's not something you can run away from."

"But...we've all worked so hard to get this far...."

"I know. And I do believe you'll come back. Destiny River will be a thriving little settlement one of these days, but it will be built with younger hands and hearts than ours."

Hannah reached around to embrace her. "I can't imagine it without you."

Eliza gave a sad smile and patted her on the back. "Yes, you can. You'll do just fine. You've got exactly the kind of spirit a place like this needs." She moved gently out of Hannah's arms.

"What will you do?"

"We don't know yet. Seth intends to contact Herr Gutmueller and see if he would be interested in a partnership. This colony will need lots of bricks if it keeps growing as it has been."

Hannah felt bereft. First they all had to leave their new homes, now Eliza and Seth were leaving for good. Giving up. And if it was true that Hugh Trask was trading illegally with the Indians, she supposed that Nancy and her children would be forced to move back East, too. That left them totally alone on a harsh frontier. The prospect didn't daunt *her,* but she wondered if it all wouldn't be enough to give Randolph second thoughts about the move west.

"I want you and Randolph to have the things we're leaving," Eliza said calmly.

"Oh. I suppose you won't be able to take much with you. I...I should talk to Randolph and see if we could buy..."

"You'll do no such thing. We've all got enough to think about this morning. Don't worry about it. Anything that's left here when you come back is yours, and welcome to it." She gave a little smile that had some of her usual spark. "Just consider it a wedding gift."

The children were back for another load, so Hannah and Eliza both helped them carry the rest of the bundles out to the horses. "You will be staying at the fort until spring, won't you?" Hannah asked. "I want you and Seth to be my witnesses at the wedding."

"Ethan says that Colonel Bouquet won't let us leave. Travel is still too dangerous. So we'd be honored. When is the wedding to be?"

"Well...we haven't actually discussed the wedding part of it. I just know that Randolph has been waiting until his year of mourning is over with."

"Pooh," Eliza huffed. "Priscilla herself would be the first to tell him to forget about that nonsense. A man has to live in the present, not the past. I'm surprised at Randolph."

Her sentiments brought back Ethan's words of the previous evening. Perhaps they both were right. Wouldn't it be nice if her prospective bridegroom showed just the tiniest bit of impatience?

They left the supplies with Jacob and Peggy and started wandering back toward Hannah's cabin. The squeals from the butchering had stopped, which meant that the fat little creatures had all been dispatched. Hannah sighed.

"You ladies planning on going somewheres?"

Hannah whirled around at the sound of Hugh Trask's raspy voice. He was standing at the edge of the clearing with another man. Each led a packhorse. "Where have you been?" Hannah asked. "We're heading out of here today. You almost missed leaving with your wife and children."

"Now wouldn't that have been a pity?" he said mockingly.

"I told ye, ye should've bought that Injun gal you was beddin' down so perty all last week," the man next to Trask drawled.

Hannah looked over at him. His buckskins were nearly black with soil and age, and his hair fell in greasy black clumps to below his shoulders. He was watching them with an oily grin. It was Silas Warren.

Eliza gripped Hannah's hand. "Just don't say anything," she advised.

Trask walked toward them. "Where are Seth and Randolph? Have they left their women to do the work?" He came close to Hannah. "'Cause you are Randolph's woman, aren't you, dearie?" He took a painful grasp on her chin. "Too good for the likes of me. You let a stinking trail guide put his hands all over you. Oh yeah, I saw you together in the woods, panting like two dogs in heat. Then you jump into Webster's bed. But you're too high-and-mighty for the likes of Hugh Trask, aren't you?"

He reeked of rum. Hannah twisted her head, trying to free herself from his brutal hold.

"Let her go, Trask, or, I swear, I'll blow you to kingdom come." Randolph had come up the little path from the corral. He held his rifle loosely, pointed at the ground, and he spoke in a deadly voice that Hannah did not even recognize.

Trask released Hannah. "Ah, there you are, Webster. We've been missing you, your little lady and I. Now why don't you put down that gun before you blow your toe off?"

Warren moved around in a circle to train his rifle on Randolph. "Should I plug him, Trask?" he asked.

"Nah. What's the need? He can't shoot worth beans. And the other one's an old man. I told you we won't have any trouble here."

Warren looked around with a nervous little tic to his neck. His empty eye socket twitched. "Let's get the rest of the rifles and get out of here." he said.

Randolph had not moved. "You're not going anywhere with any rifles, Trask. In fact, I'd say the only place you're going is a British prison," he said coolly. He looked over at his children, who were standing behind Hannah, their eyes wide. "Peggy, Jacob—get into the cabin."

Peggy grabbed Jacob's hand and pulled him in the direction of their home. When they were inside, Randolph slowly raised the barrel of his gun. "Now throw your guns on the ground," he said to Trask and Warren.

Hugh laughed. "Now I know I'm safe, Webster, 'cause you're aiming at me."

"I'm aiming at you, too, Trask."

"So am I."

Seth and Ethan stepped from behind two trees, their rifles trained on Trask.

"You didn't say Reed would be here," Warren said in an angry, whiny voice.

"Shut up!" Trask barked. He looked directly at Ethan. "If you don't want these ladies to get hurt, you'd all better throw those guns over this way." Before anyone could react, he took a quick step backward and grabbed Eliza by the arm. She gave a cry as he twisted it behind her back. Seth started toward him, but Warren, moving more quickly than his sluggish appearance would suggest, took three running strides over to Seth and, using both hands, smashed the barrel of his rifle against the side of Seth's head. The older man crumpled to the ground.

"Seth, dear God!" Eliza cried. Trask held her tightly, preventing her from going to her husband's side.

"Now, how about you other gents tossing over those rifles?" Trask said with a grin. "So's Silas here don't have to crack any more heads."

When nobody moved, Hugh reached into his belt for a hunting knife. He spit on it, then held it pressed against Eliza's throat. "I said, throw the guns, gentlemen. Gently now, over this way."

This time Ethan and Randolph tossed their weapons toward Trask. Ethan's slid to a stop directly in front of Hannah. She glanced from the weapon over to Trask, but she could see the sharp edge of his knife sinking into the wrinkly skin of Eliza's neck, and she didn't dare move.

"Well, now we got ourselves a dilemma," Trask said.

"I told you we should've come for the guns in the middle of the night," Warren complained.

"I didn't figure on Bouquet's pet scout turning up here. If we let him go, he'll have the British crawling all over these parts looking for us."

"So we shoot him," Warren said matter-of-factly.

Trask gave him an exasperated look. "In front of four witnesses?"

"So we shoot 'em all." Warren gave a demented little giggle, and for the first time Hannah realized that the man was not quite sane. A chill ran down her back.

Trask appeared to be considering. "I suppose we could make it look like the Indians had been here."

Drops of sweat were trickling down Eliza's face. "They've thrown away their guns," Hannah said. "You can let her loose now."

Trask pushed Eliza roughly toward Hannah and the two women embraced. Then he sheathed his knife and raised his rifle to aim right at Ethan's chest.

Hannah saw Ethan's eyes wandering over to where his gun lay just in front of her. She hoped he wouldn't try to jump for it. She'd seen Trask shoot, and he wouldn't miss at this range no matter how fast Ethan moved.

"I guess I'd feel a mite better if this one were out of our hair, anyway," Trask said, raising the rifle sight to his eye.

"If you get to shoot him, I get to take his scalp," Warren said with another giggle.

Hannah braced herself to jump on top of Trask. At least she could push him and spoil his aim. But before she could move, there was a movement in the bushes, and Nancy stepped into the clearing, pointing Seth's rifle at her husband.

"Stop right there, Hugh."

Hugh lowered his gun, then made a grimace of impatience. "There's no way you can fire that thing, you weak-kneed bitch. Now get out of my way, or I'll kill you, too," he said.

It seemed that Hugh was probably correct in his estimate of his wife's strength. Her arms were shaking from the effort of holding the heavy weapon, and the rifle barrel wobbled crazily. Suddenly there was tremendous blast as Nancy closed her eyes and pulled the trigger. The bullet ricocheted off a tree and into Warren's shoulder. He fell to the ground with a yelp. Nancy was knocked down amid a huge ball of smoke. The minute the shot went off, Hannah dove for Ethan's rifle. By the time the others had recovered from the surprise, she was standing to one side and slightly behind Hugh with the gun pointed at his head.

"Your wife may need a little more target practice, Hugh," she said, "but I hope you don't have any doubt that *I* can send this lead spinning into your right ear and out the left."

Warren had grabbed his arm and was rolling from side to side screaming, "I'm shot!"

Trask gave him barely a glance. He looked around for Eliza, who had slowly moved out of his way and was now too far for him to reach. "I could kill Reed before you pull the trigger," he said.

"But then you'd be dead, Hugh," Hannah said calmly. "So what good would that do you?"

He turned his head to look at her face. "You're bluffing."

"Try me." She raised the gun, looked through the sight, and held deadly still.

Out of the corner of her eye she saw Ethan watching her with an admiring grin. But she kept her gaze fixed on her target.

Finally Trask lowered the barrel of his rifle. "Drop it on the ground," Hannah told him.

He gave the rifle a shove and it clattered to the dirt. Ethan was there immediately to retrieve it. "Nice work, ladies," he said with a wink at Hannah and a nod for Nancy, who was still sprawled in confusion on the ground.

Randolph retrieved Warren's gun while Eliza went running to Seth's side. He was sitting up, holding his head and weaving. "Lucky thing I've got a hard head," he said, sounding groggy.

Eliza knelt beside him and held him in her arms, and said, "Thank the Lord."

Ethan had brought a length of rope and began tying Trask's hands. Hannah covered him with the rifle until he was finished. Then her body began to shake. She was gradually beginning to realize that she'd been a fraction of a second away from pulling the trigger and killing another human being. The shaking grew more violent, until Ethan came to her, pulled the rifle out of her hands, and put his arms around her.

"Shh, it's all over now," he murmured.

From the other side of the clearing, Randolph watched them, his face impassive.

Warren groaned and began to crawl toward his rifle. Randolph snatched it away. "What about this one, Reed?" he asked.

Ethan took his arms from Hannah and walked over to Warren. He knelt beside him to look at the man's wound. "It's just notched his arm," he said. "We'll clean it up, then tie him up, too."

Hannah took a deep breath and willed herself to regain her composure. There was poor Nancy lying on the ground, and she could see the children's little faces peering anxiously out the door of the cabin. She supposed the Trask girls, too, would be frightened. And someone should explain to them what had happened before they came running and saw their father all tied up.

Eliza was seeing to Seth, so Hannah turned to Nancy and pulled her up. "Are you all right?"

Nancy nodded. "I feel like my shoulder got blasted off," she said with a wan smile, "but I'm fine. I need to go see to my daughters."

Without a glance at Hugh, she went off in the direction of her cabin. Hannah turned toward hers, where Peggy and Jacob had now emerged. She ran to them, holding out her arms.

"Did Mr. Trask try to shoot you?" Jacob asked, his voice a mixture of disbelief and excitement.

"We think he might have," Hannah told them calmly. "But everything's all right now."

The three embraced. "I was so scared, Hannah," Peggy said with a little sob.

"I was scared, too. But we don't have to be scared anymore—it's all over."

Suddenly there was a look of panic in the children's faces as they looked past her. Hannah whirled around. While Ethan tended to Warren, Hugh had evidently cut his bonds with the hunting knife he'd still had in his belt. Hannah watched in horror as he drew back his hand and sent the deadly blade spinning straight toward Ethan's back. In almost the same instant, Randolph raised Warren's rifle and shot Trask dead center in the chest.

Trask swayed back and forth for an endless moment, then pitched face forward in the dust. Hannah cried out and ran across the clearing to Ethan, who had fallen heavily to one side, the knife buried to its hilt in his back.

Randolph retrieved Trask's rifle from Ethan's side. Then he walked over to Trask and carefully turned him over with his boot. His eyes were rolled back in his head and a crimson pool had formed in the center of his buckskin shirt. He was decisively dead. Randolph blanched at the sight and said under his breath, "Well, I didn't miss that time."

He looked over at his gaping children. "Peggy and Jacob, I want you to run down to the Trask cabin. You can tell Mrs. Trask what happened, but don't let her or the girls come up here."

The two took off running, their faces white and serious. Randolph then turned to where Hannah rocked Ethan in her arms. She looked up at him. "Tell me he's not dead, Randolph,'' she said, great tears rolling down her face. ''I couldn't bear it if he were dead.''

Hannah didn't know what they would all have done without Randolph's calm leadership after the horrible confrontation with Trask and Warren. With every other man disabled, he had taken charge without hesitation.

First he'd tied up Warren, trussed him up like a turkey so there wouldn't be any repetition of the mistake they'd made with Trask. Then he'd used detached, soothing tones to calm Hannah, and together they had removed the knife from Ethan's back. Ethan had lost so much blood that they didn't see how he could possibly live, but Eliza, who joined them after she had tended Seth's head wound, said that the blade must have missed the most vital parts, because his heart was still pumping out the blood and there was no telltale red coming from his mouth.

He was unconscious, and his body was cold and clammy. Hannah felt a tremendous sense of dread, but she forced herself to follow Randolph's calm orders.

After the knife was removed, Eliza brought her needle and thread. Randolph left the two women to stitch up the wound while he and Seth, a bandage tied around his forehead, dragged Trask's body off into the woods. ''We'll come back and bury him as soon as we make sure that everyone's all right,'' Randolph told the older man.

Hannah refused to leave Ethan's side. She clutched his moist hand and tried to force some of her own life power into his drained body.

Randolph came up behind her and tapped her gently on the shoulder. "We should get him to a bed," he said.

She nodded and stood up, but kept fast hold of Ethan's hand. Randolph lifted the wounded man's shoulders, Seth picked up his legs, and they carried him into the Webster cabin. "Put him in my bed," Hannah said.

Randolph nodded agreement, his expression inscrutable.

While Hannah and Eliza huddled over Ethan, Randolph walked to the Trask cabin. Nancy was sitting on the little front step, hugging Janie and Bridgett on each side of her. All three looked pale and frightened. Peggy was holding Janie's hand and Jacob stood nearby self-consciously.

Randolph addressed his remarks to Trask's daughters. "Your pa's dead, girls. He got involved in some bad things and with a bad man. But this is not something that's a reflection on you girls or your family or your fine mama here." He glanced at Nancy, then back to Janie and Bridgett. "The most likely thing is that the liquor got to him. Liquor's been the ruin of many a fine man, and I think it's what turned your pa."

All four children were listening intently. Randolph walked over to Jacob and put a hand on his shoulder. "Now you women got no more menfolk—at least until little Wally gets his first breeches. But Jacob and I will be pleased to help you out with whatever you need. Isn't that right, son?"

Jacob pulled himself up a little straighter and smiled at Bridgett and Janie. "Sure," he said.

"I'm going to go up with Mr. Baker and bury your pa. When we're finished, we'll come for you, so you can each be thinking of a few words you'd like to say over his grave." He rubbed his whiskers and looked at Nancy. "Are you going to be all right?" he asked gently.

She nodded, her eyes full of gratitude.

When Trask had been placed in a shallow grave, Randolph told Seth to fashion a cross while he went to fetch the family. He stopped first at his own cabin to ask Eliza if she would come out to stand with Nancy. He didn't suggest that Hannah join them, but stood for a moment watching her as she hovered anxiously over Ethan. She turned her head toward him for just a moment, then resumed her vigil.

The burial service was short and subdued. Randolph recited the Twenty-third Psalm and each of the girls placed wildflowers on the grave.

While silent tears ran down Nancy's cheek, Janie whispered, "Goodbye, Papa. I'm sorry the liquor turned you, and I hope God forgives you so we can see you in heaven."

Randolph asked Bridgett if she wanted to say anything, but she timidly shook her head. He smiled at her, then nodded once more over the grave and said, "Amen." One by one they turned and walked solemnly away.

When they came out of the trees into the clearing, Jacob said, "I'll help you pack up your horses, Mrs. Trask. I do really good knots."

Nancy acknowledged his offer with a sad smile and a pat on his head. "When do you think we'll be leaving?" she asked Randolph.

"I don't know." He glanced at the four children who had started down the path to the Trasks'. "I don't like to stay around here any longer than we have to, but we can't leave Reed, and he's hurt pretty bad."

"Is there anything I can do?"

"No. Hannah and Eliza are seeing to him." There was just a touch of bitterness in his voice as he added, "Especially Hannah."

Nancy's intelligent hazel eyes regarded him with a look of sympathy. "I don't know what we would have done without you today, Randolph."

He gave her a tired smile. "We're not through this yet. We've still got to get safely back to the fort with a prisoner and a badly wounded trail guide."

"You'll get us through," she said, putting her hand lightly on his arm. "I know you will."

Chapter Seventeen

Ethan had insisted that they start upriver only two days after the showdown with Trask. He was still feverish and weak. Hannah, who had scarcely left his side, had protested vehemently, saying that it was too soon to move him. The bleeding could start again and he could die.

She had argued first with Randolph, then with Ethan, himself, saying that the others could start back and she would stay behind with Ethan. He had shown his first signs of returning spirit when he lifted himself in the bed and told her not to be a damn fool. He had then ordered Randolph to tie him on the back of one of the horses and to keep moving, no matter what, until they reached the safety of the fort.

Randolph had made no comment to Hannah about her sudden devotion to Ethan. She had hardly slept in order to be available for anything her patient might need. Her face was drawn and her usual good humor had totally disappeared.

Randolph concentrated on the other members of the party. Seth and Eliza, now that they had made the decision to head back to Philadelphia, seemed to be quietly content. They endured the grueling pace Randolph set without complaint, and in the evening spoke with determination of starting their lives anew.

Nancy Trask, too, seemed to have found a new measure of peace. Now that she was truly alone, she no longer stayed totally in the background. She shared her opinions with Randolph when he was trying to make decisions for the group. She even spoke up more confidently with her children.

Each mile they had floated down the river seemed like ten as they worked their way back along the sometimes rough terrain of the bank. But with Ethan weakly assuring them that they were making headway, they kept moving and finally emerged one sunny afternoon to see the welcome V-shaped point of land and five-sided structure of Fort Pitt.

Randolph waited until all were settled and Ethan had been put under the care of the fort's doctor to talk privately with Hannah. He asked her to walk with him out in the yard after supper, and he went directly to the point.

"So it was true, Hannah—those ravings of Trask before he died. You were involved with Reed last spring."

Hannah looked into Randolph's honest, kind eyes. The sorrow in them made her heart ache. "Yes, I was."

"And are you in love with him?"

"I...I don't know. I didn't think I was, and, please believe me, Randolph, all this summer with you, I never thought to see Ethan again."

"And *I* thought we were building something together—you and I."

"I did, too. I wanted that. I don't think I've ever been happier in my life than these past weeks with you and the children. I was beginning to feel as if I really belonged somewhere, that I finally had a home of my own."

"But you weren't falling in love with me." His voice was quiet, pained.

They were walking along side by side, not touching. She thought of all the times through the long summer twilights that they had strolled hand in hand, content after a hard day's work at building a future.

"I don't know what to think anymore, Randolph," she answered simply.

"Because of Reed?" He stopped walking and waited for her answer. She looked down and nodded.

He winced and said, "He's not exactly the kind of man who will provide a life for you, Hannah. A home of your own the way you say you want."

"I know. I don't expect anything like that to happen."

"But he has your heart?"

Again she nodded, this time looking into his face. "I've discovered that hearts are not wise." Her eyes filled with tears.

Randolph gave her a sad smile, then broke the barrier that had grown up between them by putting a comforting arm across her shoulders. "No, I don't think love has much to do with wisdom." He resumed walking, pulling her along with him. "What do you intend to do?"

She looked over at him with surprise. "Well, I . . . I still have almost three more years to work for you. I certainly intend to honor my contract and go back with you to Destiny River next spring."

"From what I hear, the treaty the British are going to sign with the tribes might forbid settlement west of here."

"You mean we might not be able to go back?"

"It's a possibility."

"Well, then I'd go back to Philadelphia with you and the children. Or wherever else you go."

"But not as my wife."

She was blinking to keep the tears at bay. "It wouldn't be fair to you, not now, anyway. Perhaps with time..."

"Or perhaps if Reed doesn't make it," he said with his first touch of bitterness. "They say he's in pretty bad shape. I might get lucky."

Hannah turned toward him and gave a little stomp of her foot. "Randolph Webster! You know you don't mean that."

He put a hand on each side of her head and held her there, studying her face. Then he pulled away and gave a rueful smile. "I hope I don't," he said.

After some improvement when they first reached the fort, Ethan had worsened and had again lapsed into a fevered delirium. At Colonel Bouquet's insistence, he was moved to an upper bedroom in the commandant's house. With Randolph's permission, Hannah had taken over as his principal nurse, but the fort doctor had ordered that she could not spend more than half a day at the bedside without taking a break for food or rest. He wasn't about to end up with two patients instead of one, he had told her sternly.

She was too exhausted and too worried to argue, especially when Colonel Bouquet added his admonition to the doctor's. The commandant had been a frequent visitor to the sickroom and had observed Hannah's devoted nursing with some concern.

"You're quite fond of Ethan, aren't you, my dear?" he asked her on the third day of their vigil. Ethan lay on the bed semiconscious between them.

"I've never met a man quite like him," she answered.

Bouquet looked amused at her careful reply. "I've never met a braver soldier, nor a finer tracker, but those are not usually qualities that women find most appealing."

"I don't know where we'd be without him. He came back to Destiny River to save us, and it has almost cost him his life."

The colonel shook his head. "Ethan's tough. He's not going to let a knife prick kill him off."

"I hope you're right."

"Having a nurse like you's enough to make a man recover from just about anything, I would think."

Hannah gave Bouquet a weary smile. "I don't think he's even aware that we're here."

"Just make sure that you don't wear yourself out so that you can't be here when he does wake up."

"I'll be here."

He leaned across the bed and put his hand over hers on the coverlet. "You're in love with him, aren't you, my child?"

Hannah made no reply, but turned her head to study the unconscious man. Her emotions were written on her face.

Bouquet sighed. "You've not chosen an easy man to love."

"As long as he gets well, that's all I care about."

"And then what?"

She shook her head. "Nothing. You know him, Colonel. He's a free spirit. He's going to wander this beautiful West of his until it gets too crowded, then he'll move beyond to something else."

"And you?"

"And I will probably be going back to Philadelphia with the Websters. After your warnings, I don't think either Randolph or Nancy Trask intend to return to Destiny River."

Bouquet nodded. "The time's not right. In spite of the pacts we're making with the Indians, I know in my heart that someday the Ohio River valley will be settled by Englishmen. It's as inevitable as the tide. But for a time we'll try to keep the peace and hold the settlers back."

"And Destiny River will be forgotten."

"Not forgotten. Someday new settlers will find it again. A thriving community will grow from what you folks started."

"Perhaps someday I'll come back and see it happen," she said wistfully.

"I wouldn't be surprised, Mistress Hannah." The kindly colonel gave her a fond smile. "I wouldn't be surprised in the least."

Hannah had not left Ethan's side all evening, and not even the officious Dr. Fulton dared order her away. It had been over eighteen hours since he had shown any signs of consciousness. Shortly after sundown his fever had spiked dangerously. His body had convulsed violently, rattling the frame of his bed. The straw mattress he lay on was so dampened with his sweat that the room had begun to smell like wet hay.

The doctor had reluctantly decided that the patient should be bled. He didn't use the practice much himself, he had explained to Hannah, but in cases as grave as Captain Reed's there really was no other remedy left. He had left to fetch the equipment from his dispensary, leaving Hannah watching Ethan with a heavy heart.

Bleeding made no sense to her. They had bled her mother time and again, and it had only hastened the wasting process of her illness. Trask's knife had already taken more blood out of Ethan than any man should lose in a lifetime. It was the fever that was killing him now. His body was burning up.

With sudden resolution she stood and threw back the heavy goosedown tick that covered him. Dr. Fulton had draped wool wraps around his neck and chest. They were hot and wet. She pulled them away from his skin and threw them in a heap onto the floor. His shirt was soaked, too. She grasped it from the hem and started pulling it up toward his neck. "Help me, Ethan," she begged. "We need to get this wet shirt off you."

Something in his delirium responded, because his body cooperated as she drew the garment over his head. Then she lifted him in her arms and tucked a cool, dry sheet underneath his back. When she had him settled down again, she took a clean towel and began drying off his face, neck and bare chest.

She was still working over him when the doctor returned with Colonel Bouquet.

"Mistress Forrester!" he exclaimed. "Have you lost your mind?"

Ethan's ravings had already quieted. "He was too hot," she said firmly.

"Of course he was hot. He's got a terrible fever, and if you expose him to cold, he'll die on us for sure."

The doctor had an annoying habit of sniffing between every few words. When they had first arrived, she'd been utterly relieved to give Ethan over to a real doctor's care. Now she just wished he would go away. "According to you, he's going to die for sure anyway, so just let me try this. It makes more sense than sucking more blood out of him when he's already lost so much."

The doctor looked helplessly at Colonel Bouquet, who shrugged and said, "Since Captain Reed has no family here, I think we can consider Mistress Forrester as next of kin for this patient. Which means that she has the authority to approve the treatment given."

Hannah gave him a grateful look. She didn't know if she was doing the right thing, but something within her told her that Ethan was already better. Though he was still unconscious, his body was calm and his expression much more peaceful.

"If that is the case," the doctor said with one of his sniffs, "I will not be responsible for the results."

"I think Mistress Forrester understands that, Doctor."

"I'll bid you good-night then and check back in the morning," Fulton said, closing his bag with a snap.

Bouquet stayed a moment after the doctor had descended the steep stairs to the door. He watched Ethan with a worried expression. "I think I've done what Ethan would have wanted," he told Hannah.

She nodded. "I just hope *I'm* doing the right thing."

"He looks a little better than he did at supper time."

"Yes, I believe he does."

The colonel gave her a little pat of reassurance and then told her that he would be in his bedroom next door if she should need anything.

When he left, she sank down on the chair beside Ethan and took one of his hands in both of hers. His skin felt much cooler. "Am I killing you or curing you, my darling?" she asked under her breath. The endearment surprised her, but sounded right once it was out of her mouth.

With his hand still clasped in hers, she put her head down on the bed and dozed.

The bedside candle had almost burned to the bottom of its stand when she jerked awake again. She hadn't intended to actually sleep, and for a moment she felt a surge of panic. But Ethan's breathing seemed even and normal. More normal, in fact, than it had for some time. His skin felt dry, and his face had lost the red flush of fever. He looked pale but relaxed, almost as if in a regular sleep.

She let out a sigh of relief and lifted his hand to her cheek. When she looked back at his face again, his eyes were open, watching her. "What day is it?" he asked, his speech thick.

She clutched his hand in excitement and gave a shaky laugh. "I have no idea."

"But I am alive, right?"

"Aye." She wanted to burst into tears.

He twisted his head from side to side. "Where's my shirt?"

"I took it off you. You were too hot."

He looked surprised. "Where are we?"

"We're in Colonel Bouquet's house. But, Ethan, perhaps you'd better not talk. You've been gravely ill."

He closed his eyes, then opened them again and moistened his dry lips with his tongue. "And you've been nursing me?"

"Aye."

"What..." He seemed to be trying to force liquid into his mouth so that he could continue his questioning. "What does Webster say about that?"

"He... he gave me permission. We all want you to get well."

He opened his mouth several times without words. His eyes closed, and he seemed to be drifting off again. She leaned toward him to hear what he was trying to say. "—called me darling," he mumbled as he lapsed once more into unconsciousness.

In three more days Ethan had recovered so remarkably that not even Hannah could stand to be around him. Two days after the doctor had given him up as hopeless, he had rudely pushed aside the gruel they had brought to feed him and had demanded real food from the officers' mess. By the next day he was shouting for his clothes and yelling loud enough to be heard in the commandant's office downstairs that if they didn't let him get up, he would jump out the window into the middle of the yard stark naked.

Bouquet had mounted the steep steps with a stern admonishment, and had told a harried Hannah to leave her difficult patient to his sulks and take the afternoon off.

With a sigh of relief, she'd slipped out of the room and headed toward the row of barracks where the Destiny River settlers had been given housing for the winter. Now that the worry over Ethan's condition was receding, she had time to consider the reality of her current situation. She had all but declared her love for an impossible man who would no doubt be riding off to meet with some Indians or explore some new river the minute the colonel would let him get on a horse. She had turned down the devotion of one of the finest men she had ever met and had rejected his offer of marriage and a wonderful future. She had most likely lost the chance to be a mother to Peggy and Jacob, to be a part of their lives as they grew into adulthood. As she neared the barracks, her pace grew slower and slower. What was left for her?

They were all sitting around the table at one end of the long room that also served as the sleeping quarters for Randolph, Seth and Jacob. The women and girls slept in a similarly rough room adjoining. They were free to take their meals with the officers, but sometimes Nancy and Eliza, with the three girls trailing along behind, visited the fort kitchens and brought the food back so that the settlers could dine with a little bit of privacy.

They had finished the midday meal and the children had gone off to their play, but the adults were all still sitting around the table when Hannah walked in, her face pensive. They looked over at her with surprise.

Eliza stood immediately and went to her. "What is it? Is Captain Reed worse?"

Hannah shook off her gloom and smiled. "No. He's so much better that he's become quite unbearable."

Everyone smiled at the news except Randolph, who avoided Hannah's eyes.

"So now I can ease up on my nursing and resume my duties back here again."

Eliza took her arm and led her to the table. "How about if you just rest a little first. Have you eaten?" When Hannah shook her head, Eliza served her a heaping bowl of venison stew and plunked it down in front of her, setting a spoon in her hand as if she were a baby. "I want you to eat every bite. Land sakes girl, you're going to end up in the sickbed, too."

Randolph agreed, his voice sharp. "If Reed doesn't need you anymore, Hannah, you'd best see to yourself. How long since you've had a good night's sleep?"

Nancy reached across to pat Hannah's hand. She said, "Eliza, Randolph, I know you mean well. But you're badgering the poor girl. Hannah can take care of herself. She's certainly taken care of all of us well enough at one time or another. Just let her be."

Hannah flashed her a grateful and surprised smile. It wasn't like the Nancy she knew to stand up for anyone, not even for herself.

Eliza sat down next to Hannah, her eyes moving from the spoon to the stew, as if willing her friend to take a bite. Hannah couldn't remember the last time she'd felt any real appetite, but when she lifted a spoonful to her mouth, it tasted quite good. Perhaps they all were right. She had taken care of Ethan, now she needed to start taking care of herself.

"We've just had some news, Hannah. About Pontiac's alliance," Seth said, leaning backward to settle against the log wall.

Hannah looked up from her stew. In the intensity of her vigil at Ethan's side, she had almost forgotten about the rest of the world. Forgotten the reason that they were at the fort instead of back on the Destiny.

Randolph took over the telling. "The French have refused to provide him the support he was counting on, so the tribes are retreating westward."

Hannah paused with her spoon in midair. "So we can go back to our settlement?" she asked with excitement.

Randolph looked around the circle of faces. They waited for him to continue. "We're not going back, Hannah."

Eliza leaned her head on Hannah's shoulder. "Remember, I told you what Seth and I had decided," she said gently.

"But if the Indian problem is solved..."

Seth turned a loving look on his wife. "Eliza and I have realized that our enemies were not the Indians, but our memories. We're heading home so that we can make those memories into our friends."

"And I..." Randolph turned his face away from Hannah. "The children and I have decided that we will escort Nancy and her children back to Philadelphia."

Something in the way he made the statement gave Hannah pause. She looked over at Nancy, who was blushing. With her pale white skin, Nancy had blushed often when her husband had said things to embarrass her, but the expression behind this blush was pleasure rather than pain.

"You're giving up the settlement?" Hannah asked slowly.

Randolph finally met her eyes. "There's no one left to make a settlement with," he said without apology.

I'm left, Hannah wanted to say. But she had already lost the right to make that statement.

"Do the children want to go back?"

"Peggy wants to go with Janie and Bridgett, and Jacob can't wait to get home and tell his friend Benjie that he saw real Indians."

"I see."

"Of course, you'll be coming with us, too. It will be just like before."

Not just like before, Hannah thought as she pushed away the bowl of stew. She hadn't been asked her opinion about going back, because her opinion no longer mattered. She was once again a servant. She went where her master went. And now in the Webster household, she would never be more than a servant. As she watched the blush fade from Nancy's face, she noticed a new soft glow in the woman's eyes, which were fixed on Randolph. No, Hannah thought. It would decidedly not be like before.

It was evening before she made her way back to the commandant's house. She hoped that Ethan would be at least a little chastened by her long absence and be ready to behave better than he had that morning. She felt too melancholy to put up with bullying.

He was apparently asleep when she entered the tiny bedroom, but he opened his eyes immediately and gave her a smile that put a little bounce in her step as she made her way across the room. "So you've decided to come back to me," he said softly.

She approached the bed. "After all your hollering this morning, I should have stayed away until tomorrow."

He grinned. "Then you would have really heard some hollering."

He looked entirely back to normal. His skin had regained its usual ruddy color. His hair was washed and shiny. He had even shaved, or someone had done it for him. She sat alongside him on the bed. "I do believe you were spoiled as a lad, Captain Reed."

"I was not," he said indignantly.

"Well, someone has spoiled you, then."

"A few ladies, perhaps..." he began teasingly, then stopped at her expression.

"Ladies like Polly McCoy, I suppose. The commandant says she's been here asking for you. I suppose I should send word that you're ready for... visitors." She shifted from her seat on the bed to the nearby chair where she had spent so many hours over the past few days.

"Don't, sweetheart," he said with a frown. He patted the bed at the spot she had abandoned. "Sit here. I like having you close to me. And I'm just teasing about the ladies spoiling me. Most of them thought I was an ornery cuss who deserved to be thrown out on his rear."

Hannah smiled in spite of herself. She moved back to the bed, and he snatched her hand so that she couldn't move again. "I didn't see Mistress McCoy throwing you out," she said, not entirely mollified.

"Actually she did—a time or two. But none of that is of any concern to us."

Hannah looked down at their joined hands. "What exactly is of concern to us?" she asked softly.

He pulled her closer, sliding her along the feather bed. "Well, for one thing. I've been meaning to get something clear. Did I or did I not hear you calling me *darlin'* when I was so sick out of my head."

Hannah thought for a moment before answering. She had worn her emotions on her sleeve for days now. Randolph, the commandant, probably the entire fort knew of her feelings for Ethan. It didn't seem to make much sense to hide anymore. "I might have," she answered.

He sat up in bed and propped himself against the wall. "Might have?" he asked with a touch of irritation.

She gave a stubborn nod. That was all he was going to get from her. After all, *he* had never made the least declaration of *his* feelings.

"All right," he said briskly. "Let's suppose you *did* say it. Tell me something, Hannah Forrester. How many men have you called 'darling' in your lifetime?"

He sounded so self-confident that Hannah began to get irritated herself. "Dozens," she replied.

Suddenly he pulled on the hand he still held and lifted her with his other arm so that she lay sprawled against the upper part of his body, her face next to his. "Liar," he growled. Then he kissed her hard. He folded his arms around her and held her immobile while he hungrily assaulted her mouth with his lips and tongue and teeth.

Hannah struggled in his arms, which had lost none of their strength during his ordeal. "You can't be doing this," she protested. "You're not recovered."

"You're wrong," he muttered. With his mouth still on hers, he turned with her until she lay against the bed. His otherwise bare chest was still wound with a wide linen bandage. "You'll hurt yourself, Ethan," she said weakly.

He had not stopped his kisses. Hannah was starting to feel dizzy.

"Call me darling," he muttered.

"Then will you stop? Ethan, darling, let me go," she said sternly.

He threw back his head and laughed. "We can work on the tone a little, I think. But we have a lot of time for that." He gently kissed her nose, then her chin. "Because you see, Hannah Forrester, I don't *ever* intend to let you go."

Hannah's head was spinning too fast to think about what he meant by his words, but her heart gave a great thud as she heard them.

She looked toward the door, which stood open to the hall. "Please, Ethan. Be sensible. You're supposed to be resting, and the door's wide open and..."

Ethan rolled off her and turned back toward the door. "Hmm." He gave her a little push. "Why don't you just go shut the door and turn the lock?"

"I'll do no such thing."

He shrugged and pulled himself on top of her again. "All right. I doubt anyone will come by except Bouquet, oh, and maybe the doctor...."

Hannah slid out from beneath him and walked over to the door, closing it firmly and turning the iron key. She moved to face him, leaning her back against the door. Ethan lay watching her, his arms folded across his chest. There was a feral look to his dark eyes.

"I...I guess I'd better leave now," she stammered.

His teeth showed white in the dim room. "Come here," he said in a low voice.

She put her hands behind her, clutching the cold metal of the doorknob. "No. I'm leaving. And I'm not coming back until you agree to act the way a sick man should act."

Without the least appearance of being a sick man, he rolled easily off the bed and came toward her, totally naked except for the stark white strip of bandage. When he was standing practically on top of her, he bent, nipped the edge of her earlobe and whispered, "If you're so intent on leaving, why did you lock the door?"

Realizing her mistake, Hannah fumbled behind her for the key, but suddenly Ethan swept her up in his arms and turned toward the bed. "Perhaps I can relieve your conscience by..." He paused to twist one hand around to start unfastening her clothes. "By *convincing* you that I have fully regained my strength."

Hannah was already convinced. After so many days of watching him helplessly fighting the poisons of his wound, it filled her with elation to see him hearty and demanding once again. He set her down and finished removing her clothes while she stood without protest in a happy daze.

He lifted her easily onto the bed, but she saw him wince as his back hit the hard mattress. "Are you sure you're up to this?" she asked.

He laughed and ran his tongue along the edge of her jaw. "I'm definitely up to it, sweetheart," he said fiercely, and he moved his lower body against hers to leave no doubt about the issue. "But if it will make you happier, I'll let you do the work this time."

At her questioning look, he laughed again and lifted her so that she was straddling him. Soft parts of her rubbed against hard parts of him, and she felt an immediate surge of wanting. She rose up on her knees, then down again, and smiled when Ethan gave a little groan of satisfaction.

"Come here, you she-wolf, or this encounter is going to be over before it's started." He pulled her down against him and began kissing her again, methodically, skillfully, with devastating thoroughness, until she was moaning herself. Then he pulled her upward to take each breast in his mouth for the same exhaustive treatment. She cried out his name, and he quickly brought his mouth back up to hers, silencing her. "Take it easy, sweetheart. We'll have Bouquet pounding on the door in another minute."

Hannah looked horrified and for a moment her ardor cooled. Then he slid her body along his and moved in such a way that she ceased to care about Bouquet or any of the rest of the world.

"Should I stop and convalesce some more?" he teased, but his voice was thick with desire.

She shook her head and dug her nails into shoulders as he held her hips and positioned their union. When it came, coherent thought both. They moved together with one will that super-seded reason and intellect. Slowly at first, then with increasing frenzy until Hannah collapsed against him, with him, spent and changed.

For several minutes they lay without speaking. He stroked her hair, and she listened with her head on his chest to the wonderfully healthy pounding of his heart.

She expected that when either one did speak, they would sound somehow different. But Ethan's deep voice was just the same, with the same rich, teasing note. "Now will you believe me that I am recovered?" he asked. "Or do you need more convincing?"

She boosted herself up, her elbows on his chest. Joking was easier than trying to sort through the overwhelming feelings. She let out a deep breath and gave him a saucy smile. "I think your nurse is going to need more convincing, Captain Reed."

Ethan reached to give her a playful slap on her bare bottom. "How many years do you think it will take to convince you?"

"Years?"

"How about fifty?" he said, his tone suddenly serious.

The smile died from her lips. She and Ethan didn't have fifty years or even fifty days. By rights they shouldn't even have today. It wouldn't be fair to Randolph and the children for her to carry on an affair while they wintered at the fort. She wasn't a free spirit like Polly McCoy. She had other obligations. She shifted herself off him.

"What is it, sweetheart?" he asked, grabbing for her waist to pull her back to her former position.

"I can't do this, Ethan," she said, reaching for her dress and slipping it over her head.

Ethan let her go and pulled himself backward on the bed. He saw the distress in her light blue eyes, and he wanted to make it disappear as quickly as possible. He'd done a lot of thinking in the past few days, some clear, some clouded with delirium, but the conclusion had come out the same every time. He wanted Hannah. And he meant to have her. Not just once every few months when he could track her down in some settlement or trading post. He wanted her with him, by his side—tracking, hunting, exploring, mapping new rivers. He wanted her to be wherever he was. And if there were children someday, perhaps that somewhere would be a little cabin on the Destiny where they would raise a family. Children who would grow up like their mother—resilient and adventurous and strong enough to be worthy of this vast new land.

He no longer felt that she would be better off with Randolph Webster. In spite of what he had seen in their cabin that night back at the settlement, he knew with absolute certainty that Hannah was not in love with her employer. She was not a woman who could respond to Ethan the way she had just now with her heart committed to another. But he was not completely sure that love was enough. Hannah was strong-willed. Perhaps she wasn't interested in tying her future to an adventurer with a past full of women and wandering. He thought he knew her heart. But he wasn't sure, and there was only one way to find out.

"Where are my damn trousers?" he said loudly.

Hannah started. "Excuse me?" she said with a puzzled expression.

"My trousers. They've taken my clothes so I wouldn't get out of bed."

"I...think the colonel has taken them..." She backed away from the bed, looking mystified by his sudden change in subject and tone.

Ethan stood up, dragging a sheet after him. "How the hell is a man supposed to propose matrimony without any trousers?"

Hannah's face registered pure shock. "Pro... pro...pose?" she stammered.

He mumbled under his breath as he tied the sheet around his waist. "I guess this will have to do," he said grumpily. Then he dropped to one knee and reached for her hand.

Hannah couldn't help a little giggle. He looked so silly, half-naked, the sheet trailing behind him like a woman's train. He frowned. "You see! There are certain matters in life that must be settled with one's trousers on."

"Oh, no," Hannah said hastily. "Er...I... I quite like you without your trousers."

Ethan's frown turned to a suggestive grin. "The feeling is mutual, my sweet." Then he changed his tone. "Which is one of the reasons why, Hannah Forrester, I would like to request the honor of your hand in marriage. In exchange, my lady, I pledge you my heart, for in truth it is already yours."

Hannah's eyes blurred with tears as he placed a kiss on the back of her hand. Her throat was too full for words.

Ethan raised his head. "Well?" he demanded.

She nodded and pulled him up. He rose and clasped her against him, losing the sheet in the process. He looked down at her tenderly as he rocked her back and forth in his arms. "How do women do that?"

She started to recover her voice. "Do what?"

"Laugh and cry at the same time."

She laughed and cried some more and shook her head. "I don't know."

He kissed the top of her blond head, her teary eyes and her softened mouth. Then he pulled back. "Did I get an answer to my question?" he demanded to know.

"I think you knew the answer before you asked it."

"Not entirely, sweetheart. Let's just say that I was hopeful enough to talk with the fort solicitor earlier today about buying your papers from Webster."

"And what if I had said no?" she asked, feigning indignation.

"I think I would have had to buy them anyway. I wasn't about to let you go riding off with Webster. Not with the way he looks at you."

She liked the jealous note in his voice, but she did not want any more trouble between Randolph and Ethan. "I had already told Randolph that I couldn't marry him," she said gently. "And...I don't think he will be disconsolate for too long. He's planning on escorting Nancy Trask back to Philadelphia, and the two already seem to have found a great deal of affinity."

"The man's a fool. If *I* had lost you, I'd be disconsolate for a lifetime," Ethan said fervently.

She turned her face up for his kiss, which lasted longer than either expected. His breath shortening, Ethan began to move her back toward the bed. "Oh no, you don't, Ethan Reed!'' she said. She gave him a solid push and he fell backward, tripped over the dragging sheet and landed on the bed. "Not again. You're going to stay in that bed and get well if I have to tie you down."

"That might be interesting..." Ethan said, one eyebrow raised.

"And I'm going to go talk with Randolph before your solicitor does."

Ethan grew serious. "He *will* let you go, won't he?"

"Aye. But I want him to hear the news from me."

"As long as I know you'll be coming back to me, take whatever time you need."

"I'll be coming back *in the morning,*" she said sternly. "Now that you're so... healthy, I can't spend the night here with you."

"I could *pretend* to be sick," he said hopefully.

She took one look at his robust body, the signs of arousal once again fully evident. "I don't think anyone would believe you," she said dryly. Then she blew him a kiss and went out the door.

Epilogue

April 1764

Hannah had jumped out of the canoe and scampered up the gentle bank before Ethan could even secure the boat to shore. "They're here, Ethan!" she called. "Everything's here, just as we left it."

He was relieved to hear the joy in her voice. He had been afraid that even if they found the Destiny River cabins still intact, the thought of her absent friends, now on their way back to Philadelphia, would make her sad. But he should have known better. His optimistic, confident wife was a woman who knew her own mind. She had said that she wanted to return and claim the settlement. And it was partly in honor of those friends that she had come back—so that their small contribution to the opening of the West would not be entirely forgotten.

Ethan tied the canoe and walked up the bank. Hannah had disappeared into what had been the Webster cabin. If there was to be any sadness in the return, it would be there, where she had shared so many happy days with Randolph and his children.

Back at the fort, she had broken down when she'd had to say goodbye. It had started out well with fond wishes and embraces for Seth and Eliza and Nancy, but when Peggy and Jacob had both burst into tears in her arms, Hannah had faltered. It had been wrenching for her to leave the two youngsters who had become like her own. Her only consolation was that they were to have a new mother now, and fortunately, they both had already grown fond of Nancy.

Ethan, himself, had had a few difficult moments when she had gone alone for a final talk with Webster. The man had absolutely refused to take any money for Hannah's indenture papers, and he had stood up as a witness at their wedding, but Ethan couldn't entirely forget his memory of Hannah in her former employer's arms. She'd come back from her farewell with red eyes, but had gone immediately to Ethan and had turned her face up for his relieved kiss.

He followed her into the cabin. She was standing by the mantel, looking around the room. But if her memories were painful, her expression did not reveal it.

"It doesn't look like anything's been touched, does it?" he asked.

She shook her head. "It's just as we left it." She gave a little shiver, and he walked over to put an arm around her.

"Is it hard to come back?" he asked tenderly.

She leaned against him. "I was just remembering that the last time I was in this room, we had to carry you from my bed in there, and we didn't know if you were going to live or die."

He wrapped his arms around her and held her against his chest. "I'm too tough to die. You're stuck with me."

She swallowed down her emotion, then looked up at him, her blue eyes teasing. "Too bad. I believe Major Edgemont was just about ready to carry me off to a castle in England when that preacher finally arrived from Harris's Ferry."

Ethan gave her a soft pat on her rear. "Saucy wench. I should have sold you to that Indian brave when I had the chance."

"Too late. Now *you're* stuck with *me.*"

Arm in arm they walked slowly out to look around at the rest of the settlement. Nothing seemed to have been touched. Even the hams from that last frantic butchering still hung undisturbed in the smokehouse.

"Oh, look!" Hannah gave a cry of pleasure as they walked along the bank. The neat rows of fruit trees that she had thought never to see again had survived the winter intact and were covered with tiny white blossoms.

Ethan smiled at her childlike delight. He never got tired of looking at her, of hearing her merry laugh, of holding her strong, slender body next to his each night. He never ceased to be amazed that she belonged to him. "Apple trees. So now we truly have reached Eden," he said. He bent to pluck a soft blossom, then placed it tenderly in her hair.

"I believe we have," she said happily. She took his hand and led him farther along the bank to the mossy knoll where one night nearly a year ago they had made love. She wondered if he recognized the place. Probably not. Men were less sentimental about those things. She turned to him with a suggestive smile. "But I thought you said they didn't wear any clothes in paradise?"

"I believe I did," he replied casually. They had walked two more steps when all at once he lifted her off her feet and deposited her on the carpetlike grass. Before she could say a word, he dropped beside her and rolled her beneath him. He threaded his hands through her loose hair and pressed her against the bank, lavishing her mouth with several thorough kisses.

Then he drew back his head and wiggled an eyebrow at her as he asked. "How's your back?"

She gave a merry laugh and pulled him down for another long, drugging kiss. When it was over, they lay quietly in each other's arms. Around them the sound of the gentle rush of the Destiny mingled with the calls of the songbirds and the rustle of the spring winds in the tall ash trees. But for Hannah the sweetest sound of all was Ethan's voice as he put his mouth close to her ear and murmured, "Welcome home, my love."

*   *   *   *   *